George Amos Dorsey

A Bibliography of the Anthropology of Peru

George Amos Dorsey

A Bibliography of the Anthropology of Peru

ISBN/EAN: 9783337383039

Printed in Europe, USA, Canada, Australia, Japan

Cover: Foto ©Andreas Hilbeck / pixelio.de

More available books at **www.hansebooks.com**

Field Columbian Museum

Publication 23.

Anthropological Series.   Vol. II, No. 2

A BIBLIOGRAPHY
OF THE ANTHROPOLOGY
OF PERU.

BY

George A. Dorsey,
Acting Curator. Department of Anthropology.

Chicago, U. S. A.
January, 1898.

A BIBLIOGRAPHY

OF THE

ANTHROPOLOGY OF PERU.

By George A. Dorsey.

INTRODUCTION.

What was begun in 1893 as a labor of love, has been brought to a finish amid difficulties and the stress of work attendant upon new fields of investigation.

While pursuing a special course of study in the Graduate Department of Harvard University, in 1893 94, I began to form a card catalogue of the more important books which treat of the antiquities of Peru. This was done merely for my own benefit and to aid me in the particular line of investigation with which at that time I was occupied. Such a catalogue seemed all the more necessary to me, as I could find no list of books of any value which related to Peru, and my studies led me into all the many interesting problems for which that country is so justly famous.

It soon became apparent that the work of making anything like a complete list of books which relate to the Anthropology of Peru would be long and laborious, and at one time I decided to abandon the idea; but with the kindly advice of Dr. Winsor and the cordial assistance of Mr. Kiernan, both of the Harvard Library, I took hold of the work anew, and set out with the deliberate intention of making a complete list of all the books, pamphlets and magazine articles which related in any way to the anthropology of Peru. The aim has been to cover the whole ground, and from the earliest times down to the present day, to include such works as treat of the modern Indians as well of the Peruvians of ancient times, and finally to include all known editions of the early Spanish authorities. To what extent the list here presented falls short of this high aim no one knows so fully as I do. Although having at my command the extensive libraries of Harvard and Boston, yet for many titles I have had to refer to the catalogue of the British Museum Library, and to those of Sabine, Harisse, Quaritch, Dufossè, Hierseman, Winsor, etc.

On account of the additional interest which is imparted to a book when something is known of the author, I have given short biographical sketches of about fifty of the more important authors of the early Spanish times. Indeed, with many of these early writers the very

55

facts of their lives are what make their writings of so great import-
ance.   In the preparation of these biographies I am especially
indebted to the two chapters on Peru by Clements R. Markham, in
Vols. I and II of Dr. Winsor's Narrative and Critical History of
America.

This is my first attempt at bibliography; it shall be my last as
well, although I hope, in a second part, to attempt to compile an index
by subjects and topics, which will enable any one to look up such
titles as relate to special matters.   When that is finished and an
index to the literature of the most interesting country in America, as
viewed by the anthropologist, is thus rendered available for students,
I shall not feel that I have labored in vain.

ERRATA.

Page 59, line 8, *for* Acuna *read* Acuña.
" 67, " 25, " Juncos " Yuncas.
" 70, " 9, " Akad " (Kön. Akad. der Wis).
" 76, " 16, *for* Hispano-Ulkamarina *read* Hispano-Ultramina.
" 84, " 27, " Cy *read* C. y.
" " " " " del a *read* della.
" 95, " 7 (from bottom), *read* (margin) 1849 *instead of* 1595.
" 97, " 9, *for* Cronan *read* Cronau.
" " " 18, " Eleroy *read* Elroy.
" 100, " 22, " Description *read* Descripcion.
" " " " " estaditica *read* estadistica.
" 105, " 8, " Ternaux *read* Ternaux-Compans.
" 113, " 7, " Giglioli (H.H.) *read* Giglioli (E).
" 122, " 6, *for* Jarma *read* Tarma.
" 129, " 5 (from bottom), *for* Antiquadades *read* Antigüedades.
" " " 3 " " " Antiguidades " Antigüedades.
" 134, " 14, *for* Boudoin *read* Baudoin.
" 135, " 4 (from bottom), *for* Drognes *read* Drogues.
" 140, " 21, *for* Quichaus *read* Quichuas.
" " " 22, " Montana *read* Montaña.
" 143, " 23, " Acura *read* Acuña.
" 147, " 24, " Meigs (J. A.) *read* (Meigs J. Aitken).
" " " 27, *omit* Meigs (J. Aitken) *and insert* ———-
" 176, " 6, *for* Antiguadades *read* Antigüedades.
" " " 35 to end, *transfer to* Rich (Obadiah).
" 178, lines 6 and 3, (from bottom) *for* Indegenas *read* Indigenas.
" 184, line 2 from end, *for* In Mappe *read* Maps.
" 191, between lines 23 and 24 *insert* (Vol. 17. See Fernandez
Montesinos (E. L. D.) Memoires. Paris. 1840. 8°).
" 193, line 9 (from bottom), *for* Chuquiasca *read* Chuquisaca.
" 197, " 7, *for* Mapotcca *read* Mapoteca.
" 198, " 8 (from bottom), *for* Tourancen *read* Touranien.
" " " 7 " " " anciem *read* anciens.
" 200, " 24 (in margin), *insert* 1892.

BIBLIOGRAPHY.

1578   **ACOSTA** (CHRISTOVAL DE) Tractado de las drogas y medi-
cinas de las Indias Orientales, con sus plantas debuxadas al
vivo por C. A....en el qual se verifica mucho de lo que
escrivo el Dr. Garcia de Orta. *Burgos.* 1578.

1582   —— C. or Coste Aromatum et medicatorum in Orientali
India nascentium liber....C. Chisii opera ex Hispanico sermone Latinus factus in epitomen contractus, etc. 1582. 8°

1619   —— Traicté de Christophe de la Coste des drogues et
des médicament, qui naissent aux Indes, traduit par de
l'Ecluse. Figures. *Lyon.* 1619. 8 .

[Montalvo refers to a speech made by Christoval de
Acosta at the third Council of Lima, 1583.]

1588-9   **ACOSTA** (JOSÉ DE) De Natura Novi Orbis Libri duo et
de Promulgatione Evangelii apud Barbaros. *Salamanca.*
1588-9.

1595   —— (Second edition.) *Salamanca.* 1595.

1596   —— (Another edition.) *Coloniæ Agrippinæ.* 1596. 12°.

1590   —— Historia Natural y Moral de las Indias, en que se
tratan las cosas notables del Cielo, y Elementos, Metales,
Plantas y Animales dellas; y los Ritos, y Ceremonias, Leyes,
y Gobierno y Guerras de los Indios. *Sevilla.* 1590. 4 .

1591   —— (Another edition.) *Barcelona.* 1591. 8°.

1608   —— (Another edition.) *Madrid.* 1608.

1610   —— (Another edition.) *Madrid.* 1610.

1792   —— (Another edition.) 2 vols. *Madrid.* 1792. 4°.

1596   —— Historia naturale e morale della Indie novamente
tradotta....de Giovanni Paolo Gallacio. *Venetia.* 1596.
4 .

1597   ——Histoire naturelle et morale des Indes, tant Orient-alles qu' Occidentalles ; traduites en François par Robert Regnault, Cauxois. *Paris.* 1597. 8 .

1600   ——— (Another edition.) *Paris.* 1600. 8 .

1601   —— (Another edition.) 1601. Fol.

1606   ——— (Another edition.) *Paris.* 1606. 8 .

1616   —— (Another edition.) *Paris.* 1616. 8°.

1598   —— Historie naturall ende morael van de Westorsche Indien....overghent door J. Huyghen van Linschoten. *Enckhuysen.* 1598. 8°.

1727   —— Ontdekking Van West Indien....door J. D'A.... 1592 nyt het Spaans Verladd P. Van de Aa, *etc.* Deil 8. 1727. Fol.

1601   ———(Another edition.) *See* Theodor de Bry. Von Ge-legenheit der Elemente natur de Neuer Welt. J.H. Van Lin-schoten. 1601. Fol.

1602   —— (Another edition.) *See* Theodor de Bry. America nova pars....de novis orbis naturæ Acosta. America. Pars IX. *Francoforti.* 1602. Fol.

1624   ——- (Another edition.) *See* Theodor de Bry. Parali-pomena Americæ, hoe est discursus accurataque Americæ descriptio. America. Pars XII. *Frankforti.* 1624. Fol.

1604   —— The Naturall and Morall Historie of the East and West Indies....written in Spanish....translated into Eng-lish by E. G. (Edward Grimeston). 1604. 4°.

1880 .   —— (Another edition.) Reprinted from the English translated edition of E. Grimeston, 1604, with notes by Clements R. Markham. 2 vols. *London.* 1880. 8°. (Hakluyt Society, Nos. 60 and 61.)

[José de Acosta, one of the best known writers on Ameri-can history, born 1540, at Medina-del-Campo, Old Castille. Entered Society of Jesus, 1553. Taught theology at Ocana; went to Peru, 1571, and remained fifteen years. In Mexico and Antilles two years. Returned to Spain with MSS.; became rector of Salamanca. Died, 1600. Of great learning but not well acquainted with native languages.]

1848   ACOSTA (J.) *Colonel.*   Compendio historico del descubrimiento y colonizacion de la Nueva Granada en el siglo décimo
sexto. *Paris.* 1848.

1860   —— *See* BOLLAERT (D.) Antiquarian .... researches in
New Granada, *etc. London.* 1860. 8 .
(Acosta's work makes use of two unpublished parts of
Pedro Simon's MS.)

1641   ACUNA (EL PADRE CHRISTOVAL DE) Nuevo Descubrimiento
der gran Rio de las Amazonas....al qual fue, y se hizo por
orden de su Magestad, el año de 1639, por la provincia de
Quito en los Reynos del Peru. *Madrid.* 1641. 4°.
(Chaps. XXVI–XLIII describe Indian tribes. Acuna's
party were the first whites to traverse the region mentioned.)

1891   —— (Another edition.) *Madrid.* 1891. 8 .
(Vol. II. Colecion de libros que tratan de America raros y
curiosas.)

1682.   —— Relation de la rivière des Amazons, traduite par
de Gomberville sur l'original Espagnol du P. C. d'A.   Avec
une dissertation sur la rivière des Amazones pour servir de
preface. 4 vols. *Paris.* 1682. 12 .

1698   —— Voyages and Discoveries in South America.   The
first up the River of Amazons to Quito in Peru, and back
again to Brazil, performed at the command of the King of
Spain by C. d'A.   Done into English from the originals.
With Notes and Maps. *London.* 1698. 8 .

1859   —— New Discovery of the great River of the Amazons
....translated (with notes), *etc.*, by C. R. Markham. *London.* 1859. 8 .
(Hakluyt Society, No. 24, "Expeditions, *etc.*")

1729   —— Bericht von dem Strom derer Amazonen, erstlich
in Spanischer sprach herausgegeben von P. C. de Acunna
aus der Gesellschaft Jesu: nachgehends in das Franzosiche
übersetzet, durch Herrn von Gomberville .... Nunmehro
alles in Teutschen an das Leicht gestellet durch einen aus
gemeldter Gesellschaft.
(*See* FERNANDEZ (J. B.) Erbauliche und angenehme Ge-
schichten derer Chiquitos, *etc.* 1729. 8 .)

1733   —— Bericht von dem Strom derer Amazonen, *etc.*
(*Neuer Welt-Bote.* Neurer Welt-Bote, *etc.* 1733. 8'.)

1747   —— Reise auf dem Amazonen flusse. 1637–40.
         (*See* SCHWABE (J. J.) Algemeine Historie der Reisen, *etc.*,
         Bd. 16. 1747. 4°.)

         [EL PADRE CHRISTOVAL DE ACUÑA, bishop of Caracas.
         The *Nuevo Descubrimiento* is an account of an expedition, in
         1639, to see if treasure could be transported from Peru by
         the Amazon. It was suppressed that the Portuguese might
         not know of the navigability of the river to Quito.]

1878   ADAM (LUCIEN) Le Quichua, est il une langue aryenne? 1878.
         (Compte-Rendu du Congrés des Americanistes. Seconde
         session, page 75.)

1890   —— *See* LECLERC (CH.) Arte de la lengua de los Indios
         o Campas. *Paris*. 1890. 8 .

1885   ADAMS (WILLIAM HENRY DAVENPORT) Land of the Incas
         and the City of the Sun: or the story of Francisco Pizarro
         and the Conquest of Peru. Illust. *London*. 1885. 8 .

1809–17   ADELUNG (JOHANN CHRISTOPH). *See* VATER (JOHN S.) Mith-
         ridates, *etc.* Vols. II and III. *Berlin*. 1809-17.

1623   AGUILAR DEL RIO. Memorial que ofreer el lic....al Rey....
         assi en lo que toca al bien espiritual como al temporal de los
         Indios naturales del. *Lima*. 1623. Fol.
         (Valuable for history of Pizarro and the administration of
         the Indians.)

1862   AGUIRRE (LOPE DE). *See* BOLLAERT (WM.) Expedition of
         P. de Ursua and Lope de Aguirre in search of El Dorado
         and Omagua, 1560-61. *London*. 1862. 8°.
         (Hakluyt Society, No. 28.)

         [LOPE DE AGUIRRE, companion of Pedro de Ursua, on his
         expedition down the Amazon in 1560, to discover Eldorado;
         chief of the conspirators who murdered Ursua on January 1,
         1561, near Machiparo, and threw off Spanish allegiance.
         Became sovereign on murder of his companion, Fernando
         de Guzman; reached the ocean by the Orinoco or one of
         the rivers of Guiana. Landed in Venezuela to invade New
         Granada, but defeated and killed by Spanish force under
         Gutierrez de la Peña.]

1807   **ALCEDO** (ANTONIO DE).   Biblioteca Americana.   *Madrid.*
          1807.
          (MS. Jackson (J.) Bibl. géog. No. 613.)

1730?   **ALCEDO Y HERRARA** (DIONYSIO DE).   Memorial informativo,
          que pusieron en les reales manos et tribunal del consulado
          de la Ciudad de los Reyes y la junto general del comercio de
          las provincias del Peru ; sobre differentes puntos tocantes
          al estado de la real hazienda y del comercio, *etc.*   (*Madrid?*
          1730?)   Fol.

1740   ———— Aviso Historico, Politico, Geographico, con....
          Noticias....del Peru, Tierra-Firme, Chile y Nuevo Reyno
          de Granada en la Relacion de los Sucessos, de 205 años, por
          la Chronologia de los Adelantados, Presidentes, Governa-
          dores y Virreyes de aquel Reyno meridional, desde....1535
          hasta....1740, y Razon de todo lo obrada por los Ingleses en
          aquellos reynos....1567 hasta....1739.   *Madrid.*   1740.   4 ·

1741   ———— (Another edition.)   *Madrid.*   (1741.)   8 ·

1762?   ———— Aviso .... continuada hasta .... 1760.   *Madrid.*
          (1762?)   4 ·

1741   ———— Compendio historico de la provincia....de Guaya-
          quil, *etc.*   *Madrid.*   1741.   4 ·

1585   **ALCOBASA** (DIEGO DE).   Confessionario.   *Lima.*   1585.
          (Spanish, Quichua and Aymara.   Very scarce.   Markham.
          Roy. Com. ii, 200 *note.*)

1881   **ALLEN** (FREDERICK H.) Pizarro; or the Discovery and Con-
          quest of Peru.   Edited by F. H. A.   Illustrated.   *Boston.*
          (1881.)   8

1580–81   **ALMENDRAL** (MARTIN DE) and **ALVAREZ DE HOLGUIN** (PEDRO).
          Muy poderoso senor Jorge de Ortega en nombre de doña, *etc.*
          1580–81.
          (MSS. unedited.   Valuable; relates to personal services
          of M. de A. and P. A. de H. during the discovery, *etc.*, of
          Peru.)

1580–1   **ALVAREZ DE HOLGUIN** (PEDRO).   *See* ALMENDRAL (MARTIN DE)
          Muy poderoso, *etc.*   1580–1.

          [ALVAREZ DE HOLGUIN, one of Pizzaro's captains: killed
          Sept. 16, 1542, on defeat of young Almagro by Vaca de
          Castro.]

1874   ANCHORENA (JOSÉ DIONISIO).   Gramatica Quichua o del idioma del Imperio de los Incas. *Lima.* 1874.

——   ANDAGOYA (PASCUAL DE).   Narrative of the proceedings of Pedrarias Davila in Tierra firme or Castilla del Oro, *etc.* (Original MS. in Spanish in Indian Archives, Seville).

1825   —— *See* FERNANDEZ DE NAVARETTE (MARTIN) Colleccion de los Viages. Tom. iii. *Madrid.* 1825, *etc.* 4°.

1865   —— Narrative of the proceedings of Pedrarias Davila in the provinces of Tierra firme or Castilla del Oro, and of the discovery of the South Sea and the coasts of Peru and Nicaragua.   Translated and edited, with notes and an Introduction, by Cl. R. Markham. Map. *London.* 1865. 8°.
(Hakluyt Society.   No. 34.   Contains the earliest notice of Peru.)

1868   —— Pascual de Andagoya, um epysodio da historia patria.   As quatro derradeiras noites dos inconfid. de minas geraes. (1792). *Rio de Janeiro.* 1868.

[PASCUAL DE ANDAGOYA, born in the province of Alava, Spain; went to Darien, 1514; obtained information respecting the empire of the Incas on his expedition to province of *Biru* in 1522; explored further south, but returned to Panama owing to illness and turned the enterprise over to a partnership at Panama composed of Pizarro, Almagro and Luque, for whom he acted as agent until 1536. Died, 1548, at Cuzco.]

1827   ANDREWS (JOSEPH) *Captain.*   Journey from Buenos Ayres through the provinces of Cordova, Tucuman, and Salta to Potosi ; thence by the deserts of Caranja to Arica and subsequently to Santiago de Chile and Coquimbo in the years 1825-26. 2 vols. *London.* 1827. 8 .

1827   —— (Another edition). 2 vols. *London.* 1827. 12 .
(Chap. VI, Vol. 2, Potosi to Arica—describes Indians en route).

1836-7   ANGELIS (DON PEDRO DE).   Coleccion de obras y documentos relativos a la historia....del Rio de la Plata.   6 vols. *Buenos Ayres.* 1836-7. 4 .
(Vol. 5 contains Sentencia pronunciada por el Visitador Don José Antonio de Areche contra Tupac Amaru).

1856   ———— Ensayo de la historia civil del Paraguay, Buenos Ayres y Tucuman. (Edited by Dr. Don Pedro de Angelis.) 2 vols. (Second edition). 1856.

1511   ANGLERIUS (PETRUS MATYR). Legatio Babylonica. *Sevilla.* 1511.

1516   ———— (New edition enlarged). *Aleala.* 1516.

1530   ———— De Orbe nove decades (8). Prefatio Æ Antonii Nebrissensis. *Apud Michaele d'Egine. Compluti.* 1530. Fol.

1533   ———— P. M. ob Angleria de rebus oceanis et orbe nuovo decades tres (IV)....ejusdem legationis Babylonicæ libri tres. *Basilew.* 1533. Fol.

1574   ———— (Another edition). *Coloniæ.* 1574. 8°.

1587   ———— De orbe novo Petri Matyris Anglerii Mediolanensis ....Decades octo....labore et industria Richardi Hakluyti ....*Parisiis.* 1587. 8 .

1532   ———— Extraict on Receuil des Isles nouvellesment trou- vées en le grand mer Oceane....par Pierre Matyr de Millan et depuis translate en language francoys. *Paris.* 1532. ⌐

1537   ———— (Another edition). *Paris.* 1537.

1554   ———— Somario della Historia dell Indie Occidenti cavato della libri scritti da le Sig. Pietro Martire. 1554. Fol.
    See RAMUSIO (G. B.) Primo Volume....delle Navigatione et Viaggi. Vol. 3. 1554.

1563   ———— (Another edition). Vol. 3. 1563. Fol.

1606   ———— (Another edition). Somario cavato della sua his- toria del Nuovo Mondo. 1606. Fol.
    See RAMUSIO (G. B.) Vol. 3. 1606.

1555   ———— The (three) decades of the new worlde, or West India, conteyning the navigations and conquestes of the Spanyardes with the particular description of the most ryche and large landes and Ilandes lately found in the West Ocean pertayning to the inheritance of the kinges of Spayne.... Written in the Latine tounge by Petrus Matyr, of Angleria, and translated into Englysche by R. Eden. (The histories of the Weste Indies, wrytten by Gonzalus Ferdinandus Ovie- dus. A discourse of the marvellous voyage made by the Spanyardes rounde about the worlde, gathered out of a large

booke wrytten hereof by Master A. Pygafetta....)   B. L.
In aedibus Guilhelmi Powell. (End. Rycharde Jug). *London.* 1555. 4 ·

1577   —————— The History of Travayle in the West and East
Indies....Gathered in parte, and done into Englysche by
R. Eden. Newly set in order, augmented and finished by
R. Willes. B. L. R. Jugge. *London.* 1577. 4 ·

1582   —————— (Another edition). Three Decades. *Basle.* 1582.
Fol.

1809   —————— The Historie of the West Indies....Published in
Latin by Mr. Hakluyt, and translated in English by M.
Lok. 1809, *etc.* 4 · *See* HAKLUYT (R.) *Rev.* Collection
of the early voyages, *etc.* Vol. V.

1812   —————— The Historie of the West Indies (The....Decades
of the Ocean) translated by M. Lok. 1812. 4°. *See*
HAKLUYT (R.) *Rev.* A selection of....voyages, *etc.*

[PETRUS MATYR ANGLERIUS, or Peter Matyr d'Anghiera,
born about 1456, a reporter at the Spanish Court. Wrote
many letters, of which about 30 relate to America. Knew
Columbus personally. Began the *Decades,* 1493. Died,
1526.]

1866   ANGRAND (LEONCE) Antiquités Americaines : les Antiquités
de Tiahuanaco et l'origine présumable de la plus ancienne
civilization du Haut Pérou. Plates. *Paris.* 1866. 4 ·

1879   ANONYMOUS. *See* JIMÉNEZ DE LA ESPADA (MARCOS). Tres
relaciones de antigüedades péruanos. Edited by M. J. de la E.
Madrid. 1879. 8 ·

[Markham says the author was evidently a Jesuit who
went to Peru at an early date. Refers to lost works on
Peruvian civilization ; mentions ancient Incas in Montesinos'
lists and explains origin of erroneous statement that human
sacrifices were used.]

1783   ANTONIO (D. NICHOLAS). Bibliotheca Hispana Nova
sive hispaniorum scriptorum qui ab anno M. D. ad
MDCLXXXIV. floruere notitia....Tomus primus. *Madrid.*
1783. Fol.

1893   ANVERS (A. D.)   *See* Du Pouget (J. F. A.) *Marquis de Nadaillac.* Prehistoric America. Trans. by H. D. A., *etc. New York.* 1893. 8´.

1575   APIANUS (PETRUS).   La Cosmographia.   Pt. I.   *See* Lopez de Gomara (Frans.).   El sitio y descripcion de las Indias y Mundo Nuevo.   *Anvers.* 1575. 4´.

1565   APOLLONIUS (LEVINUS).   De Peruviae Regionis inter Novi Orbis provincias celeberrimae, inventione, et rebus in eadem gestis. Map. *Antverpiæ.* 1565. 8´.
          (Divided into five parts: The Expedition of Pizarro and Amalgro into the interior ; Pizarro and Atabila ; Siege of Cuzco ; arrival of Alvarado ; and the mission of Gasca.)

1566   ———— (Another edition).   *Antverpiæ.*   1566. 8

1567   ———— (Another edition).   *Antverpiæ.*   1567. 12´.

1582   ———— De Peruviæ regioni—inventioni et rebus in eadem gestis. *Basle.* 1582. Fol.
          (Third part of a German translation of Benzoni).

          [LEVINUS APOLLONIUS was a native of Ghent. His work embraces the period from the discovery of Peru to the death of Gonzalo Pizarro.]

1864   ARANA (DON DIEGO BARROS).   Colleccion de Historiadores de Chile, edited by D. B. A.   7 vols.   *Santiago.* 1864. *See* Suarez de Figueroa (Don Chris.) Hechos de Don Garcia Hurtado de Mendoza, *etc.*

1873   ———— Proceso de Pedro de Valdivia i otros documentos inéditos concernientes a este conquistador, reunidos i anotados por D. B. A. *Santiago de Chile.* 1873. 8°.
          (Gasca's despatch to the Council, describing the defeat and execution of Gonzalo Pizzaro, *etc.*, dated Cuzco, May 7, 1548, and other despatches of Gasca. Markham describes the document quoted by Prescott as " Relacion del Licenciado Gasca MS." as a mutilated copy of this despatch).

1881   ———— Histoire de la Guerre du Pacifique 1879 80. Maps. 2 vols. *Paris.* 1881. 8´.
          (General Map of Littoral (Pacific) and maps of littoral of Northern Peru and environs of Lima).

          ARIAGA (PABLO JOSÉ DE).   *See* ARRIAGA (PABLO JOSÉ DE).

1849   ARIBAU (B. C.) Biblioteca de autores Españoles. *etc.*, edited by B. C. A. 1849. 8°.

Vol. XXIV. Fernandez de Oviedo y Valdes (Gonz.) Oviedo; de la natural historia de las Indias; Castellanos (Juan de) Elegias de Varones illustres de Indias; Xeres (Fran. de) Verdadera Relacion de la Conquista del Peru.

Vol. XXVI. Zarate (Aug. de) Historia del descubrimiento y conquista del Péru y de los guerras y cosas señdades en ella; Cieza de Leon (Pedro de) La Chronica del Peru.

1883   ARONA (Juan de). (*pseud.* Pedro Paz Soldan y Unanue). Diccionario de Peruanismos (Kechua): ensayo filologico. *Lima.* 1883. 8°.

1884   —— (Another edition). *Buenos Ayres.* 1884. 8°.

1621   ARRIAGA (Pablo José de). Extirpacion de la Idolatrie del Peru. *Lima.* 1621.

[Arriaga was a priest : relates native religious beliefs and practices in minute detail.]

1833   ASPINWALL (Thomas) *Colonel.* Catalogue of Americana. *Paris.* (1833.)

1617   ATIENZA (Blas de). Relacion de los Religiosos. *Lima.* 1617.

[Blas de Atienza, a friar, son of Blas de Atienza, who served under Vasco Nuñez de Balbóa in 1513, and settled at Truxillo. His sister, Inez, accompanied Pedro de Ursua, in 1560, on his expedition in search of El Dorado.]

1592   ATTABALIPPA del Peru (*pseud* Adriano Banchieri) La Nobilta dell' Asino di A. dal Peru....Tradotta in lingua Italiana, *etc.* *Venetia.* 1592. 8°.

1599   —— (Another edition). *Venetia.* 1599. 4°.

1666   —— Quarta impressioni, con nuova aggionta. *Venetia.* 1666. 12°.

1602   AVALOS Y FIGUEROA (Don Diego d'). Primera parte de la miscelaneá austral de Don D. d'A. y F. en varias coloquias, intercolutores Delia y Cilena, con la defensa de Damas. *Lima.* 1602.

(Quichua language, Physical Geography of Peru, *etc*).

1852   AVECELLA (Pablo Alonso de la).   La conquesta del Péru. Novela historica original.   Vign.   *Paris.*   1852.   8'.

1853   ——— (Another edition).   *Caracas.*   1853.   8'.

1648   AVENDAÑO (Hernando de).   Sermones de los ministerios de nuestra Santa Fé catolica, en lengua Castellana, y la general del Inca.   Impugnanse los errores particulares que los Indios han tenido.   1648.

———   ——— Relacion de las Idolatrias de los Indios.   (MS.)

[Hernando de Avendaño, priest: wrote sermons in Quichua].

1646-8   AVILA (Francisco de) *of Cuzco.*   Tratado de los evangelios ....y general de los Indios deste reyno del Peru, y....se refutan los errores de la gentilidad de dichos Indios. (Tomo segundo....obra postuma del Dr. Don F. Davila).   2 vols. *Lima.*   1646-8.   Fol.

1873   ——— A narrative of the errors, false gods, and other superstitious and diabolical rites in which the Indians of the province of Huarochiri lived in ancient times.   Translated and edited by Cl. R. Markham.   *London.*   1873.   8°.
(Hakluyt Society, No. 48.   Narrative of the Rites and Laws of the Incas, pages 123–151).

[Francisco de Avila, priest in the province of Huaro-chiri.   Wrote in 1608.   His *Relacion* taken down in Quichua from the mouths of the natives.   Very valuable, but probably does not relate to the Juncos.   Thirty-one chapters of de Avila's work still untranslated or unpublished.]

1604   AYMARA.   Catecisme en lengua Española y Aymara.   1604.   8'.

——— *See* Quichua y Aymara.

1869   BACKER (Augustin de).   Bibliothèque des écrivains de la compagnie de Jésus ou notices bibliographiques....Nouvelle 'édition....Tome premier.   A. G.   *Liege.*   1869.   Fol.

1573   BACQUERE (R. de).   *See* Peru.   De Wonderlycke ende warachitige Historie vaut Coninskrüch va Peru, *etc.*   (Trans- lated from the Spanish by R. de B.)   *Thantwerpen.*   1573.   4'.

1826   **BALBI** (ADRIEN).   Atlas ethnographique du Globe, ou classification des peuples anciens et modernes d'après leurs
langues. *Paris.* 1826. Fol.
(Langue de la region Peruvienne, Table XXVII, and
Table XLI for brief list of words.)

——   **BALBOA** (MIQUEL CAVELLO).   Miscellanea Austral. *MS.*
(Part III relates to Peru.and was translated by M. Ternaux-Compans.)

1840   —— Histoire du Pérou (inédite). *Paris.* 1840. 8ʹ.
See TERNAUX-COMPANS (H.), Voyages de l'Amerique, Vol.
XV.

[MIQUEL CAVELLO BALBOA, first soldier, then priest; settled
at Quito, 1566; began MS. 1576, finished at Quito, 1586.
Gives Christoval de Molina as his authority for early Inca
traditions, *etc.* Account of origin of coast people; detailed
narrative of war between Huasca and Atahualpa.]

1872   **BALDWIN** (JOHN D.).   Ancient America in Notes on American Archæology.   Illustrations. *New York.* 1872. 12ʹ.
(Peru, Chap. X, pages 222–276.)

1887   **BALL** (JOHN).   Notes of a Naturalist in South America.
Map. *London.* 1887. 12ʹ.

1685.   **BALLESTEROS** (DON THOMAS DE).   Tomo primera de las
Ordenanzas del Peru....recogidas y·coordenadas por Don
Francisco de Toledo recogidas por el Lic. Don T. de B.
Lima. 1685. Fol.

1752   —— (Another edition.)...,Y Nuevamente añadidas las
Ordenanzas que para el Nuevo Establecimiento del Tribunal
de la Sta. Cruzada..... *Lima.* 1752. Fol.

1892   **BALLOU** (MATURIN M.).   Equatorial America.   Descriptive
of a visit to ....the principal capitals of South America.
Boston and New York. 1892. 8ʹ.
(Peru, pages 334–371.)

1882   **BANCROFT** (HERBERT HOWE).   History of the Pacific States
of North America.   Central America, 3 vols. *San Francisco.* 1882, *etc.* 8ʹ.
(Administration of the Indies. Vol. I, Chap. 5; Peru,
Vol. II, Chap. 7; Mines, Vol. III, Chap. 3 (Mexico)).

1749   **BARCIA** (D. ANDRES GONZALEZ DE).   Historiadores primitivos de las Indias occidentales, que juntò, traduxo en parte,
y sacò a luz, ilustrados con eruditas Notas y copiosos
Indices. 3 vols. *Madrid.* 1749. Fol.
(In Vol. I, Relacion Sumaria de la Historia natural de las
Indias, by Gonzalo Fernandez de Oviedo; in Vol. II, Historia
de las Indias, by F. Lopez de Gomara; in Vol. III, Descubrimiento del Peru, by Augustin de Zarate, and Conquista
del Peru, by Francisco de Xeres.)

1726-30   ——— *See* HERRERA TORDESILLAS (ANT. DE), Historia General de los hechos de los Castellanos, *etc.* Second edition,
with notes by A. G. B. 8 vols. *Madrid.* 1726-30. Fol.

1723   ——— *See* LASSO DE LA VEGA (GARCIA), Segunda impression....la vida de Xuli Cusi Titu Jupanqui, *etc.* Edited by
A. G. de B. *Madrid.* 1723. Fol.

1622   **BARLAEO** (G.). *See* HERRERA TORDESILLAS (ANT. DE), Novis
orbis....metaphraste G. Barlæo, *etc.* *Amsterdam.* 1622. Fol.

1868   **BARRANCA** (JOSÉ S.). Ollanta o sece la severidad de un
padre y la clemencia de un rey. Drama traducido del
Quichua al Castellano. *Lima.* 1868.

1751   **BARRERE, BOUGUER** und **DE LA CONDAMINE**. Neue Reisen
nach Guiana, Peru und durch das Südl. America. Maps and
plates. *Goettingen.* 1751.

1862-4   **BARROS ARANA** (DIEGO). Biblioteca Americana. Collection d'ouvrages inédits ou rares sur l'Amerique. (Edited by
D. B. A.) 2 pts. (all pub.). *Leipzig* (printed). *Paris.*
1862-4. 18 ·

1865   ——— Compendio de Historia de America. *Santiago.*
1865. 8°.
(Pt. I., chap. 3, El Peru antiquo. Pt. II., chaps. 14, 15,
16, Conquista del Peru.)

1826   **BARRY** (DON DAVID). *See* ULLOA (J. J. and ANT. DE).
Noticias secretas de America, *etc.* Sacadas a luz por Don
D. B. 2 vols. 1826. Fol.

BARTLETT (JOHN RUSSELL). *See* BROWN (JOHN CARTER).

1884   **BASADRE** (MODESTO). Riquezas Peruanas, Colleccion de
Articulos Descriptivos, escritos para "La Tribuna," por
Modesto Basadre. *Lima.* 1884. 12 ·

1873   BASTIAN (ADOLF). Geographische und ethnologische Bilder (aus Peru, *etc.*). *Jena.* 1873. 8°.

1878-89   —————— Die Culturlander des alten America. 3 vols. Maps and plates. *Berlin.* 1878-89. 4°.
(Vol. I, Aus Religion und Sitte des alten Peru. Vol. II, Gesehichte der Inca in Peru. Vol. III, Ethnologische Museum.)

1891   —————— Kulturhistorische und sprachliche Beiträge zur Kenntniss des alten Peru. *Wien* (Vienna). Akad. 1891.

1863   BATES (HENRY WALTER). The Naturalist on the River Amazons, a record of adventure, habits of animals, sketches of Brazilian and Indian life....during eleven years of travel. 2 vols. *London.* 1863. 8.

1873   (Third edition.) *London.* 1873. 8°.

1874   —————— Central America, the West Indies, and South America. Edited and extended by H. W. B., with Ethnological Appendix by A. H. Keane, M. A. I. Maps and illustrations. *London.* 1874. 8°.
(Part of STANFORD'S Compendium of Geography and Travel.)

1882   —————— (Second and revised edition.) *London.* 1882. 8.

1885   —————— (New edition.) *London.* 1885. 8°.
(Chaps. III and XV, Peru.)

1632   BAUDOIN (J.). *See* LASSO DE LA VEGA (GARCIA), Le Commentaire Royal, *etc.*, translated by J. B. *Paris.* 1632. 4.

1650, *etc.*   —————— (Numerous subsequent editions.) *Paris* and *Amsterdam.* 1650, *etc.*

1865   BAXLEY (H. WILLIS). What I Saw on the West Coast of South and North America and at the Hawaiian Islands. *New York.* 1865. 8°.

1808   BEAUCHAMP (ALPHONSE DE). Histoire de la Conquête et des Révolutions du Pérou. 2 vols. *Paris.* 1808. 8°.
(Portraits of Pizarro, Manco Inca.)

1835   —————— (Another edition. 2 vols. *Paris.* 1835. 8°.

1534   BENEDETTO (——————). Libro di Benedetto. *Venice.* 1534.
(Contains Italian version of Pizarro's letter announcing capture of Atahualpa.)

1565   BENZONI (GIROLAMO).   La Historia del Mondo Nuovo, laqual tratta dell' Isoli, et Mari nuovamente ritrovati, et delle nuove Città di lui proprio vedute, per acqua et per terra in quattordeci anni.   Woodcuts.   *Venetia.*   1565.   12°.

1572   ———— La Historia, *etc.*   Nuovamente ristampata, et illus- trata con la giunta d'alcune cose notabile dell' Isole di Canaria.   (Portrait.)   *Venetia.*   1572.   8°.

1578   ———— Novae novi orbis historiæ primum ab H. B. Italico sermone conscriptæ, nunc in Latinum translatæ (by U. Chauveton).   (*Geneva.*)   1578.   8°.

1578   ———— Occidentalis hactenus gestarum .... libri tres, Urbani Calvetonis opera industriaque.... Latini facti.... adjuncta est De Gallorum in Floridam expeditione... Brevis Historia.   (*Genevæ.*)   1578.   12 .

1581   ———— (Second edition.)   (*Geneva.*)   1581.   8 .

1586   ————(Third edition.)   Historiæ Indiæ occidentalis, tomis duobus comprehensa, *etc.*   2 vols.   (*Geneva.*)   1586.   8°.

1586   Historia Indiæ Occidentalis.... Hieronymo Benzone Italo, and Joanne Lerio Burgundo, testibus oculatis, autoribus ....in latinum sermonem Urbani Calvetonis and G. M. studio conversi.   (*Genevæ.*)   1586.   12°.
        (This is a reissue of the second edition (1581), with a new title.)

1590   ———— (Another edition.)   1590.

1594   ———— (Another edition.)   Historia de referta primum occidentali Indiæ a C. Columbo anno 1592.   *Frankfort.*   1594.   Fol.
        (Chauveton's translation.   De Bry, pt. IV.)

1594   ———— (Another edition.)   *Frankfort.*   1594.   Fol.
        (De Bry's America, pt. IV.   2d ed.)

1598   ———— (Another edition.)   *Geneva.*   1598.

1600   ———— (Another edition.)   Novæ novi orbis historiæ.... libri tres.   (*Geneva.*)   1600.   8 .

1612   ———— Novæ novi orbis historiæ primam ab A. H. Italico sermone conscriptæ, nunc in Latinum translatæ liber primus (—tertius).   (*Geneva.*)   1612.   8 .

1648   ———— (Another edition.)   *Hamburgh.*   1648.

1579   ———— Historie nouvelle du Nouveau Monde, contenant
en somme ce que les Hespagnols ont fait jusqu'à présént
aux Indes Occidentales, et le rude traitement qu ils font à ces
poures peuples-lá.   Extraite de l'Italien de M. Hierosme
Benzoni Milanois, qui ha voyage XIV ans en ces pays-la:
et enrichie de plusieurs Discours et choses dignes de mémoire.   Par M. Urbain Chauveton.   Ensemble, une petite
Histoire, *etc.*   (*Genève.*)   1579.   8 .

1589   ———— (Another edition.)   1589.

1579   ———— Der Neuern Weldt und Indianischen Königreichs
newe und wahrhaffte History....aus dem Latein in das
Teusch gebracht durch N. Höniger, *etc. Basel.* 1579.   Fol.

1582-3   ———— (Another edition.)   *Basel.*   1582-3.   Fol.
(*See* APOLLONIUS (LEVINUS) De Peruviæ regioni, *etc.   Basle.*
1582.)

1594   ———— Neuere und gründliche Historien von dem Nider-
gängischen Indien, *etc.*, in das Teusch gebracht durch N.
Höniger.   1594.   Fol.

1591   ———— Nova Novi Orbis Historiæ, Das ist. Aller Gesch-
ichten, so in der Newen Welt....wahrhaffter gründlicher
Bericht.   Deszgleichen .... Durch Abeln Scherdigern....
ins Deudsch gebracht, Anno 1589. *Helmstadt.* 1591.   4°.

1613   ———— Historia de referta primum occidentali India à C.
C.   1613.   Fol.
(De Bry, America, pt. IV. *German.* 2d ed.   Americæ
pars quartæ.)

1631   ———— Newe Wredt.   1631.   Fol.   (De Bry, America, pt.
XIX. *German.*)

1610   ———— De historiæ van de nieuwe weerelt, te weten de
beschryvinghe van West Indien, *etc. Haarlem.*   1610.   8°.

1663   (Another edition.)   Beschryvinghe van West Indien, *etc.*
Amsterdam.   1663.
(East Indian Voyages.   Dell. I.)

1707   ———— Scherps-togt na West Indien en het jaar 1541, *etc.*
1707, *etc.*   8°.
(P. Vander Aa, Naaukeurige versameling der Zee en
Land Reysen, *etc.*   Vol. 51.)

1727   ———— (Another edition.)   1727.   Fol.   (P. Vender Aa.
De Aanverkruswaardigste, *etc.*   Deel 7.)

1625 —— Briefe extracts translated out of Jeroni Benzos three bookes of the new world, touching the Spaniards cruell handling of the Indians and the effects thereof. *London.* 1625. Fol.

(Purchas his Pilgrim. ' Pt. 4.)

1857 —— History of the New World by G. B., showing his travels in America. 1541–56. Translated by Admiral Wm. H. Smyth. Facsimiles of old wood cuts. *London.* 1857. 8°.

(Hakluyt Soc. Pub. No. 22.)

[Girolamo Benzoni, an Italian, born about 1519. Traveled in Spanish America, 1541–1556. Not scholarly, and deals in gossip, but confirms Las Casas. Illustrations from his own drawings.]

1875 Ber (Th.) Les Indiens du Perou. *Paris and Nancy.* 1875. (Compte-Rendu de Congres des Americanistes. Vol. I, pages 449–462.)

1890 —— Ruines de Tiahuanaco. *Paris.* 1890. 8 . (Compte-Rendu de Congres de Americanistes. Eighth session, pages 533–534.)

1843 Berghaus (Dr. Heinrich Carl Wilhelm). Grundriss der Geographie....enhaltend die mathematische und physikalische Geographie, die allgemein Länder—und Völker —so wie die Staatenkunde; erläuter durch....Figuren.... Karten, *etc. Breslau.* 1843. 8°.

1845-7 —— Die Völker des Erdballs nach ihrer Abstammung und Verwandtschaft, und ihren Eigenthümlichkeiten in Regierungsform, Religion, Sitte und Tracht. 2 Bde. *Brüssel und Leipzig.* 1845-7. 8 .

1845-8 —— Dr. H. B., physikalischer Atlas, oder Sammlung von Karten auf denen die hauptsächlichsten Erscheinungen der anorganischen und organischen Natur nach der geographischen Verbreitung und Vertheilung bildlich dargestellt sind. 2 Bd. *Gotha.* 1845–8. Fol.

1848 —— Die Baudenkmäler aller Völker der Erde....Nach der zweiten Ausgabe von E. Briton's....Monumens de tous les peuples, herausgegeben von H. B. (1848), *etc.* 8°.

1850   —— Grundlinien der Ethnographie.   Enthaltend...eine allgemeine Völkertafel oder Nachweisung aller Völker des Erdbodens, *etc.*   *Stuttgart.*   1850.   8°.

BERSABITA (F.)   *See* CASTELLANI (G.)

1603   BERTONIO (P. LUDOVICO).   Arte breve de la lengua Aymara para introduction del arte grande de la misma lengua.   *Roma.* 1603.   8°.

1603   —— Arte y Grammatica muy copiosa de la lengua Aymara.   *Roma.*   1603.   12°.

1603   --——— (Same title.)   *Rome.*   1603.   8°.

1608   —— (Another edition.)   Arte y Grammatica copiosa de la lengua Aymara.   *Roma.*   1608.
(Nueva edicion, aumentada.)

1612   ——— (Another edition.)   Arte de la lengua Aymara, con una silva de frases, y su declaracion en Romance.   *Chucuyto.* 1612.   8°.

1879   ——— (Another edition.)   Publ. de nuevo por J. Platzmann.   Edicion facsimilar.   *Leipzig.*   1879.   8°.

1612   ——— Vocabularia de la lengua Aymara.   Primera parte. Donde por abecedario se ponen en primar lugar los vocables de langue Espanol para buscar los....la lengua Aymara compresto por el PL. B.   *Chucuito.*   1612.   4°.

1612   —— Vocabulario de la Lengua Aymara.   Spanish-Aymara and Aymara-Spanish.   2 Pts.   *Chucuito.*   1612.   8°.

1879   —— (Another edition.)   Publ. de nuevo por J. Platzmann.   Edicion facsimilar.   2 vols.   *Leipzig.*   1879.   8°.

1612   —— Libro de la vida y milagros de nuestro Señor Jesu Christo en dos lenguas Aymara y romance.   *Chucuyto.*   1612.

1612   —— Confessionario muy copioso en dos linguas Aymara y Españolo, con una instrucion acerca de las Siete Sacrementos de la Sancta Yglesia, *etc.*   *Chucuyto.*   1612.   8

1760   ——— Historia de los cuatra Evangelios en lengua Aymara, con varias refleciones....Sacada de un libro antiqua, que avra 160 as. dis à luz el P. L. B....Por el P. Francisco Mercier y Guzman.   1760.   8°.

[Ludovico Bertonio, an Italian and Jesuit, born near Ancona about 1551. Went to Peru, 1581. Many years at Juli, near Lake Titicaca, where studied Aymara. Died at Lima, 1625, aged 73.]

1885   Bertrand (Alejandro). Memoria sobre las Cordilleras del Desierto de Atacama i regiones limitrofes....por A. B. Maps and illustrations. *Santiago*. 1885. 4°.

1808   Bertuch (Von F. J.) Peru nach seinem gegenwärtigen Zustande dargestellt aus dem Mercurio Peruano von Skinner. Nach dem Englischen von Weyland und Er. A. Schmidt. Herausgegeben von F. J. Bertuch. 2 Maps. 2 vols. *Weimar*. 1808. 8°.
(Vol. I, translated from "Present State of Peru," by Joseph Skinner (*see*) and Vol II from the *Mercurio Peruano*).

1744   Betagh (William). Observations on the country of Peru and its inhabitants during his captivity. *London*. 1744. Fol. *See* Harris (J.) *D. D.* Navigantium atque Itinerantium Bibliotheca, *etc* Vol I.

1813   ——— (Another edition). *London*. 1813. 4. *See* Pinkerton (John) Voyages and Travels. Vol. XIX. Pages 1-29.

1880   Betanzos (Juan José de). Suma y narracion de los Incas que los Indios llamaron Capaccuna, que fueron señores de la ciudad del Cuzco y de todo lo é ella subjeto. *Madrid*. 1880. 8°. *See* Cieza de Leon (Pedro de) Segunda parte de la Cronica del Peru, sequida de la suma, *etc.*, por J. de B., la publico Jiménez de la Espada.

[Juan José de Betanzos, a soldier of the Conquest; married a daughter of the Inca Atahualpa; became a citizen of Cuzco and official interpreter to the Royal Audience and Viceroys. His *Suma y Narracion*, written by order of Viceroy Don Antonio de Mendoza; finished 1551. Only part of the MS., as referred to by Gregoria Garcia, is preserved. Comes next to Cieza de Leon as an authority].

1847   Bethune (C. R.) *Captain*. *See* Hawkins (Sir Richard). Observations on his Voyage into the South Sea, *etc*. Edited by Cap. C. R. B. *London*. 1847. 8°.

1862-4   BIBLIOTHECA AMERICANA.   Collection d'ouvrages inédites
ou rares sur l'Amérique.   3 vols.   *Paris*.   1862-4.
(I. Puren Indomito.   Poema p. F. Alvarez de Toledo.
Publ. p. D. B. Arana.   II. Voyages dans le Nord du Brésil.
1613-14.   p. Yves d'Evreux, publ. p. Denis.   III. Memoire
s. les moeurs, coustumes et religion des sauvages de l'Amérique Sept. p. N. Perrot, publ. p. Tailhan.)

1847-50   BIBLIOTECA DE AUTORES ESPANOLES.   *Madrid*.   1847-50.   *See*
CASTELLANOS (JUAN DE) Elegias de Varones illustres de
Indias;   FERNANDEZ   DE   OVIEDO   Y   VALDES   (GONZALO).
Oviedo: de la natural historia de las Indias; CIEZA DE LEON
(PEDRO DE) La Chronica del Peru.

1521   BIBLIOTECA COLOMBINA.   Early voyage to Peruvian coast.
Italian tract.   1521.
(Tract known only in German version.   *Winsor*.)

1876-82   BIBLIOTECA HISPANO-ULKAMARINA.   6 vols. *Madrid*.   1876-82.
8°.
(*Pedro Fernandéz de Quiros*, Historia del descubrimiento
de las regiones Austriales, publ. p. J. Zaragoza.   3 vols.
Cieza de Leon, Tercero libro de las guerras civiles de Peru
en cual se llama la guerra de Quito, publ. p. Marcos Jiménez de la Espada, 1877.   *Idem*, Segunda parte de la cronica del Peru que trata del señorio de los Incas Yupanquis.
1880.   *Guerra piraticas* de Filipinas, contra Mindanaos y
Joloanos, correg. p. Vincente Barrantes).

1873   BIBLIOTHECA PERUVIANA.   *London*.   1873.   (*See* Soldari, M.
P. and M. F.)

— ---   BIBLIOTHEQUE LINQUISTIQUE AMERICAINE.   7 vols.   *Paris*.

1883   BIRKEDAL (HOLGER).   Chile, Bolivia, Peru.   *San Francisco*.
1883.   8°.
(*Overland Monthly*, Vol. III, S. S., pages 627-636.)

1884   —— - Peru, Bolivia, and Chile.   *San Francisco*. 1884. 8 ·
(*Overland Monthly*, Vol. IV, S. S., pages 76, 177, 319, 411.)

(16- .)   BLAEN (W.).   Peru.   *Amsterdam*.   (16—.)
See MAPS.   PERU.

1862   BLAKE (CHARLES CARTER).   On the cranial characters of the
Peruvian races of man.   *London*.   1862.   8°.
(Trans. Ethnological Society, N. S. ii.)

1863   ————— Cranial characters of the Peruvian races of men. *London.* 1863. 8°.
(Journal of the Anthropological Institute of G. B. and Ir., Vol. II, pages 216–231.)

1878   BLAKE (JOHN H.). Notes on a collection from the ancient cemetery at the bay of Chacota, Peru. *Cambridge.* 1878. 8 .
(Report: Peabody Museum, 1878, pages 277–305.)

1751   BLANCHARDERIE (ABBÉ COURTE DE LA). Nouveau Voyage fait au Pérou (by Alonzo Carillo Lazo in 1745–49). Illus. *Paris.* 1751. 16°.

1753   ————— A Voyage to Peru; performed by the Conde of St. Malo in the years 1745....1749. Written by the chaplain (Abbé C. de la B.), to which is added an appendix containing the present state of Spanish affairs in America, in respect to mines, trade, etc. *London.* 1753. 16°.

————   BLAS VALERA. (Religion, Language, Institutions, and Chronology of the Incas.)
(Fragments preserved in Garcia Lasso de la Vega's *Commentaries.* Two fragments of Inca poetry and sayings of Inca sovereigns.)

[BLAS VALERA, son of one of the Conquerors, by Inca woman; born at Chachapoyas, 1551. As Jesuit missionary, acquired at first hand much information on native history and institutions. Wrote in Latin. Took MS. to Spain: much of it burned on capture of Cadiz by English, 1596. De la Vega preserved the rest and used it for his Commentaries.]

1853   BLOOD (REV. W.) A mission to the Indians of Orialla, South America. Portrait and plates. *London.* (1853.) 8 .

1631   BOCANEGRA (el BACH. IVAN PEREZ). Ritual, Formulario e Institucion de Curas, para Administrar a los Naturales de este Reyno, los Santos Sacramentos....con advertencias muy necessarias. *Lima.* (Spanish and Quichua.) 1631. 4

1831   BOLLAERT (WILLIAM). Peruvian Drugs. *London.* 1831.
(Paper read at the Medico-Botanical Society of London, 1831; referred to by C. R. Markham, "Royal Commentaries" (Part First), Vol. I., page 185, *note*, where list of drugs from wallet of native itinerant doctor given.)

1841   ———— Observations on the Geography of Southern Peru, including survey of the province of Jarapaca and route to Chile by the coast of the desert of Atacama.   *London.* 1841.   8 .
(Journal of the Roy. Geographical Society, 1841, pages 99 130.)

1853   ———— The pre-Incarial ruins of Tiahuanaco, in Bolivia, formerly Upper Peru.   Illus.   *London.*   1853.   8 .
(The Intellectual Observer.   Vol. III., pages 229-237.)

1854   ———— Observations on the History of the Incas of Peru, on the Indians of South America, and on some Indian remains in the province of Tarapaca.   *London.*   1854.   8´.
(Journal of the Ethnological Society.   Vol. III., pages 132-164.)

1860   ———Antiquarian, Ethnological, and other Researches in New Granada, Peru, and Chile; with observations on the Pre-Incarial, Incarial, and other monuments of Peruvian nations.   Plates.   *London.*   1860.   8°.
(Contains a translation of *Compendio historico del descubrimiento....de la Nueva Granada,* by Col. Jos. Acosta.)

1862   ———— Expedition of P. de Ursua and Lope de Aguirre in search of El Dorado and Omagua, 1560-61.   Map.   *London.* 1862.   8 .
(Hakluyt Society's Public.   No. XXVIII.)

1862   ———— On the Idol Human Head of the Jívara Indians of Ecuador.   *London.*   (18th Feb., 1862.)   8´.
(Trans. Ethnolog. Soc.   N. S. Vol. II., pages 112-15.)

1862   ———— Some observations on the Jívaros (Jíbero, Jívira) from Antiquarian, Ethnological, and other Researches in New Granada, Ecuador, Peru, and Chile, *etc.   London.* (18th February, 1862.)   8 .
(Trans. Ethnological Society, N. S.   Vol. II., pages 115-18.)

1863   ——— Antonio Raimondy on the Indian Tribes of the Great District of Loreto in Northern Peru.   Transl. from the Spanish by W. B.   *London.*   1863.   8 .
(Anthrop. Rev.   Vol. I., pages 33-43.)

1863   ———— Observations on the Past and Present Population of the New World.   *London.*   (12th May, 1863.)   8´.
(Memoirs Anthrop. Society.   Vol. I., pages 72-119.)

1864 ———— Introduction into the Palæography of America ; or Observations on Ancient Picture and Figurative Writing in the New World; on the Fictitious Writing in North America; on the Quipu of the Peruvians, and Examinations of spurious quipus. *London.* (3d May, 1864.) 8 .
(Mem. Anthrop. Society.   Vol. I., pages 169-194.)

1864 ———— Some account of the Astronomy of the Red Man of the New World, including . . . . the Stone Lunar Calendars of the Chibchas of Bogotá, and probable use of the Gnomon there ; the recently discovered Gold Calendar of the Peruvians and Telescope Tube ; their Gnomons, *etc.   London.* (15th November, 1864.) 8 .
(Mem. Anthrop. Society.   Vol. I., pages 210-280.)

1865 ———— W. R.'s Researches from 1823 to 1865, principally on South American subjects. (*London.*   1865.) 8 .
(A list of various memoirs and articles by W. R.)

1866 ———— Contributions to an Introduction to the Anthropology of the New World. *London.* (7th April, 1866.) 8 .
(Mem. Anth. Soc.   Vol. II.,   pages 92–152 ; Anthrop. Review.   Vol. IV.. Jol. Anthr. Soc. pages clxxi–xxv.)

1866 ———— On the ancient or fossil pottery found on the shores of Ecuador. *London.* (1866.) 8 .
(Mem. Anth. Soc.   Vol. III., pages 163-66.)

1866 ———— On ancient Peruvian Hieroglyphics, including the recently discovered figurated writing. *London.* (17th April, 1866.)
(Anthropological Review.   Vol. IV., page 407.)

1870 ———— On Ancient Peruvian Graphic Records. *London.* 1870. 8 .
(Mem. Anthrop. Soc.   Vol. III., pages 351–58.)

1874 ———— Sur les Signes graphiques des anciens Péruvians. *Paris.* 1874. 8 .
(Archives de la Soc. Amér. de France, N. S. Vol. I.)

1775 BOLTON (   ).   *See* D'ANVILLE.   Map of South America. 1775.

1854 BONELLI (L. HUGH DE).   Travels in Bolivia, with a Tour across the Pampas to Buenos Ayres, *etc.*   2 vols. *London* 1854. 8 .

1818   **BONNYCASTLE** (RICHARD HENRY) Spanish America ; or a Descriptive, Historical and Geological Account of the Dominions of Spain in the Western Hemisphere, Continental and Insular. 2 vols. Maps. *London.* 1818. 8°.
(Peru. Vol. II., pages 75–155.)

1809   **BONPLAND** (AIMÉ). *See* HUMBOLDT, F. H. A. VON. Voyages aux règions equinoxiales du Nouveau Continent.... 1799–1804. 14 vols. 1805-34. 4 and fol. (Plantes equinoxiales (regidé par A. B.) 2 vols. 1809).

1888   **BORSARI** (   ) La Classification chronologique des monuments architectonique de l'ancien Pérou. *Berlin.* 1888. 8 . (Title only.)
(Compte Rendu de Congres internat. des Americanistes. *Berlin*, 1888, page 753.)

1808   **BOUCHER DE LA RICHARDERIE.** Bibliothique universelle des Voyages, ou notice complète et raisonnée de tous les Voyages anciens et modernes, *etc.* 6 vols. *Paris.* 1808. 8 .
(5th Part. Critical List of Voyages to America.)

1749   **BOUGUER** (PIERRE). La Figure de la Terre, déterminée par les observations faites au Pérou. Plates. *Paris.* 1749. 4 .
(Académie Royale des Sciences, Paris. La Figure de la Terre, *etc.* 1749.)

1813   ———— An abridged relation of a voyage to Peru.... to measure the degree of the meridian near the equator, whereby to infer the figure of the earth. *London.* 1813. 4°.
See PINKERTON (JOHN). Voyages and Travels. Vol. XIV., pages 270–312.

1860   **BOWEN** (C. C.). Visit to Peru. *See* GALTON (F.). Vacation Tourist. Vol. I. 1860.

1820   **BRACKENRIDGE** (H. M.). Voyage to South America, performed by order of the American government in the years 1817 and 1818 in the Frigate Congress. 2 vols. *London.* 1820. 8 .
(Introd. Vol. I. Marriage of Spaniards with natives of Peru; Vol. II, chap. 2, refers largely to natives of Peru.)

1828   **BRAND** (CHARLES) *Lieut. R. N.* Journal of a Voyage to Peru; a passage across the Cordillera of the Andes on foot in the snow, in the winter of 1827, and a Journey across the Pampas. Plates. *London.* 1828. 8 .

1868   **BRASSEUR DE BOURBOURG** (L'ABBÉ). Manuscrit Troano. Études sur le système graphique et la langue des Mayas. 2 Tom. 1868, *etc.* (*Paris.*) +.
(Tom. I. p. 18, Quipu).

1573   **BRAUN** (GEORGIUS) and **HAGENBURG** (FRANZ). Civitatis Orbis Terrarum. *Coloniæ Agrippinæ.* 1573. Fol. (Map of Cuzco).

1582   ———— (Another edition.) *Coloniæ Agrippinæ.* 1582.

1618   ———— (Another edition.) Colored Plates. 1618.

1885   **BREHM** (R. B.). Das Inka-Reich. Beiträge zur Staats- und Sittengeschichte des Kaiserthums Tahuantinsuyu. Map and cuts. *Jena.* 1885. 8.

1890   ———— (Second edition.) Das Inka-Reich. Beiträge, *etc.* Nach d. ältesten span. Quellen bearb. *Jena.* 1890. 8.

1882   **BRINTON** (DANIEL GARRISON) *M. D.* American Hero-Myths. A study in the native religions of the Western Continent. *Philadelphia.* 1882. 8.
(Chaps. I, Introductory. II, Algonkins and Iroquois. III, Aztec Tribes. IV, Mayas. V, Qquichuas. VI, Conclusion.)

1883   ———— Aboriginal American authors and their productions, especially those in the native languages. *Philadelphia.* 1883.

1890   ———— Races and Peoples: Lectures on the Science of Ethnography. *New York.* 1890. 8°.
(Qquichuas, pages 272-5.)

1891   ———— The American Race: a linguistic classification and ethnographic description of the native tribes of North and South America. *New York.* 1891. 8°.
(The Peruvian Region, pages 202–28.)

1854–75   **BRITISH MUSEUM LIBRARY.** Index to Manuscripts, 1854–75. (P. 31, Spanish MSS. on America.)

1859, *etc.*   ———— *See* STEVENS (HENRY). Catalogues of American books, maps, *etc.*, in the B. M. L. *London.* 1859, *etc.*

1848   **BRITON** (E.). Monumens de tous les peuples. *See* BERG-HAUS (DR. H.). Die Baudenkmäler aller Völker der Erde.... nach der zweiten Ausgabe von E. B.'s....Monumens, *etc.* (1848.) 8.

1700, *etc.* **BROE** (DE). *Seigneur de Citry et de la Guëtte. See* ZARATE
(AUG. DE). Histoire de la déconverte et de la conquête du
Pérou. Tr. ad. par S. D. C. (de B. S. de Citry.) *Amster-
dam and Paris.* 1700, *etc.* 8°.

1865-71 **BROWN** (JOHN CARTER). Bibliotheca Americana: A catalogue of books relating to North and South America in the
library of J. C. B. of Providence, with Notes by John Russell Bartlett. 3 vols. 1865-71.
   (Vol. I, 1493-1600 (1865); Vol. II, 1601-1700 (1866);
Vol. III, 1701-1800. (2 pts., 1870-71.)

1875 ———— Enlarged edition of Vol. I. (1482-1600.) 1875.

1882 ———— Enlarged edition of Vol. II. (1601-1700.) 1882.

1873-6 **BROWN** (ROBERT). The Races of Mankind; being a popular description of the characteristics, manners and varie-
ties of the human family. 4 vols. Illustrated. *London.*
1873-6. 4°.
   (The Peruvians, Vol. II. pages 313-320.)

1881 ———— (Another edition.) The Peoples of the World.
4 vols. *London.* 1881, *etc.* 8°.

1887 **BRÜHL** (GUSTAV). Die Culturvölker Alt-Americas. *Cin-
cinnati.* 1887. 8°.

1808-15 **BRUUN** (MALTHE CONRAD). Annales des Voyages, *etc.* 25
vols. *Paris.* 1808-15. 8°.

1590-1634 **BRY** (THEODORE DE). Collectiones peregrinatiorum in
Indiam orientalem et Indiam occidentalem, XIII partibus
comprehenso a Theodoro, Joan-Theodoro de Bry, et a
Matheo Merian publicatæ. *Francofurti.* 1590-1634. Fol.
   (Parts I to VI, edited and illustrated by T. de Bry, parts
VII to IX by his sons. Johann Theodor and Johann Israel
de B.; parts X to XII by J. T. de B., and part XIII by M.
Merian.)

1596 ———— (America. Part VI.) Historiæ ab A. Bezono ....
scriptæ, sectio tertio....in hac reperies qua natione His-
pani....Peruani regni provincias occuparint, capto rege
Atabaliba, *etc.* (3d part of G. Benzoni's Historia del Mondo
Nuovo.) Map and plates, 2 parts. *Frankfurt.* 1596. Fol.

1617 ———— (Second edition.) *Oppenheimii.* 1617. Fol.

1595 ———— (German edition.) *Frankfurt.* 1595. Fol.

1613   —— (Second German edition.) *Frankfurt.* 1613. Fol.

1599   —— (America.   Part VII.)   Descriptionem trium itin-erum....equitis F. Draken....J. Hauckens....G. Ralegh ....in Latinum sermonem conversa auctore G. Artus.   Maps and plates.   3 pt.   *Francofurti.*   1599.   Fol.

1625   —— (Second edition.) *Francofurti.*   1625.   Fol.

1602   —— (America.   Part IX.)   De novi orbis natura (by J. de Acosta).   Accessit....S. de Weert and....O. a. Noort ....Plates.   5 pt.   *Francofurti.* 1602.   Fol.

1633   —— (Second edition.)   *Francofurti.*   1633.   Fol.

1601   (German edition.) Von Gelegenheit der elemente natur de Neuer Welt.   J. H. v. Linschoten.   *Frankfurt.*   1601. Fol.

1602   —— (Latin and German edition.)   *Frankfurt.*   1602.

1620   —— (Latin and German edition.)   *Frankfurt.*   1620.

1624   —— (America.   Part XII.)   Descriptio Indiæ Occidenta-lis, auctore A. de Herrera.   Accesserunt....J. de More.... P. Ordonnez de Cevallos....Paralipomena Americæ (com-piled from J. de Acosta's work "De novi orbis natura"). *Francofurti.*   1624.   Fol.

1623   —— (German edition.)   *Frankfurt.*   1623.   Fol.

1634   —— Historia Americæ, sive Novi Orbis, continens in XII distinctis partibus....descriptionem....Indiæ Occidentalis ....com exegesi ulteriore....Ornata....tabulis geographi-cis, et figures....Accessit Elenchus Sectionem et Index capitum, *etc. Sumptibus M. Meriani. Francofurti.* 1634. Fol.

1763   **BUENO** (COSME).   Descripcion del Reyno del Peru, *etc.,* que....div a luz....Don C. B.   (1763, *etc.*)   8°.

1763   —— Descripcion de las Provincias de el Peru, por el cosmografo mayor el Vireynato don C. B. *Lima.* 1763. 16 .

1786   —— Coleccion de las descripciones de obiejiados i pro-vincias publicadas en sus almanaques.   *Lima.*   1786.   16 .

1886   **BUREAU OF ETHNOLOGY** (Washington.)   Fourth Report of the B. of E.   *Washington.*   1886.

       (Quipu, page 79.)

1864   BURGHOLZHAUSEN (COUNT MARSCHALL VON). On Ethno-
graphical Objects presented to the Novara Museum, Vienna.
London. 1864. 8.
(Anthrop. Review. Vol. II. Jol. Anth. Soc. p. ccxxxv.
—Mummy from Atacama, Peruvian skulls, *etc.*)

1873   BUSK (GEORGE), *F. R. S.* Remarks on a collection of 150
ancient Peruvian skulls presented to the Anthropological
Institute by T. J. Hutchinson, H. M. Consul at Callao.
2 plates. *London.* 1873. 8.
(Journal Anthrop. Inst. Vol. III., pages 86 94.)

1863   BUSSIERRE (MARIE THEODORE RENOURD LE). Le Perou et
Sainte Rose de Lima (Sainte-Rose de Sainte Marie.) *Paris*
1863. 8.
(Compiled account of Peru, pages 5-167.)

1850   BYAM (GEORGE). Wanderings in some of the western
republics of America. Illust. *London.* 1850. 12°.
(Chap. XII. Republic of Peru; Lima and Guayaquil.)

1775-89   BYER (WOLFGANG). Aymara cum versione latina. *Nürn-
berg.* 1775, *etc.* 8°. *See* MURR (G. G. VON). Journal für
Kunst und Literatur. 17 vols. 1775-89.
Vol. I., pages 112-21; II., pages 277-334; III., pages
55-104.)

1892   BYRNE (JAMES). General Principles of the Structure of
Language. "Grammatical Sketches." 2 vols. *London.*
1892. 8.
(Quichua, Vol. I., pages 205-8.

1870   CY SOBRON (DE FÉLIX). Los idiomas del a America latina.
Etudios biografico-bibliograficos. *Madrid.* 1870. 8.

1638   CALANCHA (FRAY ANTONIO DE LA). Coronica moralizada del
orden de San Augustin en el Peru, con sucesos egenplares
en esta monarquia. *Barcelona.* 1638. Fol.

1639-53   ——— Coronica moralizada, *etc.* 2 vols. *Barcelona.*
1639-53. Fol.
(Vol. I. is a duplicate of Vol. I. of the edition of 1638,
with the date 1639.)

1653   ———— Coronica moralizada, *etc.*, continued by Fray Diego de Cordova. *Lima.* 1653. Fol.

    (This continuation forms Vol. II. of the last preceding edition, and is unfinished.)

1651   ———— Coronica moralizada, *etc.* Latin translation (so-called) under the title of *Historia Peruana ordinis ermitarum, S. P. Augustini libri octodecim. Antuerpiæ.* 1651.

1653   ———— Coronica moralizada, *etc.* French translation. *Toulouse.* 1653.

    [PADRE ANTONIO DE LA CALANCHA, an ecclesiastic, wrote between 1638 and 1653. His *Coronica Moralizada* is "a prec ious storehouse of details respecting the manners and cus toms of the Indians and the topography of the country." Gives the most accurate Inca calendar, and the "Confession" of Lejesama.]

1825   CALDCLEUGH (ALEXANDER). Travels in South America, during the years 1819-20-21 ; containing an account of the present state of Brazil, Buenos Ayres and Chili. 2 vols. Illus. *London.* 1825. 8 .

    (Peru: Lima described, chap. XIV.)

1578   CALVETON (URBANIS). *See* BENZONI (GIROLAMO). Novæ novi orbis, *etc.* Nunc in Latinum translatæ. (*Geneva.*) 1578. 8 . *See* BENZONI (GIROLAMO). Occidentalis hactenus gestarum....libri tres, Urbani Calvetonis opera industriaque....Latini facte, *etc.* (*Geneva.*) 1578. 12 .

    (Numerous editions in various languages.)

1888   CAMACHO (S. B.) *See* PAZ SOLDAN (M. F.) Historia del Peru independiente. Edited by C. Paz Soldan, with a biography of the author by S. B. C. *Buenos Aires.* 1888. 8°.

1875   CAMPBELL (JOHN). The traditions of the ancient races of Peru and Mexico identified with those of the historical peoples of the old world. *Nancy* and *Paris.* 1875. 8 .

    (Compte-Rendu de Congrès des Americanistes. Vol. I., pages 348 367.)

1744–8   CAMPBELL (JOHN). *See* HARRIS (JOHN) *D. D.* Navigantium atque Itinerantium Bibliotheca, *etc.* Carefully revised.... by Dr. J. C. 2 vols. *London.* 1744 8. Fol.

1764   ———— (Another edition.) 2 vols. *London.* 1764. Fol.

1775   CANO Y OLMEDELLA (JUAN DE LA CRUZ.) Mapa geografico de America Meridional. *Madrid.* 1775.

1799   ——— (Another edition.)   *London.*   1799.

1614   CANTO (FRANCISCO DEL.) *See* TORRES RUBIO (DIEGO DE.)
Arte y Vocabulario en la lengua general del Peru llamada
Quichua, y en la lengua Española....En *los Reyes.* (*Lima.*)
1614.   4 .
(Biblioteca Herberiana, VI., 35; No. 572. X, 18; No. 522.)

1889   CARLI (F. ANTONIO.)   Compendio de gramatica quichua.
Santiago.   1889.

1780   CARLI (GIOVANNI RINALDO.)   Delle · lettere Americane.
Cosmofali.   1780.   12°.
(Letters VII. and VIII. of Vol. I.)

1785   ——— Briefe über Amerika.   Transl. by Christian Gott-
fried Hennig.   3 vols. *Gera.* 1785.   16 .
(Letters VII. and VIII. of Vol. I.)

1787   ——— Lettres Americaines, dans lesquelles on examine
l'origine....les moers, les usages des anciens habitans de
l'Amerique....pour servir de suite aux mémoires de D.
Ulloa. Avec des observations et additions du tradacteur
Jean Baptiste Lefebre de Villebrune.   2 vols. *Boston,*
Paris. 1787.   8 .
(Letter VII., L'immortalité de l'âme chez les divers
peuples d'Amerique surtout chez les Incas. Letter VIII.,
Rits divers :....Simplicité de la religion des Incas.)

1791   ——— (Second edition.)   2 vols. *Paris.* 1791. 8°.

1857   CARMOY (PAUL DE).   D'Arequipa á Cuzco, souvenirs de
voyage dans l'Amerique du Sud. *Paris.* 1857.
(Revue Contemporaine, 1st series, 31, pages 322–361.)

1876   CARRASCO (CONSTANTINO).   Ollanta. Drama quichua en tres
actos y en verso.   Puesto en verso castellano por C. C.
Lima. 1876. 8 .

1644   CARRERA (DON FERNANDO DE LA).   Arte de la lengua yunga
de los valles del Obispado de Truxillo del Peru, con un
Confessonario, y todas las Oraciones Christiana, traducidas
en la lengua, y otras cosas. *Lima.* 1644. 8 .
(Only three copies in existence, one in Madrid, one in
London and one in Lima.)

1880   ——— (Another edition.)   Edited by Dr. Gonzalez de la
Rosa.   Reimpresso (bajo la direccion de C. Pas Soldan).
Lima. 1880. 8 .
(Reprinted in parts in the *Revista de Lima.*)

1856   **CARREY** (PIERRE EMILE).   L'Amazone.   Huit jours sous l'Equateur.   *Paris.*   1856.   12 ·

1875   ———— Le Pérou.   Tableau descriptif, historique et analytique des Êtres et des choses de ce Pays.   *Paris.* 1875.   8 ·

1877   **CARTAS DE INDIAS.**   Publicalas por primera vez el Ministro de Fomento.   Facsimile plates and maps.   *Madrid.*   1877. Fol.   *See* GASCA (PEDRO DE LA); VACA DE CASTRO (CRISTOBAL).
(With facsimiles of autograph letters of the early discov. erers, *etc.*, of America.)

CARTER-BROWN.   *See* BROWN (JOHN CARTER).

1552   **CASAS** (BARTOLOMÉ DE LAS) *Bishop of Chiapa.*   Brevissima relaccion de la destruycion de las Indias, *etc.*   Coligeda por B. de las Càsas....G. L.   *Sevilla.*   1552.   4 ·

1812   ———— (Another edition.)   Breve relacion de la destruc- cion de las Indias Occidentales, *etc.*   *Sevilla.*   1552.   (Reim- presa en Londres.)   1812.   12'·

1822   — —— (Another edition.)   Breve relacion, *etc.*   (Edited by S. T. de Mier, Noriega y Guerra).   *Mexico.*   1822.   16 ·

1626   ———— Istoria, ó brevissima relatione della destruttione dell'Indie Occidentali....Con la traduttione in Italiano di F. Bersabita (*i. e.* G. Castellani.)   *Spanish and Italian. Venetia.*   1626.   4 ·

1643   ———— (Another edition.)   *Venetia.*   1643.   4 ·

1579   ———— Tyrannies et cruautez des Espagnols perpetrées és Indes Occidentales.... descrites en langue Castellane par B. de las Casas....traduites par J. de Miggrode.   *Anvers.* 1579.   8 ·

1630   ———— (Another edition.)   *Rouen.*   1630.   4 ·

1852   ———— (Another edition.)   *Paris.*   1852.   8 ·

1583   ———— The Spanish Colonie, or Briefe Chronicle of the Acts and gestes of the Spaniardes in the West Indies.... written in the Castilian tongue....by B. de las Casas.... and now first translated into English (from the French translation by J. de Miggrode).   By M. M. S.   *London.* 1583.   4 ·

1625   ———— A briefe Narration of the destruction of the Indies by the Spaniards. (Translated from the Spanish.) *London.* 1625. Fol. *See* PURCHAS (S). "Purchas his Pilgrimes, *etc.*," pt. IV.

1656   ———— The tears of the Indians : being an historical.... account of the cruel massacres....of about twenty millions of innocent people, committed by the Spaniards in the islands of Hispaniola, Cuba, Jamaica, *etc.*, as also in the continent of Mexico, Peru, and other places of the West Indies.... Written in Spanish by Casaus, and made English by J. P[hillips]. *London.* 1656. 8°.

[BARTOLOMÉ DE LAS CASAS, born at Seville, 1474 ; son of Antoine las Casas, who accompanied Columbus on his first voyage of discovery. Went west with Columbus in 1498 and 1502 ; ordained priest in San Domingo by Bishop of Hispaniola, 1510 : accompanied expedition under Velasquez for occupation of Cuba, 1511, when he began his opposition to Spanish cruelty. Devoted his life to the service of the Indians, crossing the ocean twelve times in his almost fruitless attempts to ameliorate their condition. Wrote his History of the Destruction of the Indians, while in Spain, about 1540, advising the Council of the Indies on a new code of laws for the government of the colonies then being framed. Consecrated Bishop of Chiapa, 1544, to secure authority to enforce the new code, and went to Hispaniola same year. Resigned bishopric, 1547, and returned to Spain ; resided at Dominican College at Valladolid. Wrote a work on Peru, 1564. Died at Madrid, July, 1566, during visit "in service of the Indians," aged 92. |

1880   CASTAING (ALPHONSE). Les sources de l'histoire du Pérou antique. *Paris.* 1880. 8°.

— —   — Les Fêtes, offrandes et sacrifices dans l'Antiquité peruvienne.
            (Archiv. de la Soc.-Américaine de France. N. S. iii., 239.)

————   — Le Système religieux dans l'Antiquité peruvienne. (Archiv. de la Soc.-Américaine de France. N. S. iii., 86, 145.)

1626   CASTELLANI (G.) *See* CASAS (BARTOLOMÉ DE LAS). Istoria, obrevissimo relatione, *etc.*, tradittione in Italiano di F. Bersabita (*i. e.* G. Castellani). *Venetia.* 1626. 4°.

1589   CASTELLANOS (JUAN DE).   Elegias de Varones illustres de Indias.   Portrait.   *Madrid.*   1589.

(Metrical version of the expedition of Ursua and Aguirre, *etc.*, by a contemporary; made use of by De Bry in eighth part of *Grand Voyages.*   Contains only Pt. 1 of Castellanos' "metrical chronicle.")

1847-50   —— Elegias de Varones, *etc.*, edited by Buenaventura Carlos Aribau.   *Madrid.*   1847-50.   *See* BIBLIOTECA DE AUTORES ESPAÑOLES.

(Contains the three first parts of Castellanos' poem; parts 2 and 3 give the adventures of the Germans in search of El Dorado, and refer to the expeditions of Lugo, Belalcazar, *etc.*; a fourth part of the poem treated of the conquest of New Granada, and is lost, though used by Piedrahita.)

1850-61   CASTELNAU (FRANCIS DE).   Expédition dans les parties centrales de l'Amérique du Sud, de Rio de Janeiro à Lima et de Lima au Para, 1843-47.   Seven parts, in 6 vols., 8°; and 9 vols., 4°.   *Paris.*   1850-61.   8° and 4°.

(Part I.   Histoire du Voyage. 6 vols., 8°.)
(Part II.   Vues et scénes, avec 60 pl.   4°)
(Part III.   Antiquités des Incas et autres peuples anciens, avec 61 pl.   4°)
(Part IV.   Itinéraires et coupe géologique, avec 76 cartes. 4°)
(Part V.   Géographie, avec 30 cartes.   4°)
(Part VI.   Botanique, 2 vols., avec 90 pl.   4°)
(Part VII.   Zoologie, ou Animaux nouveaux et rares, avec 176 pl.   4°)

1850   —— (Same work, but without the 4° volumes.)   6 vols. *Paris.*   1850.   8°.

(Vol. I.   Histoire du Voyage.   France to Rio and to Araguay river.)
(Vol. II.   To Uliranda near Paraguay.)
(Vol. III.   To Potosi, La Paz, Tiauhuanaco, Puno, Arequipa, Callao.)
(Vol. IV.   Lima, Paseo, Huanca velica, Cuzco, Ucayli, Nauta.)
(Vol. V.   To Tabitinga, to Para, to Gugava.)
(Vol. VI.   Gran Chaco to Cuzco.)
(*See* WEDDELL (H. ALGERNON) and D'OSERY (M.)).

1852   —— Expédition dans les parties centrales de l'Amérique du Sud; Itinéraires et coupe géologique à travers le continent de l'Amérique du Sud, de Rio de Janeiro à Lima. 76 colored maps. *Paris.* 1852. Fol.

1852   —— Antiquités des Incas et autre Peuples anciens. Col. plates. *Paris.* 1852. 4 .

1891   CEZAR (F. DE OLIVEIRA). La vida en los bosques Sud-Americanos. Viaje al oriente de Bolivia. Portrait and plates. *Buenos-Aires.* 1891.

1853   CHAIX (PAUL). Histoire de l'Amerique meridionale au seizième siècle. Premier partie. Pérou. Avec cinq cartes géographiques. 2 vols. *Geneve.* 1853. 12 .

1882   CHALON (P. F.). El arte de construir de los antiguos Peruanos. *Lima.* 1882. 8 .

1851   CHAMBERS (ROBERT). Papers for the People. 1851. (Vol. XII. Incas.)

1841   CHAMPOLLION (A.). *See* SILVESTRE (JOS. BALT.), Paleographie Universelle, *etc. Paris.* 1841. Fol.

1841   CHAMPOLLION-FIGEAC (M.) *See* SILVESTRE (JOS. BALT.), Paleographie Universelle, *etc. Paris.* 1841. Fol.

1887   CHARENCEY (H. DE). Deux poésies péruvien (dans le dialect quichua). *Paris.* 1887.

1823   CHASE (WASHINGTON). A voyage from the United States to South America, performed during the years 1821, 1822 and 1823. Portrait. *Newbury.* 1823. 8 .
     (Peru; Arica, Santos and Tumbos, pages 59–72.)

     CHAUVETON (URBANIS). *See* CALVETON (URBANIS).

     CHAVES (FRANCISCO DE). Narrative of the Conquest of Peru.

     [FRANCISCO DE CHAVES, of Truxillo, companion of Pizarro and friend of Atahualpa's brother, tried to save the Inca's life. Slain, 1541, while defending the staircase against Pizarro's assassins. His MS. went to his relation, Luis Valera, but was lost.]

1891   CHILD (THEODORE).   The Spanish-American Republics.
Illus. Maps. *New York.* 1891. 4 ·
(Impressions of Peru, pages 183–227.)

1891   ———— Les Républiques Hispano - Américaines. Illus.
Maps. *Paris.* 1891.

1812   CHILTON (J.). Voyage to Peru, 1568. *London.* 1812. 8 ·

1877   CHURCH (GEORGE EARL). A Report to the Government of
Bolivia and Brazil. The Route to Bolivia via the River
Amazon. *London.* 1877. 8 ·
(Contains information as to products of Alto-Peru and
trade-routes to Bolivia, pages 153–189.)

1732   CHURCHILL (A. AND J.) Collection of Voyages and Travels,
etc. London. 1732, *etc.* Fol.
(Vol. III. An Historical Relation of the Kingdom of
Chili. By Al. de Ovalle.)

1744   ———— (Another edition.) *London.* 1744. Fol.
(Vol. V. General Observations, *etc.* By Antonio de Herrera Tordesillas.)

1752   ———— (Another edition.) *London.* 1752. Fol.

n. d.   CHURRON (LE LICENCIADO). Cartilla, Catecismo y Sermones traducidos en la lengua general del Peru. Fol.
(MS. Viñaza: Bibl. Españ.: No. 1,032.)

1553   CIEZA DE LEON (PEDRO DE). Parte primera de la chronica
del Peru. Que tracta la demarcacion de sus provincias: la
descripcion dellas. Las fundaciones de las nuevas cui-
dades. Los ritos y costumbres de los indios. Yotras cosas
estrañas dignas de ser sabidas. *Sevilla.* 1553. Fol.

1554   ———— (Another edition.) Parte primera de la chronica
del Peru. *Anvers.* (Juan Steelsio.) 1554. 8 ·

1554   ———— (Another edition.) Map and wood cuts. *Anvers.*
(Juan Bellero.) 1554. 8ᵒ.
(A duplicate of the preceding, with a different publisher's
name and device.)

1554   ———— (Another edition.) *Anvers.* (Martin Nucio.)
1554. 8ᵒ.

1849   ———— La Chronica del Peru. Edited by Aribau (B. S.).
Madrid. 1849. 8 ·
(Biblioteca de Autores Espagnoles. Vol. XXVI.)

1555   ——— La prima parte dell'istorie del Peru: dove si tratta
l'ordine delle Provincie, della Città nuoue in quel Paese
edificate, i riti et costumi de gli Indiani, con molte cose
notabile, i degne che uengano à notitia. *Rome*. 1855. 8°.
(First Italian edition. Translated by Valiero and Luigi
Dorici.)

1556   ——— (Second Italian edition.) Translated by Aug. de
Cravaliz. *Venetia*. 1556. 8°.

1556-7 ——— (Another edition.) 2 vols. *Venetia*. 1556-7. 12°.

1560-4 ——— (Another edition.) *Venetia*. 1560-4. 8 .
(Pt. I. La prima parte. Pt. II. La seconda parte dell
historie dell' India. Pt. III. Le Historie di Fernando Cor-
tez, by Gomarra.)

1560   ——— (Another edition.) *Venetia*. (Giord. Ziletti.)
1560. 12°.

1560   ——— (Another edition.) *Venetia*. (Lor. da Turino.)
1560. 12 .

1564   ——— Cronica del gran regno del Peru, con la descrit-
tione di tutte le Provincie, e costumi, e riti, et con le nuova
Citta edificate, et altre strane e maravigliose notitie. Parte
Prima. *Venetia*. (G. Bonadio.) 1564. 8 .
(Two other volumes containing Secunda Parte delle His-
torie dell' India, and Historia di Don Ferd. Cortes.)

1576   —— (Another edition.) *Venetia*. (C. Francheschini.)
1576.

1873   —— Segunda parte de la Cronica del Peru. Edited by
Dr. Manuel Gonzales de la Rosa. *London*. 1873.
(Edition of the Escurial MS.; printed, but not published.)

1880   ——— Segunda parte de la Cronica del Peru....seguida
de la suma y narracion do los Incas....por J. de Betánzos.
La publico M. Jiménez de la Espada. *Madrid*. 1880. 8 .
(Part of the Biblioteca Hispano-Ultramarina.)

1708   · Travels of Peter de Cieza through the mighty king-
dom of Peru and the province of Popayan, in South America.
(By Captain John Stevens.) *London*. 1708. 4 .
(Gives only 94 out of 119 chapters.)

1709   ——— (Another edition.) *London*. 1709. 4 .

1711 ——— (Another edition.) *London.* 1711. 4 .
(STEVENS (JOHN). A new Collection of Voyages and Travels. Vol. I.)

1864 ——— The Travels of Pedro de Cieza de Leon, 1532–50, contained in the first part of his Chronicle of Peru, translated and edited, with Notes and Introduction, by Cl. R. Markham. Map. *London.* 1864. 8°.
(Hakluyt Society. Pub. No. 33.)

1883 ——— The second part of the Chronicle of Peru. Translated with notes by Cl. R. Markham. *London.* 1883. 8 .
(Hakluyt Society. Pub. No. 68.)

1725 6 ———— General History of the vast continent and islands of America....from the first discovery thereof : with the best accounts the people could give of their antiquities, translated into English by Capt. John Stevens. 6 vols. Maps and plates. (*London?*) 1725–6. 8°.

1842 ——— Guerras civiles del Peru. *Madrid.* 1842. 8 .
(Vol. LXVIII. Coleccion de documentos ineditos, *etc.*, edited by Navarette.)

1877 ——— Tercero libro de las guerras civiles del Peru, et cual se llama la guerra de Quito (1543-4), y publicadas por M. Jiménez de la Espada. *Madrid.* 1877. 4°.
(Vol. II, Bibliotheca Hispano-Ultramarina. The Guerras Civiles is Bk. III of Pt. IV of Cieza de Leon's History. Jiménez de la Espada supposes Bk. I and II to exist in MS. The MS. of Bk. IV and V, treating of the War of Huarina and the War of Xaquixaguana, is lost.)

[CIEZA DE LEON, born 1519; in Peru, 1532–50. History written between 1541 (Popayan) and 1550 (Lima). Bk. I relates to the Geography of Peru and its Inhabitants; Bk. II, History of the Incas; Bk. III, Spanish Conquest; Bk. IV, Civil Wars of the Conquerors. Cieza de Leon was present at the defeat of Gonzalo Pizarro, 1548; visited Cuzco to obtain information from surviving descendant of Inca Huayna Ccapac; died at Seville, 1560.]

CITRY (DE). *See* BROÉ (DE) *S. de Citry.*

1891 CLARK (E. B.). Twelve Months in Peru. Illus. *New York.* 1891. 16 .

1874   **CLARKE** (HYDE).   Researches in Prehistoric and Protohistoric Comparative Philology, Mythology and Archæology, in connection with the origin of culture in America, and its propagation by the Sumerian or Akkad families.   *London.* 1874.   8 .
(Jol. Anthrop. Inst.   Vol. IV, pages 148–214.)

1803   **CLARKE** (J. S.).   The Progress of Maritime Discovery, *etc.* 1803.   4 .
(Vol. 1, Appendix, Galvano's *Discoveries of the World, etc.*)

1879   **COBO** (FATHER BERNABÉ).   Historia de Lima.   Edited by Dr. M. Gonzalez de la Rosa.   *Lima.*   1879.
(Written between 1610 and 1629.)

1859   **COCHRANE** (THOMAS) *Earl of Dundonald.*   Narrative of Services in the Liberation of Chili, Peru and Brazil from Spanish and Portuguese Domination, by Thomas, Earl of Dundonald.   Vol. I.   *London.*   1859.   8°.

1884   **COLE** (G. R. FITZ-ROY).   The Peruvians at Home.   1884.   8 .

1842. *etc.*   **COLECCION DE DOCUMENTOS** ineditos para la historia de España, por de Pidal, de Miraflores y M. Salva.   103 vols. *Madrid.*   1842, etc.   8 .
(Vols. V, XIII, XLIX, L and LI, matter relating to Peru.)

1864, *etc.*   **COLECCION DE DOCUMENTOS** ineditos relativos al descubrimiento, conquista y colonizacion de las posesiones Españoles en America y Oceania, sacados, en su mayor parte, del Real Archivo de Indias.   Edited by Joaquin F. Pacheco, Francisco de Cárdenas, and Luis Torres de Mendoza.   40 vols. *Madrid.*   1864, *etc.*

1891 2   **COLECCION DE LIBROS** que tratan de America raros y curiosos.   7 vols. *Madrid.*   1891–2.   8 .
(Vol. I.   Xeres.   Conquista del Peru.   1534.)
(Vol. II.   Acuña.   Nuevo descubrimiento del gran Rio de las Amazonas.)
(Vol. III, IV.   Rocha. Tratado del origen de las Indios occidentales del Perú, Méjico. Santa Fé y Chile.   2 vol.)
(Vol. V, VI.   Fern. Colon.   Historia del Almirante de las Indias don Cristóbal Colon.   Reimpr. c. un extenso estudio acerca del autor y sus obras.   2 vol.)
(Vol. VII.   Ruir Blanco.   Conversion del Piritu, de Indios Cumanagotos y Palenques.)

(Vol. XIII. Varias relaciones del Peru y Chile, *etc.*
1535 1658.
(Vol. XVI. Montesinos. Memorias antiquas....del Peru.
1570–2.)

1825-37 Coleccion de los Viages y Descubrimiento, *etc.* 5 vols.
Madrid. 1825–37. 4 . *See* FERNANDEZ DE NAVARETTE
(MARTIN).

——— COLLAHUASO (JACINTO). Historia de las guarras civiles del
Inca Atahualpa, con su hermano Atoco comunemente llamado
Huascar Inca.
(MS. lost—referred to by Juan de Velasco.)

1619. *etc.* COLLIN (M.). Oost-Indische onde West-Indische Voyagien, *etc.* 1619, *etc.* 4
See HAWKINS (SIR JOHN). Voyagie von....Sir Jan Hawkins, *etc.*

1875-6 CONGRÈS INTERNATIONAL DES AMÉRICANISTES (COMPTE-RENDU
DE). 2 vols. Maps and plates. *Paris and Nancy.* 1875–76.
8 . *See* ZEGARRA (GAV. PACH.) Alphabet phonétique de la
langue Quéchua.

1878 ——— (Compte-Rendu de). Sec. Session. 2 vols. Maps
and plates. *Luxembourg.* 1878. 8 .

1879 ——— (Compte-Rendu de). Trois. Session. 2 vols.
Maps and plates. Atlas of 40 colored plates. *Bruxelles.*
1879. 8 and 4 . *See* RENAUD (J.) La Céramique péruvienne, *etc.* JIMÉNEZ DE LA ESPADA (MARCOS) Del hombre
blanco, signo de la Cruz precolombianos en el Peru.

1826 CONSTABLE (A.). Constable's Miscellany. (Vols. II. and
III.) *Edinburgh and London.* 1826, *etc.* 12 . *See* HALL
(BASIL.) *Captain.* Extracts from a journal written on the
coasts of Chili, Peru, *etc.*

1595 COOLEY (W. D.) *See* DRAKE (SIR FRANCIS). His voyage,
1595, by Thomas Maynarde, edited from the original manuscripts by W. D. C. *London.* 1849. 8 .

1630 CORDOVA Y SALINAS (FRAY DIEGO DE). Vida del Apostol
del Perú el Venerable Fray Francisco Solano. *Lima.* 1630.

1643 ——— (Another edition). Augmented by Alonzo de
Mendista. *Madrid.* 1643.

1650   —— Chronica Franciscana. *Lima.* 1650.

1653   —— *See* Calancha (Fray Antonio de). Coronica Moralizada, *etc.* Continued by F. D. de C. y S. *Lima.* 1653. Fol.

1893   CORNWALLIS (Kinahan). The conquest of Mexico and Peru, an historical narrative poem. *New York.* 1893. 12 .

1869   CORREA (Gaspar). The three voyages of Vasco da Gama and his viceroyalty. From the Lendas da India. Trans. with original documents, notes and introduction, by H. E. J. Stanley. With portrait, plan and facsimile plates. *London.* 1869. 8°.
            (Hakluyt Society's Public. No. 42).

1553?   CORTES (Hernando). Copia delle lettere del Prefetto (H. C.) della India, la Nuova Spagna detta, *etc.* (1553?). 8°.
            (Account of the capture of Atabalipa by Pizarro.

1875   CORTES (José Domingo). Bolivia apuntes geograficos, estaduticos, de costumbres, descriftivos e historicos. *Paris.* 1875. 8 .

1660-71   COSTE (N. de la). *See* Herrera Tordesillos (Ant. de). Histoire générale des voyages, *etc.*, trad....par N. de la C. 3 vols. *Paris.* 1660–71. 4°.

1847   COULTER (John) *M. D.* Adventures on the Western Coast of South America and the Interior of California....With an account of the Natural Productions and the manners and customs in Peace and War of the various savage tribes visited. 2 vols. *London.* 1847. 8 .
            (Tacames. Vol. I., pages 33 87).

            COURTE DE LA BLANCHARDERIE. *See* Blancharderie (Courte de la).

1560   CRAVALIZ (A. de). *See* Cieza de León (Pedro de). Cronica del gran regno del Peru, *etc.* Trans. by A. de C. *Venetia.* 1560. 8 .

1884   CRAWFORD (Robert). Across the Pampas and the Andes. Map and Illus. *London.* 1884.

—— ·   **Crespillo** (Fr. Sebastian). Catecismo y oraciones en lengua general del Peru.

(Leon Pinelo: Epitome, t.ii. col. 728 ; Viñaza: Bibl. Español. No. 1147).

1883   **Crevaux** (Jules). Voyages dans l'Amerique du Sud, contenant . . . . II. de Cayenne aux Andes (1878–9), exploration de S'Oyapoch, du Parou, de l' Ica and du Japura. Maps and Illus. *Paris.* 1883. 4 ·

1892   **Cronan** (Rudolf). Amerika, die Geschichte seiner Entdekung von der ältesten bis auf die nueste Zeit. 2 vols. Illus. *Leipzig.* 1892. 8 ·

(Vol. I., pages 79–94. Die alten Kultur völker Südamerikas. Vol. II, pages 81–134. Francisco Pizarro und die Eroberung von Peru).

1775   **Cruz Cano y Almeda** (Juan de la). *See* Maps. *London.* 1775.

1895   **Cunow** (H.) Die soziale Verfassung des Inkareichs. (*See* No. 298 review in Petermann's Mittheilungen for 1895).

1888   **Curtis** (William Eleroy). The capitals of Spanish America. Map and Illus. *New York.* 1888. 8°.

(Lima, pages 354–415.)

1572   **Cuzco.** View of the town of Cuzco (bird's-eye view) from Braun and Hogenburg's Staedtebuch. 1572. Copper plate 27 x 24 cm.

(Sometimes colored.)

1844   **Dahlgren** (Madelaine Vinton) *Mrs.*   South Sea Sketches. A narrative by Mrs. M. V. D. *Boston.* 1884. 8 ·

(Peru, pages 22 90).

1744   **Dalibard** (———). *See* Lasso de la Vega (Garcia). Histoire des Yncas, Rois du Pérou. Translated by Dalibard. 2 vols. *Paris.* 1774. 8 ·

1893   **Dall** (W. H.) *See* Du Pouget (J. F. A.) *Marquis de Nadaillac.* Prehistoric America. Edited by W. H. D. *New York.* 1893. 8 ·

1897   **Dalton** (O. M.) An Ethnographical Collection from Ecuador. Illustrated. *London.* 1897. 8 ·

(Jol. of Anth. Inst., G. B. and Ir.   Vol. 27, No. 1, pages 148–155.

1697–1709 DAMPIER (WILLIAM.)   A New Voyage Round the World, describing particularly the Isthmus of Panama, several coasts and islands in the West Indies, the Isles of Cape Verd, the Passage of Terra del Fuego, the South Sea coasts of Chili, Peru and Mexico, *etc.*   3 vols.   Maps and illus. *London.*   1697–1709.   8°.

(Voyage began in 1679. Coast of Equador, California and Peru above Poyta.)

1697   —— (Second edition, corrected.)   3 vols.   *London.* 1697.   8°.

1698   —— (Third edition, corrected.)   2 vols.   *London.* 1698.   8°.

1699   —— (Fourth edition, corrected.)   2 vols.   *London.* 1699.   8°.

1703–09   —— (Another edition.)   3 vols.   *London.*   1703–09.   8°.

1705   —— An account of Capt. B.'s Voyage round the World. *London.*   1705.   Fol.

(Harris (J.) *D. D., etc.*   Navigantium atque Itinerantium Bibliotheca, *etc.* Vol. II.)

1797   —— (Another edition.)   A New Voyage round the World.... *London.*   1797.   8°.

1776   —— The Voyages and Adventures of....W. B., *etc.* 2 vols.   *London.*   1776.   8°.

1698   —— Nouveau voyage antour du monde, on l' on decrit en particulier l' isthme de l' Amérique, plusieurs costes et isles des Indes occidentales, les isles du Cap Verd, le passage par la Terre del Fuego, les côtes meridionales du Chili, du Pérou et du Mexique....2 vols.   Maps and illus.   *Amsterdam.*   1698.   12°.

1701–5   —— (Another edition.)   4 vols.   *Amsterdam.*   1701 5. 12 .

1698–1700 —— Nieuwe Reystogt rondom de Werreld.   2 vols. *Gravenhage.*   1698–1700.   4 .

1702   —— Neue Reise um die Welt.   *Leipzig.*   1702.   8 .

1748   D'ANVILLE (.)   *See* MAPS.   South America.   *Paris.* 1748.

1775–9   —— (Other editions.)   1775 and 1779.

1880   DAVIS (JOHN.), *the Navigator*. Voyages and Works of John Davis, the Navigator. With notes and introduction by C. L. Markham. Facsimile map of the world, plates, *etc.* *London*. 1880. 8 .
(Hakluyt Society's publications, No. 59.)

1873   DAVIS (JOSEPH BARNARD.) On Ancient Peruvian Skulls and Pottery. Plate. *London*. (April 1, 1873.) 8°.
(Jol. Anthrop. Inst. Vol. III., pages 94–100.)

1867   ——. Thesaurus Craniorum. Catalogue of the skulls of the various races of men in the collection of J. B. D. *London*. 1867. 8°.

1875   ——— Supplement to Thesaurus Craniorum. *London*. 1875. 8 .

——   DÉCADAS ABREVIADAS de los descubrimientos, conquistos, fundaciones y otras cosas notables, acaecidas en las Indias occidentales desde 1492 á 1640. *See* DOCUMENTOS INÉDITOS, *etc.* Vol. VIII., pages 5–52.

1886   DEFORMITIES OF BONES among the ancient Peruvians. *New York*. 1886. Fol.
(*Science*. Vol. VII., Feb. 5, 1886, pages 130–31.)
(Remarks on bones found by Tschudi near Pachacamac. Said by Virchow to show multiple exostosis.)

1805   DELAMETHERIE (J. C.) Reise der Herren v. Humboldt und Bonpland, nach den Wendekreisen in den Jahren 1799–1804. Ein Auszug aus ihren Memorien Von J. C. D. Aus dem Franzosischen. *Erfurt*. 1805. 8 .

DELECLUSE (CHARLES.) *See* L'ECLUSE (CHARLES DE).

n. d.   DELISLE (GUILLAUME.) *See* MAPS. Carte de la terre ferme du Pérou. *etc.* *Amsterdam*. *n. d.*

1875   DENIS (JEAN FERDINAND.) Arte plumaria—Les Plumes dans les Arts au Mexique, au Perou, au Brézil, *etc.* *Paris*. 1875. 8 .

1858   DESJARDINS (E.) Le Pérou avant la conquête espagnole. d'après les principaux historiens originaux et quelques documents inédits sur les antiquités de ce pays. *Paris*. 1858. 8 .

1835–47   DESSALINES D'ORBIGNY (ALCIDE.) Voyage dans l' Amérique Meridionale (Le Brésil, Uruguay, l' Argentine, Chile, Bolivia, Perou, *etc.*), executie pendant les années 1823 à 1826. 9 vols. (Vols. VIII. and IX. Plates, chiefly colored.) *Paris*. 1835–47. 4 .

1853   —— Voyage dans les Deux Amériques, augmenté de renseignements exacts jusqu'en 1853 sur les différentes Etats du Nouveau Monde.   Nouvelle édition, publié sous la direction de M. A. d'O.   *Paris.*   1853.   8°.

1859   ——— (Another edition.) *See* DUMONT D'URVILLE (J.S.C.) Histoire générale des Voyages, *etc.* 1859. 8°.

1836   ——— Voyage pittoresque dans les deux Amériques, résumé générale de tous les voyages de Colomb, Las-Casas, Oviedo, Gomara, Garcilazo de la Vega, Acosta, la Condomine, *etc.*, publié sous la direction de M. A. d'O.   Plates and maps.   *Paris.*   1836.   8 .

1841   ——— (Another edition.) *Paris.* 1841. 8'.

1839   —— L'Homme Americain (de l' Amérique méridionale) considéré sous ses rapports physiologiques et moraux.   2 vols.   Atlas and plates, with ethnological map.   *Paris.*   1839.   8° and 4 .

1845   ——— Fragment l' un histoire de l' Amérique meridionale, contenant des considerations sur la navigation de l' Amazone et de la Plata, et sur les anciennes missions des provinces de Chiquitos et de Moxos (Bolivia).   *Paris.*   1845. 8 .

1845   —— Description geográfica, historica y estaditica de Bolivia, *etc.* *Paris.* 1845, *etc.* 8 .

1846   ——— Atlas, Primera entrega. 1846. 8 . (No more published.)

1879   DIRKS (GERVAIS.)   Explorations du fleuve des Amazones, faites par les Franciscains du Pérou (1633–1650.) *Bruxelles.* 1879. 8 .
(Compte-Rendu de troisiéme Congrés des Américanistes. *Bruxelles.* 1879.

D'OCAMPO (BALTASAR.)   *See* OCAMPO (BALTASAR D').

1814   DOLORES LECETA (FRAY JERONIMO DE LOS.) Cuaderno que contiene el Vocabulario en Lengua del Inca, segun se habla en le Obispado de Maynas y Ucayali.   Mayo 21, 1814.
(MS. del Convento de Santa Rosa de Ocopa, provincia de Jauja ; Viñaza.   Bibl. Espagn., No. 408.)

1560   DOMINGO DE SAN THOMAS (FRAY.) Grammatica, o Arte de la lengua general de los Indios de los Reynos del Peru.   (Impresso por Francisco Fernandez de Cordova.)   B. L. *Valladolid.* 1560. 8 .

1891 —— (Another edition) Grammatica, o Arte....com-
puesta por Fr. D. de S. T. publicado de nuevo por Julio
Platzmann. Edicion facsimilar. *Leipzig.* 1891. 8 .

1560 ——— Lexicon, o Vocabulario de la lengua general del
Peru, *etc.* B. L. *Valladolid.* 1560. 16 .

1586 —— (Another edition.) Grammatica o Arte-Lexicon o
Vocabulario. *Lima.* 1586.

D'ORBIGNY (ALCIDE DES.) *See* DESSALINES D'ORBIGNY
(ALCIDE).

1850 **D'OSERY** (M.) Itineraire de M. D'Osery d'Arequipa a
Lima. *Paris.* 1850.
(By the Coast. Castelnau's "Expedition, *etc.*" Vol. IV.,
Chap. LXVI.)

1626 **DRAKE** (SIR FRANCIS) *Baronet.* Sir Francis Drake revived
....by this relation of....a third voyage....set forth by Sir
F. D., Baronet (his nephew), *etc. London.* 1626. 4 .

1628 ——— The World encompassed by Sir F. D., being his
next voyage to that to Nombre de Dios. *London.* 1628. 4 .

1854 —— (Another edition.) The World encompassed. By
Francis Fletcher. Edited by Wm. Sandys Wright Vaux.
Map. (Hakluyt Soc. Pub., No. 17.) *London.* 1854. 8 .

[Mentions end of Lower Chile, Arica and Lima. Sir
Francis Drake appeared on the coast of Peru, 1579, during
the government of Don Francisco de Toledo.]

1877 **DUFFIELD** (ALEXANDER JAMES.) Peru in the guano age ;
a short account of a visit to the guano deposits. *London.*
1877. 8 .

1859 **DUMONT D'URVILLE** (J. S. C.) Histoire genérale des Voyages, *etc.* 1859. 8°. *See* DESSALINES D'ORBIGNY (Alcide).
Voyage dans l'Amerique Meridionale, *etc.*

1707 **DU PERIER** (———).. Histoire Universelle des Voyages
faits par mer et par terre dans l'ancien et dans le nouveau
monde. (By J. B. Morvan de Bellegarde, edited by Du P.)
Paris. 1707. 8°.

1708 ——— (Another edition.) *Amsterdam.* 1708. 12

1708 ——— A General History of all Voyages and Travels....
made English. *London.* 1708. 8 .

1711   —— (New edition.) *London.* 1711. 8°.
(Early Spanish Voyages to America.)

1564   DU PINET (ANT.) Plantz, Pourtraitz et Descriptions de plusieurs Villes, *etc. Lyons.* 1564.
(Large wood cut map of Cuzco.)

1841   DUPONCHEL (A.) Nouvelle Bibliothéque des Voyages, *etc.* Vol. XII., 1841, *etc.* 8 . *See* HALL (BASIL.) *Captain.* Voyage aux Etats-Unis de l'Amérique septentrionelle, *etc.*

1893   DU POUGET (JEAN FRANÇOIS ALBERT) *Marquis de Nadaillac.* Prehistoric America. Translated by H. D'Anvers. Edited by W. H. Dall. Illus. *New York.* 1893. 8 .
(Peru. chap. VIII.)

1881   — — — Les premiers hommes et les temps préhistoriques. ....Illus. 2 vols. *Paris.* 1881. 8°.

1884   —— — Die Ersten Menschen....herausgegeben von W. Schlösser und E. Seler, *etc.* 1884. 8 .

1720   DURRET (LE SIEUR). Voyage de Marcille a Lima et dans les autres lieux des Indes Occidentales, avec une exacte description de ce qu'il y a de plus remarkable tant pour la Geographie, que pour les Mores, les Coutumes, le Commerce, le Gouvernment. et le Religion des Peuples ; avec des notes et des figures....Par le Sieur D....Maps, illus. and plans. *Paris.* 1720. 16 .

1777   EBELING (———) *Professor.* Amerikanische Bibliothek (2 Stücke). *Leipzig.* 1777.

1795-1816   —— Erdbeschreibung und Geschichte von America. 7 vols. *Hamburg.* 1795–1816.

1797   —— Americanisches Magazin. *Hamburg.* 1797.

1555   EDEN (RYCHARDE). The Decades of the New Worlde or West India ....by Petrus Matyr of Angleria, and translated into Englysche by R. E. *London.* 1555. 4 .
(*See* ANGLERIUS (PETRUS MATYR). *London,* 1555, *etc.*

1577   ———— (Another edition.) Newly set in order....by R. Willis. *London.* 1577. 4 .

1791   EDER (FRANZ XAVER). Descriptio provinciæ Moxitarum in regno Peruano. Map and plates. *Budæ.* 1791. 8°.

1861   **Edwards** (William H.).   A Voyage up the River Amazon, including a residence at Para. *London.* 1861. 8°.

1875   **Ellis** (Robert).   Peruvia Sythica, the Quichua language of Peru: its derivation from Central Asia with the American languages in general, and with the Turanian and Iberian languages of the old world, including the Basque, the Lycian and the Pre-Aryan language of Etruria. *London.* 1875. 8°.

1816–17   Ensayo de la historia civil del Paraguay, Buenos Ayres y Tucuman. 3 vols. *Buenos Ayres.* 1816–17.

1856   —— (Second edition.) 2 vols. 1856. *See* Angelis (Dr. Don Pedro de).

1776   **Ercilla y Zuñiga** (Don Alonso de).   La Araucana. Parte I. *Madrid.* 1776.

1872   **Estete** (Miguel).   The Narrative of the journey made by el Sr. Capitan Hernando Pizarro, by order of the governor, his brother, from the city of Coxamalca to Parcama, and thence to Xaixa. *Loudon.* 1872. 8°.
     (Markham's Translation of Xeres : Hakluyt Society's Publications, No. 47: Reports on the Discovery of Peru.)

     [Miguel Estete accompanied Hernando Pizarro to Pachacamac, which he describes.]

1851–60   **Evans** (W. W.).   Peruvian Antiquities. *See* Schoolcraft (H. R.).   Historical....Information, *etc.* *Philadelphia.* 1851–60. Series V, pages 657–659.
     (A letter to Gillis concerning opening of a tomb in Arica.)

1859   Expeditions into the Valley of the Amazons, 1539, 1549, 1639 (by Pizarro, Orellana and Acuna). Translated and edited with notes by C. R. Markham. Map. *London.* 1859. 8°.
     (Hakluyt Society's Publications, No. 24.)

1883.   **Falb** (Rudolf).   Das Land der Inca in seiner Bedeutung für die Urgeschichte der Sprache and Schrift. *Leipzig.* 1883. 8°.

1888   —— Die Andes-Sprachen in ihrem Zusammenhange mit dem semitischen Sprachstamme. *Leipzig.* 1888. 8°.

1840–44   **FALBE** (C. T.).   Vases antiques du Pérou.   *Copenhagen.*
1840–44.
(Mem. de la Société Royale des Antiquaires du Nord,
pages 131–38.)

——   **FALCON** (DIE LICENTIATE).   Apologia pro Indis.   *Winsor.*

1847–59   **FAYE** (H.)   *See* HUMBOLDT (F. H. A. VON).   Cosmos....
trad. par H. F.   (Vols. 1 and 3).   4 vols.   *Paris.*   1847–
59.   8 .

1881–90   **FEATHERMAN** (A.)   Social History of the Races of Mankind.
London.   1881–90.   8°.
(Peruvians.   Third division.   Vol. 1, 1890, pages 373–415.)

1872   **FERGUSSON** (JAMES).   Rude Stone Monuments in all countries, their age and uses.   With two hundred and thirty-
four illustrations.   *London*   1872.   8°.
(Chap. XIV., pages 518–19.)

1865–7   —— History of Architecture.   2 vols.   *London.*   1865–7. 8 .
(Peru, Vol. II., page 775. Tiahuanaco.)

1571   **FERNANDEZ** (DIEGO).   Primera y Segunda Parte, de la Historia del Peru....Cõtiene la primera, lo succedido en le
Nueva España y en el Peru, sobre la execucion de las nuevas
leyes : y el allanamiento, y castigo, que hiro el Presidente
Gasca, de Gonçalo Piçarro y sus sequaces.   La Segunda,
contiene la tyrannia y alçamiento de los Contreras.   2 Parts.
Sevilla.   1571.   Fol.

[Only edition.   Its original publication prohibited by
order of the Royal Council of the Indies.   Order revoked in
1729, but reissued in 1731.]

1729   **FERNANDEZ** (J. B.)   Erbauliche und angenehme Gechsichten
derer Chiquitos, *etc.*   1729.   8°.

——   **FERNANDEZ MONTESINOS** (EL. LIC. DON).   Memorias Antiguas
Historiales dal Peru Seguidas de los Anales del Mismo
Reyno.   2 parts.   MS.

[MS. in the Archives of the Real Academia de Historia de
Madrid.   *First Part:* History of Peru from B. C. 4000 to
discovery of America by Columbus.   *Second Part:* the Anales
from 1493–1546.]

1882   —— Memorias antiguas historiales y politicas del Perú por....Fernando Montesinos, seguidas de las informaciones acerca del señorio de los Incas, hechos por mandado de D. Francisco de Toledo, virey del Perú. (1570–72). Edited by Don Marcos Jiménez de la Espada. *Madrid.* 1882. 8 .

1840   —— Memoires historiques sur l'ancien Pérou. *Paris.* 1840   8°
(Vol. 17.   Ternaux' Voyages de l'Amérique.)

[Licentiate FERNANDEZ MONTESINOS went to Peru 1629; traveled 1,500 leagues from Quito to Potosi; subsequently chaplain at Lima; afterwards Visitador General at Quito. Gives ancient records acquired from *quipus* through learned natives.   The "Anonymous" authority edited by Marcos Jiménez de la Espada incidentally confirms Montesinos' statements by referring to ancient Incas given in his lists.]

1825–37   **FERNANDEZ DE NAVARETTE** (MARTIN).   Coleccion de los Viages y Descubrimientos que hicieron por mar los Espanoles, desde fines del siglo XV.   Con varios documentos ineditos concernientes à la Historia de la marina Castellana y de los establecimientos espanoles en Indias.   5 vols.   Portrait and Maps. *Madrid.*   1825–37.   4 .

[Very important.   Extends from 1393 to 1540.   Two other volumes were left unfinished at de Navarette's death.]

1837–80   —— Second edition (of Vols. 1, 2 and 3).   5 vols. *Madrid.*   1837–80.   4°.

1828   —— French translation of Vols. 1 and 2. *Paris.*   1828.

1840–41   —— Italian translation of Vols. 1 and 2. *Prato.* 1840–41.

1868?   **FERNANDEZ NODAL** (JOSÉ).   Los Yncas del Imperio Tahuantinsuyo. *Paris.*   (1868?)   Fol.

1872   —— Elementos de Gramática Quichua ó Idioma de los Yncas, bajo los Auspicios de la Redentora Sociedad de Filantropos para Mejorar la Suerte de los Aborijenes Peruanos. *Cuzco, Aylesbury y Londres.* (Printed 1872.) 8°.

1875?   —— Elementos de Gramática Quichua ó idioma de los Yncas. *Cuzco.* (1875?) 8 .

1874   ———— Los Vinculos de Ollanta y Cusi-Kcuyllor. Drama en Quechua. *Ayacucho* (*Londres*). (1874.) 8 .

1878   ———— Legislation civile comparée des Mexicains sous le Empereurs Aztecs et des Peruviens a l'époque des Incas. *Luxemburg* and *Paris*. 1878. 8°.
(Compte-rendu de Congrés des Américanistes. Sec. Sess. Pages 235-37.)

1879   ———— Comparaison de l'Aymara du Quichua et du dialecte de Quito. *Bruxelles*. 1879. 8 .
(Compte-rendu de Congrés des Américanistes. Trois. Sess. Pages 511-24. Lists of words and bibliography.)

1526   **FERNANDEZ DE OVIEDO Y VALDES** (GONZALO). Oviedo de la natural hystoria de las Indias. 2d Title. Sumario de la natural y general istoria de las Indias. *Toledo*. 1526. Fol.
(The original of the second book of the Italian "Summario della historia delle Indie.")

1749   ———— (Another edition). Relacion sumario de la Historia natural de las Indias, *etc*. *Madrid*. 1749. Fol.
(Vol 1 of Historiadores primitivos, *etc*. of D. Andres Gonzalez de Barcia).

1534   ———— *See* XERES (F. DE). Veradera relacion de la conquista del Peru y Provincia del Cuzco. With stanzas relating to the author by G. F. de Q. y V.? (1534.) Fol.

1535   ———— La Historia general de las Indias. (Primera parte, siguen una carta missiva, *etc*.) *Sevilla*. 1535. Fol.

1557   ———— Coronica de las Indias. La Hystoria general de las Indias. Agora nuevamente impressa corregida y emendada. 1547. Y con la conquista del Peru. 1547. (Por Francisco de Xeres). *Valladolid*. 1557. Fol.

1557   ———— Libro xx de la Segunda parte de la historia de las Indias. *Valladolid*. 1557. Fol.

1851-55   ———— Historia general y natural de las Indias, islas y tierra-firme del Mar Oceano. Cotejada con el códice original, enriquecida con las enmiendas y adiciones del autor, é ilustrada con la vida del mismo por José Amador de Los Rios. (Life of Oviedo. Plates and facsimile maps). 4 vols. *Madrid*. 1851-55. Fol.
(First publication of Bks. XXI-L. Historia general y natural).

1858 —— —— De la natural hystoria de las Indias. 1858. *See* VEDIA. Hist. prim. de Indias. Vol I.

1554 —— —— La historia generale et naturale delle Indie occidentali. 1554. Fol.
(RAMUSIO (G. B.) Primo volume delle navigatione et viaggi. Vol. 3. 1554).

1563 —— —— (Another edition.) 1563. Fol.
(RAMUSIO. Navigatione et viaggi. Vol. 3. 1563.)

1555 —— —— L' Histoire naturelle et generalle des Indes....
Traduicte de Castellane en François. (By Jean Polem).
Paris. 1555. Fol.

1556 —— —— L' Histoire, *etc.*, translated....by Jean Polem.
Paris. 1556. Fol.
(Duplicate of preceding with new title page.)

1849 —— —— (Another edition.) *See* ARIBAU (B. C.). Biblioteca de autores Españoles, *etc.* Tom. 22. 1849. 8 ·

1555 —— ——— The Historie of the West Indies. *See* ANGLERIUS (P. M.) The (three) decades of the new worlde, *etc.*
1555. 4 ·

1577 —— —— (Another edition.) *See* EDEN (R.) The History of Travayle in the West and East Indies, *etc.* 1577. 4 ·

1625 —— —— Decades of the New World. *See* PURCHAS (SAMUEL) *the Elder.* Purchas his Pilgrimes, *etc.* 4 pt.
London. 1625. Fol.
(A condensed version of Eden's *Decades.*)

[GONZALO FERNANDEZ DE OVIEDO Y VALDES, born in Asturia, Spain, about 1478; resided 34 years in America; was at Panama when Pizarro and Almagro fitted out their first expedition. Afterwards Chronicler of the Indies.
Died, 1557.]

1571 **FERNANDEZ DE PALENCIA** (DIEGO). Primera y Secunde Parte de la Historia del Peru, que se mando escrétir á Diego Fernandez, vecino de la ciudad de Palencia. 2 pts. *Seville.*
1571. Fol.

[FERNANDEZ DE PALENCIA, usually called "El Palentino" from his place of birth, served in Peru against Giron, 1544; Chronicler of Peru under Viceroy Cañete.]

1816-34   FERRARIO (GIULIO).   Il Costume Antico e Moderno, o storia dell governo, della milizia, della religione, delle arti, scienze ed usanze di tetti i popoli antichi e moderni provata coi monumenti dell' antichita e rappresentata cogli analoghi designi del dottore, G. F. (assisted by A. Levati, R. Gironi and C. Magnetti).   18 vols.   *Milano.*   1816-34   4 .

1826-8   ——— Edizione seconda. . .accresciuta.   26 vols.   *Firenze*   1826-8.   8°.

1763   FEYZOO DE SOSA (DR. MIGUEL).   Relacion descriptiva de la ciudad, y provincia de Truxillo del Peru, con noticias exactas de su estado politico.   Map and plan of city.   *Madrid.*   1763.   Fol.

1700   FIGUERREDO (PADRE JUAN DE).   Vocabulary of the Chinchaysuyu Dialect.   *Lima.*   1700.   8°.
(Attached to Torres Rubio's Arte de la lengua Quichua.)

1754   ——— Arti i vocabulario de la lengua quichua general de los india del Perú, que compaso el padre Diego de Torres Rubio i añalida por P. J. de F., with vocabulary of the Chinchaysuyu dialect.   *Lima.*   1754.   16 .

[JUAN DE FIGUERREDO, missionary priest, born at Huancavelica, of Spanish parents, 1648.   Died at Lima, 1724.]

1892   FISKE (JOHN).   The discovery of America, with some account of ancient America and the Spanish conquest.   2 vols.   Maps.   *Boston.*   1892.   8 .
(Peru and Conquest, Chaps. IX and X.)

1854   FLETCHER (FRANCIS).   The World encompassed by Sir Francis Drake, by F. F.
See DRAKE (Sir FRANCIS), The World encompassed, *etc.*   *London.*   1854.   8 .

1870   FORBES (DAVID).   On the Aymara Indians of Bolivia and Peru.   Plates.   *London.*   1870.   8°.
(Journal of the Ethnological Society of London, Vol. II, N. S., pages 193-305.)

1778   FORSTER (JOHANN REINHOLD).   Observations made during a voyage round the world on Physical Geography, Natural History and Ethic Philosophy.   *London.*   1778.   4°.

1778   ———— Observations faites pendant le second voyage de
M. Cook sur la Géographie, l'histoire naturelle et la phil-
osophie moral.   (Tom. V of Cook's Voyage dans l'Hemis-
phère Austral, *etc.*)   1778.   + ·

1783   ———— (German edition.)   *Berlin.*   1783

1799   FRAGGIA, *etc.*   Indice de la Coleccion de manuscritos perti-
necientes a la historia de las Indias.   *Madrid.*   1799.
(Jackson (J.), Bibl. Geogr., No. 612.)

1577   FRAMPTON (J.).   *See* MONARDES (NICHOLAS), Joyfull Newes
out of the newe founde Worlde, *etc.*   Englished by J. F.
London.   1577.   4 ·

1885   FREUZEL (KARL WILHELM).   Der Schuck des Inka.   *München*
and *Leipzig.*   1885.   16′ ·
(Incas are Celts.   Neuer Deutcher Novellenschatz, Bd.
XII, pages 73–183.)

1716   FREZIER (AMEDÉE FRANCOIS).   Relation du Voyage de la
mer du Sud aux côtes du Chily et du Pérou fait pendant
les années 1712, 1713 and 1714.   With plates and maps.
Paris.   1716.   4°·
(First described the Quippu.)

1717   ———— (Another edition.)   2 vols.   *Amsterdam.*   1717.   12 ·

1732   ———— (Another edition.)   *Paris.*   1732.   4 ·

1717   ———— A voyage to the South Sea and along the coasts of
Chile and Peru in....1712, 1713 and 1714.   Cuts.   *London.*
1717.   4 ·

1747   ———— Reise an den Küsten von Peru, 1713.   1747.   + ·
(Schwabe, Allgemeine Histoire der Reisen, Vol. XV.
1747.)

1707   FRITZ (SAMUEL).   Map of the Amazons, *Quito*, 1707.   *See*
STOCKLEIN, Reise Beschreibungen; MARKHAM (C. R.), Valley
of the Amazons, page xxxiii.

1889   FRY (CARLOS).   La gran region de los bosques rios Peruanos
navegables Urubamba, Ucayli, Amazonas, Pachitea y Palcaza.
Diario de viajes y exploraciones por Carlos Fry en 1886, 1887
y 1888.   Maps and illus.   *Lima.*   1889.   + ·

1859   FUENTES (DON MANUEL).   Memorias de los Vireyes que han
gobernado el Perú, durante el tempo del Coloniaje Español.
Edited by Don M. F.   6 vols.   *Lima.*   1859.   + ·

1867   ——— (Another edition.) Relaciones de los Vireyes y Audiencias que han gobernado el Peru. *Lima.* 1867. Fol.

1866   ——— Lima, or Sketches of the Capitol of Peru; historical, statistical, administrative, commercial and moral. Portraits and plates. *Paris.* 1866. 8 .
(Part VI (pages 75–219), Natives, with illustrations.)

1568   FUMÉE (MART.). *See* LOPEZ DE GOMARA (FRANCISCO), Histoire Générale des Indes occidentales....trad. par M. F. *Paris.* 1568. 8°.

1868   GABRIAC (COMTE DE). Promenade à travers l'Amérique du Sud. Nouvelle Grenade, Equateur, Pérou, Brésil. Maps and illus. *Paris.* 1868. 8°.

1547.   GAHORY (JACQUES). L'Histoire de la terre nueve du Péru en l'Indie occidentale, trad., par J. G. *Paris.* 1547.

[Pretends to be a summary of Oviedo, but is a translation of Xeres' *Relacion*.]

1880   GALLENGA (ANTONIO), pseud. MARIOTTI (L.). South America. *London.* 1880.
(Peru and Bolivia, pages 45–143.)

1596   GALLUCIO (GIOVANNI PAOLO). Historia naturale e morale delle Indie nov. trad....de G. P. G. *Venetia.* 1596. 4 .

1860   GALTON (FRANCIS). Vacation Tourist. Vol. I. 1860. *See* BOWEN (C. C.), Visit to Peru.

1865   ——— *See* RISING (*Lieut.*). On the artificial eyes of certain Peruvian mummies, with Notes by F. G. *London.* 1865. 8°.

1847–59   GALUSKY (C.). *See* HUMBOLDT (F. H. A. VON). Cosmos ...trad. par C. G. (Vols. II and IV.) 4 vols. *Paris.* 1847–59. 8 .

1601   GALVANO (A.). The Discoveries of the World from their first original unto the yœre....1555....corrected, quoted and now published in English by R[ichard] H[akluyt]. *London.* 1601. 4 .

1862   ——— (Another edition.) Edited by Admiral Bethune. *London.* 1862. 8 .
See HAKLUYT SOCIETY. No. XXX.

1803 —— —— *See* CLARKE (J. S.), The Progress of Maritime Discovery, *etc.* Vol. I. Appendix. 1803. 4°.

1729 **GARCIA** (FRAY GREGORIO). Origen de los Indios de el Nuevo Mundo e Indias Occidentales, Averiguado con Discurso de Opiniones. *Madrid.* 1729. Fol.

(Peru, the Ophir of Solomon; gives the earliest notice of Betanzo's narrative. Gregorio Garcia traveled extensively in the Spanish Colonies.)

—— —— —— — Monarquia de los Incas del Peru. MS.

(Lost. Referred to by D. Nicholas Antonio. Bibl. Hist.)

GARCILASSO DE LA VEGA. *See* LASSO DE LA VEGA (GARCIA.)

1877 **GASCA** (PEDRO DE LA). *See* CARTAS DE INDIAS. *Madrid.* 1877. Fol. Letter LXXXVI. Carta del licenciado Pedro de la Gasca al Consejo de Indias, dando cuenta de su llegada al puerto de Santa Marta y de las noticias alli recibedas sobre el esteido de los asuntos del Perú. Santa Marta de Julio de 1546.

LXXXVII. a Miguel Dies Armendariz, dandale noticia de la expedicion que disponia contra Gonzalo Pizarro. Panama, 27 de Feb., 1547.

LXXXVIII. al Consejo de Indias, participando que enviaba à Espagña, con personas de confianza, los leyos de Juan y Gonzalo Pizarro, para que cuidar de en educacion los parientes que tenian en Castillæ. Los Reyes, 15 de Feb., 1549.

LXXXIX. al Consejo de Indias, recomendando à Fray Pedro de Ulloa. Los Reyes, 22 de Febro. de 1549.

XC. al Consejo de Indias proponiendo dobear el salario a los oidores, para que en todo pudieran proceder con rectitud è inde prudencia. Los Reyes, 20 de Julio de 1549.

XCI. al Consejo de Indias, avicando las desposiciones que se habian adaptado respecto al repartimiento de coca, que tuvo Francisco Pizarro. Los Reyes, 16 Septiembre de 1549.

XCII. From Ondegardo to Gasca.

XCIII. al Consejo de Indias, remitiendo alar ordenanza que hizo sobre la presentacion de apelaciones interpuestas ante aquella Chancielleria, avisando lo acordaba respecto de la tasa de tributos, y del envio de un cargamento de barras de plata y dando cuenta de otros acuntos de aquella gobernacion. Puerta de la ciudad le Los Reyes, 8 de Noviembre de 1549.

XCIV. a los principales de Hungria y Bohemia, Maximiliano y Maria, gobernadores de Espagna, dandoles cuenta del estado de los asuntos en el Peru.   Puerto de Ciudad de Los Reyos, 6 de Deciembre de 1549.

XCV. al precidente y señores del Conseyo de Indias, sobre lo conveniente que seria anmentar los repartimientos de la Corona en el Peru.   Rio de Sevella, 22 de Setiembre de 1550.

XCVI. Condition of country on the departure of Gasca. Aug. 11, 1550.

1873   —— See ARANA (D. B.).   Proceso de Pedro de Valdivia i otros documentos, etc.   Santiago (Chile).   (1873.)   8 .

(Gasca's despatch of May, 1548, describing defeat and execution of Gonzalo Pizarro, with other despatches dated Lima, Sept. 25 and Nov. 26, 1548.)

1880   —— Instructions to Lorenzo de Aldana, Letters to Gonzalo Pizarro, and detailed Report of his agent, Panigua. Revista de Lima.   Lima.   1880.

[LICENCIADO PEDRO DE LA GASCA sailed from Spain May 26, 1546, with title of President of the Audencia, to carry out order revoking the "New Laws," which led to Gonzalo Pizarro's rebellion, which he put down with great cruelty. Left Peru suddenly, January, 1550, on receipt of order that all personal service of Indians should be abolished, leaving affairs in great confusion.   Many of his papers preserved by the family and made use of by Helps for his Spanish Conquest. Gasca's Report, dated Andahuaylas, March 7, 1548, written on his way to attack Gonzalo Pizarro, has not been published.]

1620   GAVILAN (FRAY ALONZO RAMOS).   Historia de Copacabana y de su milagrosa imagen.   1620.

1860   (Another edition.).   Edited by Fr. Rafael Sans. La Paz.   1860.

[Throws light on the movements of the Inca colonists, Mitionaes; gives version of Inca calendar.]

1875   GAYANGOS (PASCUAL DE).   Catalogue of the Manuscripts in the Spanish language in the British Museum.   London. 1875, etc.   8°.

(America.   Vol. II.)

1535   **GAZTELU** (DOMINGO DE). *See* XERES (FRANC. DE). Libro primo de la conquista del Peru, *etc.* (Translated by D. de G.) *Vinegia.* 1535. 4 ·

1853   **GHILLANY** (F. W.). Geschichte des Seefahrer's Ritter. 1853. Fol. *See* HUMBOLDT (F. H. A. VON). Uber die ältesten Karten des Neuen Continent, *etc.*

1891   **GIGLIOLI** (H. H.). On two ancient Peruvian masks made with the facial portion of human skulls. Plate. *Leiden.* 1891. (Internat. Archiv. für Ethnologie. IV, 83–87.)

1891   ———— Maschere fatte colla parte faciale d'crani umani proventienti dal Yunca-Suyu. *Firenze.* 1891. (Archiv. für l'Anthropologie. XXI, 41–45.)

1855   **GILLIS** (J. N.). The United States naval astronomical expedition to the southern hemisphere during the years 1849–50– 51–52. Maps and plates. *Washington.* 1855. 4°· (Vol. 1, Chile; Vol. II, The Andes and Pampas.)

1851, *etc.*   ———— *See* SCHOOLCRAFT (H. R.). Historical and Statistical Information....of the Indian Tribes. Vol. V. *Philadelphia.* 1856, *etc.* 4 · *See* EVANS (W. W.). Peruvian Antiquities.

1857   **GLIDDON** (GEORGE R.). *See* NOTT (J. C.). Indigenous Races of the Earth, *etc.* *Philadelphia.* 1857. 4 ·

1889-90   **GOLDSMITH** (E.). *See* HAKLUYT (R.). Principal Navigations, Voyages, *etc.* Edited by E. G. 55 Parts. *Edinburgh.* 1889–90. (Vol. XII–XVI. America and Voyages of circumnavigation.)

        GOMARA (LOPEZ DE). *See* LOPEZ DE GOMARA (FRANCISCO).

1586   **GONZALEZ HOLGUIN** (PADRE DIEGO). Vocabulario de la lengua general de todo el Peru llamada lengua Qquichua, o del Inca....corregido y renovado conforme a la propriedad cortesana del Cuzco. *Ciudad de Los Reyes.* (*Lima.*) 1586. 8·

1608   ———— (Another edition.) *Ciudad de Los Reyes.* 1608. 4 ·

1603   ———— Gramatica y Vocabulario de la lengua del Peru. *Seville.* 1603.

        [Supposed first edition of the Gramatica of 1607 and the Vocabulario of 1608.]

1607   ——— Gramatica y Arte nueva de la lengua general de todo el Peru, llamada Qquichua, ó lengua del Inca. *Los Reyes del Peru.* (Lima.) 1607. 4·

1614   ——— Arte y Vocabulario en la lengua general del Peru llamada Qquichua, y en la lengua Española....en *los Reyes.* (Lima.) 1614. 12°.

[Usually ascribed to its publisher, Francisco del Canto.]

1842   ——— (Another edition) Gramatica y Arte, *etc.*, Añadida y cumplida....Nueva edicion revista y corregida. *Geneva.* 1842. 4·

1842   ——— (Another edition) revista y corregida. *Lima.* 1842. 8°.

[DIEGO GONZALES HOLGUIN, born in Estremadura, Spain, about 1552; became Jesuit, 1568; went to Peru, 1581. Studied Quichua at Juli, near Lake Titicaca, where established printing press. Became interpreter. Died at Ascencion, Paraguay, 1618.]

1873   **GONZALES DE LA ROSA** (DR. MANUEL). *See* CIEZA DE LEON (PEDRO DE). Segunde parte de la Cronica del Peru. *London.* 1873.

1879   ——— *See* COBO (FATHER BERNABÉ) Historia de Lima, edited by Dr. M. G. de la R. *Lima.* 1879.

1880   ——— *See* CARRERA (DON FERNANDO DE LA.) Arte de lengua Yunga, *etc.* Edited by Dr. G. de la R. *Lima.* 1880. 8°.

1863   **GOSSE** (L. A.) Dissertation sur les races qui composaient l'ancienne population du Pérou. Plates. *Paris.* 1863. 8°.
(Mem. Soc. d'Anthropol. de Paris (1860–63). Vol. I, pages 149–176.)

1819   **GRAHAM** (JOHN) AND **RODNEY** (C. A.) *See* RODNEY (C. A.). Report on the present state of the United States of South America, *etc. London.* 1819.

1861   **GRANDIDIER** (ERNEST) Voyage dans l'Amérique du Sud, Perou et Bolivie. *Paris.* 1861. 8°.

1888   **GRATECAP** (L. P.) Peruvian civilization. Chicago. 1888. 8°.
(American Antiquarian. Vol. X, pages 95–115.)

GRAVALIZ (AUGUSTINO DE).   *See* CRAVELIZ (AGOSTINO).

1604   GRIMSTON (EDWARD).   *See* ACOSTA (JOSÉ DE).   The naturall and morall Historie of the Indies....translated by E. G. 1604.   4°.

1888   GROSSI (N.).   Le Mummie nell' antico e nel nuovo mondo. *Torino.*   1888.

1612   GUALDO (DIEGO DE).   Arte de la lengua Aymara con una sylva de frasis de la misma lengua, y su declaracion en romance.   1612.   8°.

1540   GUAZZO (MARCO) Historie di tutte le cose degne di memoria qual del anno MDXXXIV.   *Venice.*   1540.

1545   —— (Another edition.)   *Venice.*   1545.

1546   —— (Another edition.)   *Venice.*   1546.

1614   GUERRO (LOBO) *Archbishop.*   Constituciones Synodales. *Lima.*   1614.

1754   —— (Another edition.)   *Lima.*   1754.

GUETTE (DE LA).   *See* BROÉ (DE) *Seig. de Citry et de la G.*

1817   GUEULLETTE (THOMAS SIMON).   *See* HUMPHREYS (SAMUEL). Peruvian Tales, *etc.   London.*   1817.   16°.

1888   GUILLAUME (H.).   The Amazon provinces of Peru as a field for European emigration.   A statistical and geographical review of the country and its resources, including the gold and silver mines, together with a mass of useful and valuable information, with map and illustrations. *London.*   1888.   12°.

1862   GUZMAN (ALONZO ENRIQUEZ DE).   Life and Acts of.   1518-43.   Translated by C. L. Markham.   *London.*   1862.   8°. (Hakluyt Society Pub.   No. XXIX.)

[ALONZO ENRIQUEZ DE GUZMAN, friend of Almagro, born about 1500; went to Peru, 1534.   A principal actor in events between Almagro's expedition to Chili, 1535, and his execution, 1538.   His autobiography extends to 1543; includes letter to the Emperor on the conduct of Hernando Pizarro.]

1582   HAKLUYT (RICHARD).   Divers Voyages touching the Discovery of America, *etc.* (by R. H.).   B. L.   2 parts. *London.* 1582.   4°.

1850   ———— (Another edition.) Edited by J. Winter Jones. *London.* 1850. 8°.
                (Hakluyt Soc. Pub.   No. VII.)

1587   ———— *See* ANGLERIUS (P. M.). De orbe novo decades octo. Annotationibus, illustratæ, labore R. H. 1587. 8°.

1620?   ———— *See* ANGLERIUS (P. M.). The Historie of the West Indies....published in Latin by Mr. Hakluyt, *etc.* (1620?) 4°.
                (R. H. collection of the early voyages, *etc.* 1809. Vol. V.)

1589   The principall navigations, voyages and discoveries of the English nation, made by sea or over land....within the compasse of these 1500 yeeres; divided into three parts.... Whereunto is added the last most renowned English navigation (*i. e.* Thomas Cavendish) round the....earth. B. L. *London.* 1589. Fol.

1598–1600   ————The principal navigations, voyages, traffiques and discoveries of the English nation, *etc.* 3 vols. B. L. *London.* 1598–1600. Fol.

1809-12   ———— (Another edition.) 5 vols. *London.* 1809–12. 4°.
                (American Voyages, Vol. III.)

1812   ———— A collection of curious, rare and early voyages and histories of interesting discoveries, chiefly published by Hakluyt, or at his suggestion, but not included in his....compilation, to which, to Purchas, and other general collections, this is intended as a supplement. *London.* 1812. 4°.

1884–90   ———— Principal navigations, voyages, *etc.*, collated by R. II., edited by E. Goldsmid. 55 parts. *Edinburgh.* 1884–90. 4°.
                (America and Voyages of Circumnavigation. Vols. XII.–XVI.)

1601   ———— *See* GALVANO (A.) The Discoveries of the World ....corrected....and now published in English by R. H. *London.* 1601. 4°.

1803   ———— *See* CLARKE (J. S.). The Progress of Maritime Discovery, *etc.* Vol. I. Appendix. 1803. 4°.

1862   ———— (Another edition.) The Discoveries of the World by A. Galvano. Edited by Admiral Bethune. *London.* 1862. 8°.
                (Hakluyt Soc. Pub., No. XXX.)

1880   —————   The Voyages of the Elizabethan Seamen to America.   Thirteen original narratives from the collection of Hakluyt, selected and edited, with historical narratives, by E. J. Payne. *London.* 1880. 8°.

HAKLUYT SOCIETY (*London.*)   Publications.

1847   I. HAWKINS (SIR RICHARD). Observations on his Voyage into the South Sea in 1593, 1622. Edited by Cap. C. R. Bethune. *London.* 1847. 8°.

1849   IV. DRAKE (SIR FRANCIS), his Voyage, 1595, by Thomas Maynarde. Edited from the original manuscripts by W. D. Cooley. *London.* 1849. 8°.

1850   VII. HAKLUYT (RICHARD). Divers voyages touching the Discovery of America and the Islands adjacent, 1582; edited by J. Winter Jones. Facsimile and two maps. *London.* 1850. 8°.

1854   XVII. FLETCHER (FRANCIS). The World encompassed by SIR FRANCIS DRAKE; edited by W. S. W. Vaux. Map. *London.* 1854. 8°.

1857   XXI. BENZONI (GIROLAMO). History of the New World, Travels, 1541–56. *Venice,* 1572. Translated and edited by Admiral W. H. Smyth. Facsimile wood-cuts. *London.* 1857. 8°.

1859   XXIV. EXPEDITIONS into the Valley of the Amazons, 1539, 1540, 1639: translated and edited by C. R. Markham. *London.* 1859. 8°.

1862   XXVIII. EXPEDITION of URSUA and AGUIRRE in search of El Dorado. Translated by Wm. Bollaert. *London.* 1862. 8°.

1862   XXIX. Life of DON ALONZO ENRIQUEZ DE GUZMAN. Translated by C. R. Markham. *London.* 1862. 8°.

1862   XXX. The Discoveries of the World by A. GALVANO ....corrected by.... Richard Hakluyt. Edited by Admiral Bethune. *London.* 1862. 8°.

1864   XXXIII. PEDRO DE CIEZA DE LEON. Travels, A. D. 1532–50, contained in the first part of his Chronicle of Peru; translated and edited by C. R. Markham. Map. *London.* 1864. 8°.

1865   XXXIV. NARRATIVE of PASCUAL DE ANDAGOYA, containing the earliest notice of Peru.   Translated by C. R. Markham. *London.* 1865. 8 .

1869.   XLI. and XLV. ROYAL COMMENTARIES of the Yncas, by the Ynca GARCILASSO DE LA VEGA.   Translated by C. R. Markham. Vols. I. and II. *London.* 1869. 8°.

1872   XLVII. REPORTS on the Discovery of Peru.   Translated by C. R. Markham. *London.* 1872. 8 .

1873   XLVIII. NARRATIVES of the Rites and Laws of the Yncas.   Translated from the Spanish MSS. by C. R. Markham. *London.* 1873. 8°.

1877   LVII.   The Hawkins Voyages.   Observations of SIR J. HAWKINS on his voyage into the South Sea in 1593, *etc.*, by C. R. Markham. *London.* 1877. 8 .

1878–80   LIX. Voyages and Works of JOHN DAVIS, the navigator.   By Cap. A. H. Markham.   Facsimile map of the world, A. D. 1600, called the "Mollineux Map." *London.* 1878–80. 8 .

1878–79   LX. and LXI.   ACOSTA'S Natural and Moral History of the Indies, from the English edition of E. Grimston. 1604. By C. R. Markham. 2 vols. *London.* 1878–79. 8 .

1883.   LXVIII. CHRONICLE OF PERU, by PEDRO DE CIEZA DE LEON. Second part. Translated with notes by C. R. Markham. *London.* 1883. 8°.

1844   HALE (HORATIO).   United States Exploring Expedition.... Ethnography and Philology. By H. H. *See* WILKES (C.) *Comm. U. S. N.* Narrative of the U. S. Exploring Expedition, *etc.* Vol. 6. 1844, *etc.* 4°.

1824   HALL (BASIL) *Captain.* Extracts from a journal written on the coasts of Chili, Peru and Mexico, in the years 1820, 1821, 1822. Map. 2 vols. *London.* 1824. 8°.

1824   —— (Second edition.) 2 vols. *Edinburgh.* 1824. 8°.

1824   —— (Another edition.) 2 vols. *Philadelphia.* 1824. 8°.

——— (Third edition.)

1825   —— (Fourth edition.) 2 vols. *Edinburgh.* 1825. 8°.

1826   —— (Another edition.)   2 vols. *See* CONSTABLE (A.) Constable's Miscellany, vols. 2 and 3.   1826, *etc.*   12°.

1835   ——— Voyage au Chili, au Pérou et au Mexique, entrepris par ordre du gouvernment anglais. Map. 2 vols. *La Haye*. 1835. 12´.

1841   ——— Voyage aux États-Unis de l'Amérique septentrion-elle, d'après B. H., *etc. See* Duponchel (A.): Nouvelle Bibliothéque des Voyages, *etc.* Vol. 12. 1841, *etc.* 8°.

1849   Hall (J. C.) *See* Pickering (Charles). The Races of Man ....New edition, to which is prefixed an Analytical Synopsis of the Natural History of Man, by J. C. H. *London.* 1849. 8°.

1850   ——— New edition (Bohn's Illustrated Library.) *London.* 1850. 8°.

1705   Harris (John) *D. D.* Navigantium atque Itinerantium Bib-liotheca ; or a compleat collection of Voyages and Travels, consisting of about four hundred of the most authentick writers. 2 vols. *London.* 1705. Fol.
     (*See* Betach (Wm.) I ; Dampier (William.) II.)

1744–48   ——— (Another edition.) Carefully revised, with large additions, and continued down to the present time, by Dr. John Campbell. 2 vols. *London.* 1744–48. Fol.

1764   ——— (Another edition.) Revised, with large additions, (by Dr. John Campbell). 2 vols. *London.* 1764. Fol.

1866–72   Harrisse (Henry). Bibliotheca Americana Vetutissima. A description of works relating to America, published between ....1492 and 1551 (additions). *New York ; Paris.* (Addi-tions–*Paris*). 1866–72. 8°.
     (Copies of MSS. preserved in New York and Boston, pages 320–22.)

1875   Hartt (C. F.) Amazonian Myths. *Rio de Janeiro.* 1875. 8°.

1830–34   Harvard College. General catalogue of the College Li-brary. 5 vols. 1830-34.
     (Includes the American Library of Prof. Ebeling and the Americana collected by David B. Warden.)

1867   Hassaurek (F.) Four years among the Spanish Ameri-cans. *New York.* 1867.
     (Chap. XVI, epitome of history of Quito.)

1569   HAWKINS (SIR JOHN) *Rear Admiral.* A true declaration of
the troublesome voyage of M. J. Hawkins to the parties of
Guyney and the West Indies, in the yeares of our Lord 1567
and 1568. *London.* 1569. 8°.

1598   ——— The first voyage of....Sir J. H....made to the
West Indies, 1562. The second voyage made by J. H....
to the coast of Guinea and the Indies of Nova Hispania,
begun in An. Dom. 1564. The third troublesome voyage
made....to the parts of Guinea, and the West Indies in the
years 1567 and 1568.
        See Hakluyt (R.): Collection of Early Voyages.   1598,
etc. Fol.
        (Coast of Chili, Peru and Ecuador.)

1809   ——— (Another edition.) Hakluyt. Vol. 3. 1809, *etc.* 4°.

1847   ——— Observations on his Voyage into the South Sea in
1593–1622. Edited by Capt. C. R. Bethune. *London.* 1847.
8°. (Hakluyt Soc. No. 1.)

1877   ——— (Another edition.) Voyages during the reigns of
Henry VIII, Elizabeth and James I. Observations, *etc.*,
with introduction by C. L. Markham. Portrait. *London.*
1877. 8°
        (Hakluyt Society's publications, No. 57.)

1619   ——— Voyagie von Siere F. Draeck, en Siere Jan Hau-
kins, *etc. See* COLLIN (M.) Oost–Indesche onde West–Indesche Voyagien, *etc.*, pt. 6. 1619, *etc.* 4°.

1643   ——— Der Schif–Vaert van....F. Draeck en....J. H....
West Indien. Journalen van de Voyagien, *etc.* 1643. 4°.

1599   ——— Die letzte Reysz der Edlen....F. Draeck und J.
H., *etc. See* BRY (T. DE). (America, Pt. VII. German).
Americæ achter Theil, *etc.* 1599. Fol.

1853   HAWKS (F. L.) *See* RIVERO Y USTARIZ (M. ED. DE) and
TSCHUDI (J. D. DE). Peruvian Antiquities. Translated....
by F. L. H. *New York*, 1853. 8°.

1605   HAYUS (JUAN). De Rebus Japonicis, Indicus et Peruanis
Epistolæ recentiores. *Antuerpiæ.* 1605.

1878   HEATH (E. R.) Peruvian Antiquities. Kansas City Review.
Vol. I (1878), pages 455–69.
        (General account of Peruvian ruins—coast and interior.)

1847   **HELLWALD** (FRIEDRICH VON) Die Erde und ihre Völker. *See* STANFORD (————) Compendium of Geography and Travel (based on Hellwald's *Die Erde und ihre Völker*). *London.* 1874, *etc.* 8°.

1798   **HELMS** (ANTON ZACHARIAS). Tagebuch einer Reise durch Peru von Buenos Ayres au dem groszen Plataflusse, über Potosi nach Lima. *Dresden.* 1798 8°.

1806   ———— Travels from Buenos Ayres, by Potosi, to Lima. With notes by the translator, containing topographical descriptions of the Spanish possessions in South America, drawn from the last and best authorities. (Two maps.) *London.* 1806. 12°.

1807   ———— (Second edition.) *London.* 1807. 8°.

1805   ————(Another edition.) *See* A Collection of Modern.... Voyages and Travels, *etc.* Vol. 5. 1805, *etc.* 8°.

1812   ———— Voyage dans l'Amérique meridionale, commençant par Buenos Ayres et Potosi qusqu' à Lima. Translated from the English. *Paris.* 1812. 8°.

1855–61   **HELPS** (SIR ARTHUR). The Spanish Conquest in America and its relation to the history of slavery and to the government of the colonies, *London.* 1855–61. 8°.

(Inca civilization, Vol. III., Bk. XIII., Chap. III., pages 468–513).

1869   ———— The Life of Pizarro, with some account of his associates in the conquest of Peru. *London.* 1869. 8°.

1877   **HENRY** (V.). Le Quichua est-il une langue aryenne ? Examine critique du livre de V. F. Lopez: Les races aryennes du Perou. *Paris and Luxemburg.* 1877.

(Compte-Rendu de Congrés des Americanistes, ii, pages 75–157.)

n. d.   **HEREDES** (HOMANIANOS). *See* MAPS. Tabula Americæ specialis geographica regna Peru. *n. d.*

1652   **HEREMITE** (JACQUES D') *Admiral.* Journal van de Nassauche Vloot. *Amsterdam.* 1652. *See* MADRIDA (PEDRO DE) Observations, *etc.*

1620?   **HERNANDEZ** (MELCHIOR). Memorial de Chirique del padre presentado Fr. M. H. (*Madrid?* 1620?) Fol.

1853-4   HERNDON (WM. LEWIS) and GIBBON (LARDNER).   Exploration of the Valley of the Amazon, made under the direction
of the Navy Department.   Maps and illus.   4 vols.   *Washington.*   1853-4.   8°.
>   (Part I (Herndon) Lima, Pasco, Huallaga.   Part II (Gib-
bon) Jarma, Cuzco, La Paz, *etc.*)

1854   —— (Another edition of Herndon's Report).   1 vol.
(Different title page and additional map.)   *Washington.*   1854.
8°.

HERRERA (ANTONIO DE).   *See* HERRERA TORDESILLAS (AN-
TONIO DE).

——   HERRERA TORDESILLAS (ANTONIO DE).   Vida y elojio del licenciado Vaca de Castro Gobernador del Peru.

1601-15   —— Historia General de los hechos de los Castellanos
en las Islas i Tierra firme del Mar Oceano.   8 Decads.
Descripcion de las Indias Ocidentales.   9 parts.   Portraits.
14 Maps.   5 vols.   *Madrid.*   1601-15.   Fol.

1726-30   —— (Second edition.)   With notes by A. G. Barcia.
8 vols.   *Madrid.*   1726-30.   Fol.
>   (Usually cited as of 1730.)

1728   —— (Another edition.)   *Antwerp.*   1728.
(No maps, and with DeBry's instead of Herrera's engravings.)

1738   —— (Another edition.)   Sigué á la ultima decada la
description de las Indias.   4 vols.   *Amberes.*   1738.   Fol.

1852   —— Historia de la Indias Ocidentalis, *etc.*   (Lib. i–vi.
Las Glorias Nacionalis.)   *Madrid.*   1852.   4°.

1622   —— Novus Orbis, sive descriptio Indiæ Occidentalis....
metaphraste G. Barlæo.   Accesserunt et aliorum Indiæ
Occidentalis Descriptiones, et Navigationes nuperæ Australis
Jacobi Le Maire Historia, uti et navigationum omnium per
Fretum Magellanicum succinta narratio.   *Amsterdam.*   1622.
Fol.

1624   —— Descriptio Insularum et Continentis....quæ vulgo
India Occidentalis vocantur.   (Bry (T. de) America, Part
xii.   Novi Orbis pars duodecima, *etc.*)   *Francofurti.*   1624.
Fol.

1622 ————Description des Indes Occidentales, qu' on appelle
• aujourdhuy le Nouveau Monde.... Traduite d'Espagnol en
François. A la quelle sont adjoustées quelques antres descriptions des mesmes pays.... Illustrations and 17 maps.
Amsterdam. 1622. Fol.

(*Journal* of Jacques Le Maire; *Relation* of Cap. Don Jean
de More; abridgment of the voyages of Magellan, Gutierres,
Carvajal, Fray Garcia de Loaysa, Francis Drake, Pedro
Sarmiento, Thos. Candios, Jaques Mahu, Semion de Cordes,
and Olivier du Nort. Particulière description del' Inde Occidentale, par Pedro Ordonnez de Civallos; et description
d'Amérique tiré des tableaux géographiques de Petrus
Bertonio.)

1660–71 ———— Historie generale des Voyages et conquestes des
Castellans, dans les Indes et Terra-firme des Indes occidentales. Traduite de l'Espagnol.... par. N. de la Coste.
3 vols. *Paris.* 1660–71. 4 .
(Comprises only the first three decades.)

1622 ———— Nieuwe Werelt. *Amsterdam.* 1622. Fol.

1725–6 ———— The General History of the vast continent and
Islands of America, commonly called the West Indies....
with the best accounts the people could give of their antiquities.... Translated by John Stevens. 6 vols. *London.*
1725–6. 8°.

1740 ———— (Another edition.) Cuts and maps. 6 vols. *London.* 1740. 12°.
(Same edition as that of 1725–6, with fresh titles.)

1744 General Observations, etc. (Churchill's Collection of
Voyages, etc. Vol. 5.) *London.* 1744. Fol.

1752 ———— (Another edition.) Churchill's Collection. *London.*
1752. Fol.

1859 *See* ORELLANA (FRANCISCO DE). Expedition into the Valley of the Amazons. 1540. Translated by C. R. Markham.
London. 1859. 8 .

[ANTONIO DE HERRERA or HERRERA TORDESILLAS, born 1549,
died 1625. Appointed by Philip II of Spain historiagrapher,
which office he held under the two following reigns. Herrera is
regarded as an annalist rather than historian; copied largely

from Las Casas. His works display great "research, candor, and justness," although his method is considered too strictly chronological. Gives portraits of the Incas supposed to have been copied from those on the pedigree of the Incas, inscribed on cloth, sent to Spain by the Viceroy Don Francisco de Toledo.]

1834   HERRERO (PAD. F. ANDRÉS). Doctrina y oraciones cristiana en lengua mosetana traducitas en español, palabra por palabra. *Roma.* 1834.
(Follows text adopted by the Council of Lima.)

1784   HERVAS Y PANDURO (D. LORENZO). Catalogo delle langue conosciute e notizia della loro affinitá é diversitá. *Cesena.* 1784. 4°.

1800 5   —— Catalogo de las lenguas de las naciones conocidas, *etc.*.....6 vols. *Madrid.* 1800-5. 4°.
(Vol. II (1801) Lenguas y naciones de las Islas de los mares Pacifico è Indiano austral y oriental, y del continente de Asia.)

1785   —— Origine, formazione, meccanismo, ed armonia degl' idiomi. *Cesena.* 1785. 4°.
(Vol. 18 of Idea del Universo (*Cesena*), 1778-81. 21 vols. 4°) and also part of Vol. 22 of the same work, published in 1792.)

1786   —— Aritmetica delle nazioni e divisione del tempo fra l'orientali. *Cesena.* 1786. 4'.
(Vol. 19 and part of Vol. 22 (1792) of the Idea del Universo.)

1787   —— Vocabulario poligloto con prolegomeni sopra piu C. L. lingue dove sono delle scoperte nuove, ed utili all' antica storia dell' uman genere, ad alla cognizione del mecanismo delle parole. *Cesena.* 1787. 4°.
(Vol. 20 and part of Vol. 22 (1792) of the Ideal del Universo.)

1787   —— Saggio pratico delle lingue con prologomeni, e una raccolta di orazione Dominicali in piu di tricento lingue.... *Cesena.* 1787. 4'.
(Vol. 21 of the Ideal del Universo and contained in Vol. 22 (1792)).

——— ——— Gramaticas obreviadas de los diez y ocho lenguas principales de America.
(MS. appears to be lost.)

1860   HILL (S. S.).   Travels in Peru and Mexico.   2 vols.   *London.*   1860.   4 .

1890   HITTEL (JOHN S.).   Looking Backward in Peru.   *San Francisco.*   1890.   8 .
(The Overland, Vol. XV, s. s. pages 630–38.)

1860   HOEVEN (JAN VAN DER).   Catalogus craniorum divers. gentium.   Lugd. *Batavia.*   1860.   8°.

——— ——— Omtrent eenige menschlijke Schedels.   8 .

HOLGUIN (DON PEDRO GONZALEZ).   *See* GONZALEZ HOLQUIN (DON P.).

1884   HOLMES (W. H.)   Burial masks of the ancient Peruvians.   *Cambridge* (Mass.).   1884.
(Science.   Vol. IV. pages 10–11.)

1889   ———- Textile Fabrics of Ancient Peru.   Illustrated.   *Washington.*   1889.   8°.
(Smithsonian Institution.   Bureau of Ethnology.)

——— HOMER (ARTHUR).   Bibliotheca Americana.   12 vols.
(MS. Sir Thomas Phillips' Library, Middlehill (Eng.) Copy in Cornell Library, Ithaca (N. Y.).)

1579   HÖNIGER (N.).   *See* BENZONI (G.).   Der Neuern Weldt and Indianischen Königreichs, *etc.*, auss dem Latein in das Teusch gebracht durch N. H., *etc.   Basel.*   1579.   Fol.

1887   HORSLEY (VICTOR).   Trephining in the Neolithic period.   *London.*   1887.   8 .
(Jol. Anthrop. Inst., November, 1887.   Vol. xvii.)

1616   HUERTA (ALONSO DE).   Arte de la lengua Quechua general de los Yndios de este Reyno del Peru.   *Los Reyes (Lima).*   1616.   4 .

1844   HUEVAL (J. A. VAN).   El Dorado.   *New York.*   1844.
(Appendix vi, page 166.)

1598–1650   HULSIUS (LEVINUS).   Collection of Voyages and Travels. Edited by Levinus Hulsius and his successors.   (German.) 26 Thle.   *Franckfurt am Mayn, Norribergae, Oppenheim, Hanaw.*   1598–1650.   8 .

1603   Theil VI.   Kurtze, warhafftige Relation und Beschreibung
der Wunderbarsten vier Schiffarten....F. Megellani....mit
C. de Cano, F. Draconis....T. Candisch...O. von Noort
....Maps and Plates.   *Noribergae.*   1603.   4°.

——— (Second edition.)

1620   ——— (Third edition.)   *Frankfurt.*   1626.   4°.

1623   ——— Theil XVIII.   Grundliche volkommene Entdeckung
aller der West Indianischen Landschafften....durch A. de
Herrera.   *Frankfurt am Mayn.*   1623.   4°.

1805-34   **Humboldt** (**Friedlich Heinrich Alexander von**)   *Baron,*
and **Bonpland** (Aimé).   Voyages aux Regions Equinoxiales
du Nouveau Continent, faits dans les années 1799 á 1804.
Redigé par A. de H.   14 vols.   Maps and plates.   *Paris.*
1805-34.   4° and Fol.
    (Part I, Sec. 1 (1814-19), Relation Historique; 3 vols., 4°.
Part I, Sec. 2 (1810), Vues des Cordillères, et Monumens
des Peuples indigènes de l'Amerique ; 69 col. plates, fol.
Part I, Secs. 3 and 4 (1814-19-34), Examen critique de
l'Histoire de la Géographie du Nouveau Continent, with Atlas
Géographique et Physique; 37 maps, *etc.,* 2 vols., fol.   Part
III (1811), Essai politique sur la Royaume de la Nouvelle
Espagne ; maps, 3 vols., 4° and fol.   Part IV (1808-10),
Recueil d'Observations Astronomiques, *etc.*; 2 vols., 4°.
Part V (1808), Essai sur la Geographie des Plantes, with
"Tableau Physique des Andes," 4°.   Part VI, Sec. 1 (1809).
Plantes equinoxiales (rédigé par A. Bonpland).   144 plates.
2 vols.   1809.)

1816-31   ——— (Another edition.)   13 vols.   *Paris.*   1816-31.   8°.

1805   ——— Reise der Herren V. H. and B. nach den Wende-
kreisen in der jahren 1799-1804.   Ein Auszug aus ihren.
Memorien von J. C. Delametherie.   Aus dem Franzosischen.
Erfurt.   1805.   8°.

1815-32   ——— Reise en die .Equinoctial Gegenden des neuen Continent in dem jahren 1799-1804.   6 thle.   *Stuttgart and
Tübingen.*   1815-32.   8°.

1822-29   ——— Personal Narrative of Travels to the Equinoctial
Regions of the New Continent, during the years 1799-1804,
by A. von H. and A. B., translated by Helen Maria Williams.
Maps and plates.   7 vols.   *London.*   1822-29.   8°.

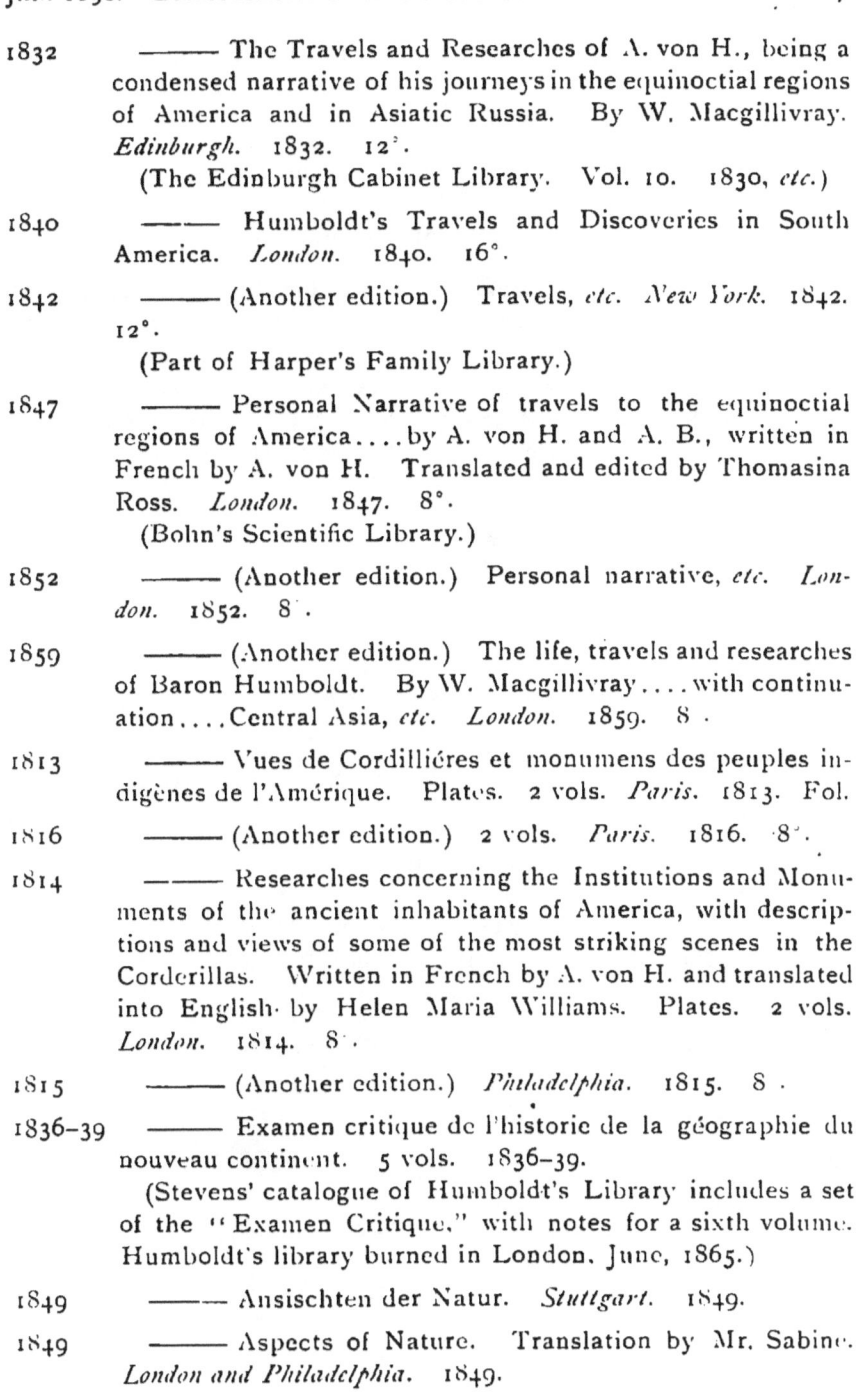

1832   ———— The Travels and Researches of A. von H., being a condensed narrative of his journeys in the equinoctial regions of America and in Asiatic Russia.   By W. Macgillivray. *Edinburgh.*   1832.   12°.
            (The Edinburgh Cabinet Library.   Vol. 10.   1830, *etc.*)

1840   ——— Humboldt's Travels and Discoveries in South America. *London.*   1840.   16°.

1842   ———— (Another edition.)   Travels, *etc.   New York.*   1842. 12°.
            (Part of Harper's Family Library.)

1847   ———— Personal Narrative of travels to the equinoctial regions of America....by A. von H. and A. B., written in French by A. von H.   Translated and edited by Thomasina Ross. *London.*   1847.   8°.
            (Bohn's Scientific Library.)

1852   ———— (Another edition.)   Personal narrative, *etc.   London.*   1852.   8.

1859   ———— (Another edition.)   The life, travels and researches of Baron Humboldt.   By W. Macgillivray.... with continuation....Central Asia, *etc.   London.*   1859.   8.

1813   ———— Vues de Cordillières et monumens des peuples indigènes de l'Amérique.   Plates.   2 vols. *Paris.*   1813.   Fol.

1816   ———— (Another edition.)   2 vols. *Paris.*   1816.   8°.

1814   ———— Researches concerning the Institutions and Monuments of the ancient inhabitants of America, with descriptions and views of some of the most striking scenes in the Corderillas.   Written in French by A. von H. and translated into English by Helen Maria Williams.   Plates.   2 vols. *London.*   1814.   8.

1815   ———— (Another edition.)   *Philadelphia.*   1815.   8.

1836-39   ———— Examen critique de l'historie de la géographie du nouveau continent.   5 vols.   1836-39.
            (Stevens' catalogue of Humboldt's Library includes a set of the "Examen Critique," with notes for a sixth volume. Humboldt's library burned in London, June, 1865.)

1849   ——— Ansischten der Natur. *Stuttgart.*   1849.

1849   ———— Aspects of Nature.   Translation by Mr. Sabine. *London and Philadelphia.*   1849.

1850   ——— Views of Nature. Translation by E. C. Otté.
London. 1850.
(Inca roads.   Vol. II., page 270.)

1853   ——— Uber die altesten Karten des Neuen Continents und
den Namen Amerikar, *etc.* *See* GHILLANY (F. W.) Geschichte
des Seefahrer's Ritter.   M. Behaim, *etc.*   1853.   Fol.

1817   **HUMPHREYS** (SAMUEL).   *See* GUEULETTE (THOMAS SIMON).
Peruvian Tales related in 1001 hours by one of the select
virgins of Cuzco to the Ynca of Peru....interspersed with
curious and historical remarks ; explaining the religious and
civil customs and ceremonies of the ancient inhabitants of
that great empire.   Translated from the French by S. H.,
Esq., and continued by John Kelly, Esq.   *London.*   1817.   16°.

1873   **HUTCHINSON** (THOMAS J.).   Two Years in Peru, with exploration of its antiquities.   Maps, by D. Barrera, and illus.
2 vols.   *London.*   1873.   8°.

1874   -——— *See* LOBO (M.).   Un hijo de Inglaterra, *etc.*   1874.   8°.
(Criticism of Hutchinson's work.)

1873   ——— Some fallacies about the Incas.   *Liverpool.*   1873.
(Proc. of Literary and Philos. Soc. of Liverpool, 1873–74,
page 121.)

1873-4   ——— Explorations amongst ancient burial mounds,
chiefly in the sea-coast valleys of Peru.   Part I., 11th November, 1873.   Part II., 10th February, 1874.   *London.*   8°.
(Part I., Jol. Anth. Inst., Vol. III., pages 311–26 ; Pt. II.,
Jol. Anth. Inst., Vol. IV., pages 2–13.)

1873   ——— *See* BUSK (GEORGE).   Remarks on a collection of 150
ancient Peruvian skulls, presented to the Anthropological
Institute by T. J. H., *etc.*   *London.*   1873.   8°.

1875   ——— Anthropology of pre-historic Peru.   *London.*
1875.   8°.
(Jol. of Anthrop. Institute, Vol. IV. (1875), pages 438–57.)

1866   **ICAZBALCETA** (JOAQUIN GARCIA).   Apuntes para un Catalogo
de Escritores en lenguas indigenas de America.   *Mexico.*
1866.   12°.

1850   —— — *See* PRESCOTT (W. H.) Historia de la Conquista del Perú.... Traducida al Castellana por J. G. I. con un appendice del traductor.   2d ed.   (Relacion de la Conquista del Peru, escrita por P. Sancho, *etc.*) 2 vol. *Mexico.* 1850. 8°.

1868-9   INMAN (THOMAS).   Ancient Faiths embodied in Ancient Names; or an attempt to trace the religious belief, sacred rites, and holy emblems of certain nations, *etc.*   2 vols. *London.* 1868-9. 8°.

1872-3   ——— (Second edition.) 2 vols. *London.* 1872-3. 8°.

1876   ———— Ancient faiths and modern ; a dissertation upon worships, legends and divinities in Central and Western Asia, Europe and elsewhere, before the Christian era, showing their relations to religious customs as they now exist. *New York.* 1876. 8°.
     (Peru, pages 47–62.)

1884   INWARDS (RICHARD).   The Temple of the Andes.   *London.* 1884. 4°. p. 32.

n. d.   JANSSON (JOAUN).   *See* Maps.   Peru.   *n. d.*

1853   JENKINS (JOHN S.) Voyage of the United States exploring squadron commanded by Captain Charles Wilkes, of the United States Navy, in 1838.... 1842, together with the explorations and discoveries made by.... other navigators, *etc.* Illustrated. *Detroit.* 1853. 8°.
     (Peru, Chap. VI., pages 108–54.)

1877   JIMÉNEZ DE LA ESPADA (MARCOS).   *See* CIEZA DE LEON (PEDRO DE).   Tercero libro de las guerras civiles del Peru el cual se llama la Guerra de Quito.   Edited by M. J. de la E. *Madrid.* 1877. 8°.

1879   ——— *See* SANTA CRUZ PACHACUTI-YANQUI SALCAMAYHUA (JUAN DE).   Relacion de la Antiquadades deste Reyno del Peru.   Edited by M. J. de la E.   *Madrid.* 1879. 8°.

1879   ——— Tres relaciones de antiguidades peruanas.   Edited by M. J. de la E.   Publicadas el Ministerio de Fomento. *Madrid.* 1879. 8°.

1879   —— del hombre blanco, signo de la Cruz precolumbi-
anos en el Peru. Atlas of Plates. *Bruxelles.* 1879. 8°.
and Fol.
(Compte-rendu de Congrès internat. des Américanistes,
troisiéme Session.)

1880   —— *See* Cieza de Leon (Pedro de). Segunde parte de la
Cronica del Peru, *etc.* Seguida de la Suma y Narracion de
los Incas....por Juan de Betanzos. *Madrid.* 1880. 4°.

1881   —— Yaravies Quiteños. *Madrid.* 1881. 8°.
(Collection of popular tunes, some with words.)

1881   —— Relaciones géográficos de Indias. Edited, with
introduction, by M. J. de la E. El Ministerio de Fomento de
. Peru. *Madrid* (printed). 1881.
(Vol. I. contains 12 documents of 16th century, now first
published.)

1882   —— *See* Fernandez Montesinos (El. Lic. Don).
Memorias antiguas....del Peru, *etc.* Edited by Don M. J.
de la E. *Madrid.* 1882. 8°.

1882   —— *See* Toledo (Don Fr. de), *Viceroy.* Informaciones
acerca, *etc.* 1570-72. Edited by Don M. J. de la E.
Madrid. 1882.

1850   Jones (J. Winter). *See* Hakluyt (Richard). Divers
voyages touching the discovery of America, *etc.*   1582.
Edited by J. W. J. *London.* 1850. 8°.
(Hakluyt Soc. Pub., No. 7.)

1868   Kalb (Cortenay de). Possibilities in Eastern Peru.
Nation. Vol. VI. (1868), page 48.

1874   Keane (A. H.) *See* Stanford (—). Compendium of
Geography and Travel, *etc.* Translated by A. H. K. *London.* 1874, *etc.* 8°.

1880-7   —— *See* Reiss (Wilhelm) and Stübel (Alphonse).
The Necropolis of Ancon, *etc.* Translated by Prof. A.H.K.
3 vols. Illust. Maps, *etc.* *Berlin.* 1880-7. Fol.

1894-5   —— *See* Reclus (J. J. E.) The earth and its inhabitants. South America. Edited by A. H. K. 2 vols. *New
York.* 1894-5. 8°.

1713   KENNETT (WHITE), *Bishop.* Bibliothecæ Americanæ Primordia. *London.* 1713.

1811-24   KERR (ROBERT). A general history and collection of voyages and travels arranged in systematic order....from the earliest to the present time. 18 vols. *Edinburgh and London.* 1811-24. 8°.
(Peru, Vol. IV., pages 328-518 ; Vol. V., pages 1-217.)

1830   KING (EDWARD), *Viscount Kingsborough.* Antiquities of Mexico, *etc.* 1830, *etc.* Fol.
(Quipu, Vol. IV.)

1874   KIRK (J. F.) *See* PRESCOTT (WM. H.) History of the conquest of Peru, *etc.* 2 vols. *Philadelphia.* 1874. 8°.

1889   KOPPEL (B.) *See* STÜBEL (A.), REISS (W.) and B.K. Kultur und Industrie südamerikanischer völker, *etc.* 2 Bde. Plates. *Berlin.* 1889. Fol.

1843   KULB (P. H.). *See* XERES (FR. DE). Geschichte den Entdeckung und Eroberung Peru's. Translated by P. H. K. *Stuttgart.* 1843. 8°.

1803-4   KUTSCHER (F. J.). America, ein beitrag zur geographie, natur - und Volkergeschichte Von Westindien. 2 vols. 1803-4. 8°.
(Mexico and Peru).

——   LABARTHE (CHARLES). La civilisation peruvienne avant l'arrivée des Espagnols.
(Archives de la Soc. Amér. de France. n. s. i.)

1861   ——Documents inédits sur l'empire des Incas. *Paris.* 1861.
(Annuaire Ethnographique.)

1751   LA CONDAMINE (CHARLES MARIE DE). Journal du Voyage fait par Ordre du Roi à l'Equator; Mesure de trois premiers degrés du Meridien dans l'Austral. Map, *etc.* 2 vols. *Paris.* 1751. 4°.

1745   —— Relation abrégée d'une voyage fait dans l'interieur de l'Amérique Meridionale....en descendant la riviére des Amazones chart. (*Paris?*) 1745. 8°.

1778   ———— (New edition.)   Relation abrége d'une voyage fait dans l'intérieur de l'Amerique Méridionale.   Augm. de la relation de l'émeute populaire de Cuenca.   Map and plate. *Maestricht.*   1778.   8°·

1779   ———— Relation abrégée d'un voyage fait dans l'interieur de l'Amerique Meridionale en descendant la riviére des Amazones, depuis la cote de la Mer du Sud, jusqu 'aux cotes du Brazil et de la Guyane.   Par. M. de la C. de la Academie des Sciences avec une carte du Maraguon, onde la Riviere des Amazones, levee par le meme: et d'un lettre de M. Godin des Odonais, contenant la Relacion du Voyage de Madame Godin, son espouse, *etc.*   Maps.   *Frankfort au Mein.*   1779. 8°·
(Read in Paris before the Academy of Sciences, 1745.)

1747   ———— Succinct abridgement of the voyage made within the inland parts of South America, from the coasts of the South Sea to the coasts of Brazil, *etc.*   Map.   *London.* 1747.   8°·

1813   ———— Abridged narrative of travels through the interior of South America, from the shores of the Pacific Ocean to the coasts of Brazil and Guyana, descending the river of Amazons.   *London.*   1813.   4°·   *See* PINKERTON (WM.) Voyages, *etc.*   Vol. XIV., pages 211–270.

1747   ————Reise nach Peru. 1735–42. 1747. 4°· *See* SCHWABE (J. J.) Allgemeine Historie der Reisen.   Bd. 15.

1747   ———— Reisen in Quito.   1747. 4°· *See* SCHWABE (J. J.) Allgemeine Historie der Reisen.   Bd. 16.

1746   ———— Quelques anciens monumens du Perou du temps des Incas.   *Berlin.*   1746.
(Berlin Acad. de Wissen.   Abh.   1746.)

1751   ———— Histoire des Pyramides de Quito élevées par les Academiciens énvoyes sous l'Equateur par ordre du Roy. (*Paris.*)   1751   4°·

1883   LAMBERT (T. H.).   Origin of the name America from the native name for Peru.   1883.
(Bull. of the Amer. Geog. Society, No. 1 of 1883.)

1873   LANG (ANDREW).   The Aryan Races of Peru.   Macmillan's Magazine. Vol. 27 (1873), pages 424–27.
(Quichua language; criticism of V. P. Lopez.)

            LAS CASAS.   *See* CASAS (BARTOLOMÉ DE LAS).

1609   **LASSO DE LA VEGA** (GARCIA), *El Inca.* Primera. (-Segunda) Parte de los Commentarios Reales que tratan del origin de los Yncas, Reyes que fueron del Peru, de su idolatria, leyes y gobierno....y de todo lo que fue aquel imperio....autes que los espagñoles pascaron a el. 2 parts. *P. Crasbeeck. Lisboa.* 1609. (Part I. 1608.) Fol.

1609–17   ——— Primera parte de los Comentarios Reales, 1609. (Segunda Parte) Historia del Peru, 1617. *Cordova.* 2 vols. Fol.

1616   ——— Historia general del Peru. *Cordova.* 1616 (1617).

1722–3   ——— Primera Parte de los Commentarios Reales de el Origen de los Incas, su idolatria, leies, y govierno, vidas y conquistas, 1723. (Segunda Parte) Historia general del Peru, guerras entre Pizarros y Almagros, 1722. La Florida del Inca, 1723. 3 vols. *Madrid.* 1722–3. Fol.

1722   ——— Histoire generale del Peru, trata, el descubrim., de el; y como lo Ganaron, los Espanoles: las guerras civiles, que huvo entre Pizarros y Almagros s. la partija de la tierra, *etc.* Segund impression, enmendada y añædida. *Madrid.* 1722. Fol.

1723   ——— Segunda impression, enmendada y añædida la vida de Xuli Cusi Titu Jupanqui, penultimo Inca (Historia general). Edited by A. G. de Barcia. 2 parts. *Madrid.* 1723. Fol.

1800   ——— (Another edition.) *Madrid.* 1800.

1829   ——— (Nueva edicion.) (Historia de la Conquista del Nuevo Mondo.) Tom. 2–5. *Madrid.* 1829. 8°. (Part of a series in 9 vols. *Conquista del Nuevo Mondo.*)

1625   ——— Observations of things most remarkable, collected out of the first part of the Commentaries Royall, written by the Inca G. de la Vega. *London.* 1625. Fol. (*See* PURCHAS (SAMUEL). Purchas his Pilgrimes. Pt. 4.)

1688   ——— The Royal Commentaries of Peru in two parts. The first part treating of the original of their Incas....The second part describing the manner by which the new world was conquered by the Spaniards, and of their civil wars, written in Spanish by the Inca Garcilasso de la Vega. Rendered English by Sir Paul Rycaut. Portrait of Rycaut and ten plates. *London.* 1688. Fol.

1859   —————— Expedition of Gonzalo Pizarro to the land of cin-
namon,. translated from second part of Royal Commentaries
of Peru.   Edited by C. R. Markham.   *London.* ' 1859.   8°.
(Hakluyt Society publications, No. 24.)

1869   —————— First part of the Royal Commentaries of the Yncas.
Translated with notes, etc., by Cl. R. Markham.   Map.
2 vols.   *London.*   1869.   8°.
(Hakluyt Society public., Nos. 41 and 45.)

1632   —————— Le Commentaire Royal, ou l'Histoire des Yncas,
Roys du Peru ; contenant leur Origine, leur Idolatrie, leurs
Sacrifices, leurs Loix, leurs Conquestes ; les Merveilles du
Temple du Soleil ; les incroyables richesses, *etc.*   *Paris.*
1632.   4°.

1633   —————— Le commentaire royal.   Translated by J. Boudoin.
Paris.   1633.

1650   —————— Histoire des Guerres civiles des Espagnols dans les
Indes.   Mise en françois par I. Baudoin.   Suitte des Guerres
civiles des Espagnols dans le Peru.   Traducion par I.
Baudoin.   2 vols.   *Paris.*   1650.   4°.

1658   —————— Histoire des Guerres civiles des Espagnols dans
les Indes, causées par les Soufleuemens des Picarres et des
Almagres, escritte en Espagnole par l'Ynca Garcilasso de la
Vega, et mise en Francois par I. Baudoin.   2 vols.   Paris.
1658.   4°.

1672   —————— (Another edition.)   Histoire des Guerres Civiles,
etc.   Paris.   1672.

1706   —————— Histoire des Guerres civiles des Espagnols dans les
Indes, entre les Picarres et les Almagres qui les avaient con-
quises.   (Commentarios, pt. 2).   Traduite de l'Espagnol
par J. Baudoin.   2 vols.   *Amsterdam.*   1706.   12°.

1715   —————— Histoire des Yncas, rois du Pérou.   Traduite de
l'Espagnol, par J. Baudoin.   2 vols.   *Amsterdam.*   1715.   8°.

1737   —————— (Another edition.)   2 vols.   *Amsterdam.*   1737.   4°.

1744   —————— (Another edition.)   Translated by Dalibard.   2
vols.   *Paris.*   1744.   8°.

1830   ——— (Another edition.)   Baudoin's translation.   3 vols.
        Paris.   1830.   8°.

1704   ——— (Dutch translation.)   *Amsterdam.*   1704.

1798   ——— (German translation.)   1798.

[GARCIA LASSO DE LA VEGA, usually known as Garcilasso
de la Vega, or The Inca, son of one of the early Spanish conquerors, of noble lineage, by an Inca princess, was born at
Cuzco, 1539.   In 1560 went to Spain, where thirty years
afterwards he began the compilation of "The Commentaries."   The work was composed chiefly from memory,
aided by information obtained from his surviving half-caste
schoolfellows, and from the works of preceding Spanish
writers, whose mistakes he corrects.   Besides Blas Valera,
he quotes from Cieza de Leon, Acosta, Lopez de Gomara
and Zarate.   Notwithstanding its serious errors, the Commentaries is one of the chief sources of our knowledge of the
times of the Incas.   Garcia Lasso died at Cordova, Spain,
1617.]

        LAZO (ALONZO CARILLO).   *See* BLANCHARDERIE (ABBÉ COURTE
DE LA).

1879   LECLERC (CH.).   Bibliotheca Americana and Supplement.
        Paris.   1879, *etc.*

1890   ——— Arte de la lengua de los Indios Antis o Campas,
varias preguntas, advertencias i doctrina crist. conf. al MS.
orig. hall. en ciudad de Toledo por C. L. Con Vocabulario
metod. i una introduccion comparat, par L. Adam.   *Paris.*
1890.   8°.

1619   L'ECLUSE (CHARLES DE).   Histoire des simples Médicaments
apportés de l'Amérique.   3 vols.   1619.   8°.   *See* MONARDES
(NICHOLAS) De Simplicibus Medicamentis ex Occidentali
India delatis....   *Antverpia.*   1574.   8°.

        ——— *See* ORTA (G. DE) Due libri dell' historia del sem-
plici, aromati....   1576.   4°.

        ——— *See* ORTA (G. DE) Histoire des Drognes, Espeçeries,
etc.   1619.   8°.

1619   ——— *See* ACOSTA (CHRISTOPHER DE L') Traicte de Christophe de la Coste, *etc.* traduit par de l'Écluse.   1619.   8°.

1883   LEIGH (F. STUDDY).   Peruvia, Bolivia and Chile. *San Francisco.* 1883.
(Overland Monthly, Vol. III., pages 527–41.)

1589   LEJESAMA (MANCIO SERRADE).   Confession or Preamble to the Will of M. S. L., dated 15th Sept., 1589. *See* MILLER (N.) *General.* On the state of the Peruvian Empire previous to the arrival of the Spaniards. 1844. 8°.

[Lejesama, or Leguisamo, Alcalde of Cuzco, was the last survivor of the first body of Spanish invaders.]

——   LENOX LIBRARY Catalogue. *New York.*
(The Lenox Library is rich in Americana.)

1653   LEON-PINOLO (DON ANTONIO).   Vida del Illustrisimo Reverendissimo D. Toribio Alfonso Mogrovejo, Urcobispo de la ciudad de los Reyes. 1653.

1557   LEVINUS (APOLLONIUS).   De Peruviæ regionis inter Novi Orbis provincias celeberrimæ inventione, et rebus in eadem gestis. Libri V. *Antverp.* 1557. 12°.

1863   LIEBIG (JUSTUS VON).   The Natural Laws of Husbandry. (A translation of Part II. of the 7th edition of " Die Chemie in ihrer Anwendung auf Agricultur und Physiologie.").... Edited by J. Blyth. *London.* 1863. 8°.
(Chapter VII.)

1879   LILIENFELD (P. VON).   Gedanken über die Socialwissenschaft der Zukunft. Thl. IV: Die Sociale Physiologie. *Mitau.* 1879.

1748   LIMA AND CALLAO.   A true and particular relation of the dreadful earthquake which happened at Lima, the capital of Peru, and the neighbouring Port of Callao, on the 28th of October, 1746, with an account of everything material that passed there afterwards.   Published at Lima by command of the Viceroy, and translated from the original Spanish; to which is added a description of Callao and Lima, before their destruction, and of the Kingdom of Peru, with the manners and customs of the inhabitants, *etc.* Maps and plates. 1748. 8°.

1598   LINSCHOTEN (J. HUYGHEN VAN).   Historie naturael ende morael Van de Westersche Indien....overghent doo J. H. V. L. *Enckhuysen.* 1598. 8°.

1574   **Lobo Guerrero.** Constituciones Synodales de Arçobispads de los Reyes (Lima) en el Perù. *Lima.* 1574. Fol.
(Some pages are in Quichua.)

1809   **Lok** (M.). *See* Anglerius (P. M.) The History of the West Indies, *etc.* Translated into English by M. L. *London.* 1809. 4 .
(Hakluyt (R.) Collection of the Early Voyages, *etc.*, Vol. V.)

Lopez de Caravantes (Francisco). Inedited MS.
(Contains Pedro Sancho's note of the distribution of Atahualap's ransom, with a list of the conquerors.)

1552-3   **Lopez de Gomara** (Francisco). Primera y segunda parte de la historia general de las Indias con todo el descubrimiento y cosas notables, que han acæcido dende que se ganaron ata el año de 1551. Con le Conquista de Mexico y de la nueva España. 2 vols. Map of the world. *Caragoça*, Agustin Millan. 1552-3. Fol.

1553   —— Hispania Victrix. Primera y segunda parte de la historia general. Con la Conquista de Mexico. 2 parts. *Medino del Campo.* 1553. Fol.

1553   —— Sa Historia General de las Indias con todos los descubrimientos, y cosas notables que han acæcido dende que se ganaron hasta agora escripta por Gomora Anadiose de nuevo la descripcion y traca de los Indias con una Table alphabetica de los Provincios, Istos, Puereos, Ciudades y nombres de conquistadores y vorones principales que alla bon passado. *Anvers.* (Steelsio). 1553. 16°.

1554   —— (Another edition.) La Historia General. Cronica de la Nueva España con lo Conquista de Mexico. 2 parts. *Caragoça.* (A. Millan). 1554. Fol.

1554   —— (Another edition.) Historia General. Conquista de Mexico. 2 pt. *Anvers. M. Nuncio.* 1554. 8°.

1554   —— (Another edition.) La Historia general de las Indias. *Anvers.* (*J. Bellero*). 1554. 8°.

1555   —— (Another edition.) *Carogoça.* 1555.

1575   ——— El sitio y descripcion de las India y Mundo Nuevo sacada de la historia de F. Lopez de G. *Anvers.* 1575. 4°.
(La Cosmographia of Petrus Apianus. Pt. I.).

1749   ——·— Historia de las Indias. *Madrid.* 1749. Fol.
            (De Barcia's Historiadores primitivos, *etc.* Vol. II.)

1849   ——·— Historia general. Conquista de Peru. *Madrid.*
            1849. 8°.
            (Biblioteca de Autores Espagñoles. Edited by B. C.
            Aribau. Vol. 22.)

1852   ——·— Historia de la conquista del Peru. *Madrid.* 1852. 4°.
            (Extracted from pt. I. of La Historia de las Indias y Con-
            quista de Mexico.)

1555-56 La Historia generale delle Indie Occidentali. Tradotta
         per A. de Cravaliz. V. & L. Dorici. *Roma.* 1555-1556. 4°.

1560   ——— (Another edition.) *Venetia.* 1560. 12ᶜ.

1564   ——— (Another edition.) *Venetia.* 1564.

1565   ——·— (Another edition.) *Venetia.* 1565.

1566   ——·— (Another edition.) *Venetia.* 1566.

1570   ——— (Another edition.) *Venetia.* 1570.

1573   ——— (Another edition.) *Venetia.* 1573.

1576   ——·— (Another edition.) *Venetia.* 1576.

1599   ——— (Another edition.) *Venetia.* 1599. 8°.

1568   ——·— Histoire générale des Indes occidentales et Terres
            Neuves, qui....traduite par Mart. Fumée. *Paris.* 1568. 8°.

1569   ——·— (Another edition.) *Paris.* 1569. 8°.

1577   ——— *Paris.* 1577. 8°.

1578   ——— *Paris.* 1578. 8°.

1580   ——— *Paris.* 1580. 8°.

1584   ——— (Another edition, enlarged.) *Paris.* 1584. 8 ·

1587   ——·— *Paris.* 1587. 8°.

1588   ——— *Paris.* 1588. 8°.

1597   ——·— *Paris.* 1597. 8°.

1604   ——— (Another edition.) 1604.

1605   ——·— *Paris.* 1605. 8°.

1606   ——— *Paris.* 1606. 8°.

1555   ——·— General History abridged in Eden's Orcades. 1555.

1577 ——— (Another edition.) Eden's History of Travayle. 1577.

1578 ——— The pleasant Historie of the conquest of the Weast India, now called New Spayne, atchieved by the worthy Prince Hernando Cortes, Marques of the Valley of Huaxacac, most delectable to reade, translated.... by T[homas] N[icholas]. *London.* 1578.

1596 ——— (Another edition.) 1596.

[Francisco Lopez de Gomara, born about 1510; became in 1540 chaplain and secretary of Hernando Cortes. The second part of his *Historia General*, entitled *La Conquista de Mexico*, appeared in 1552, and the *first* part, relating the conquest of Peru, which he never visited, the following year. His book suppressed by the Spanish government, and edict maintained until 1729.]

1871 Lopez (Dr. Don Vincente Fidel).   Les Races aryennes du Perou, leur langue, leur religion, leur historie. *Paris.* 1871. 4°·
(Home of ancient Peruvians in Central Asia.)

1883 ——— Poesia dramatica de los Incas. Ollantay, por Cl. R. Markham traducido del Ingles por Adolfo F. Olivares, y seguido de una carta critica del D. Don V. F. L. *Buenos Ayres.* 1883.

1860 Lorente (Don Sebastian). Historia antigua del Peru. *Lima.* 1860.

1861 ——— Historia de la conquista del Peru. *Lima.*   1861.

1863 ——— Historia del Peru bajo la dinastia austrica.   1542–1598. *Lima.* 1863. 8°·

1870 ——— (Another edition.) *Paris.* 1870.

1871 ——— Historia del Peru, bajo los Borbones.   1800–1821. *Lima.* 1871. 8°·

1876 ——— Historia del Peru desde la Proclamacion de la Independencia. Tomo I. 1821–1827. *Lima.* 1876. 12'·

1880 ——— Historia de la civilization Peruana. Revista de Lima. *Lima.* 1880.

1851–55   LOS RIOS (J. A. DE).   *See* FERNANDEZ DE OVIEDO Y VALDES (GONZALEZ).   Historia general y natural, *etc.*, cotejada con el códice original .... por J. A. de L. R.   4 vols.   *Madrid.* 1851–55.   Fol.

1780   LOUR (BRION DE LA).   *See* MAPS.   South America.   *Paris.* 1780.

1836   LOWE (F.).   *See* SMYTH (W.) *Lieut.*   Narrative of a journey from Lima to Para, *etc.*   1836.   8°.

1733   LOZANA (Pedro).   Descripcion chorografica del Gran Charco.   *Cordova.*   1733.
(Missions to cannibal Chirihuanas.)

——   LUCERO (P. JUAN).   Gramaticas y Catecismos de muchas lenguas de Quito, y principalmente de los idiomas Parana-puro y Cocamo.
(Hervas : Cat. de las lenguas, t. i. p. 271 ; Viñaza : Bibl. Espan. No. 931.)

1858.   LUDEWIG (HERMAN ERNST).   The Literature of American aboriginal languages.   With additions and corrections by Professor Wm. M. Turner.   Edited by Nicholas Trübner. *London.*   1858.   8°.
(Quichaus, Yuncas, *etc.*, pages 158–63.)

1864   LYMAN (J. HUNTINGDON).   The Montana of the Andes. *New York.*   1864.
(Hunt's Magazine.   Vol. 50, pages 261–69.)

1883   MACEDO (DR. ——).   Comparison of the Inca and Aztec civilizations.   *Philadelphia.*   1883.
(Proc. Numismatic and Antiquarian Society.)

1832   MACGILLIVRAY (W.).   *See* HUMBOLDT (F. H. A. VON).   The travels and researches of A. von Humboldt, being a condensed narrative, *etc.   Edinburgh.*   1832.   12°.

1859   —— (Another edition.)   With continuation, *etc.   London.*   1859.   8°.

1878   MACKENNA (V——).   Historia de la jornada del 20 de Abril de 1851, una batalla en las calles de Santiago.   Con 4 retratos.   *Lima.*   1878.

1850   MADDEN (SIR FRANCIS).   *See* SILVESTRE (JOSEPH BALTHAZAR)
Paleographie universelle, *etc.*   Translated....and edited,
with corrections and notes, by Sir F. M.   2 vols.   *London.*
1850.   8°.

1652   MADRIDA (PEDRO DE).   Observations (appended to "Journal Van de Nassausche Vloot," by Admiral Jacques d'Heremite).   *Amsterdam.*   1652.

——   MAGAZINE OF AMERICAN HISTORY.   Record of copies of MSS.
preserved in New York.   Mag. Am. Hist. I., page 254.

1877   MALDONADO (FRANCISCO).   Carta de....regidor de la ciudad
del Cuzco, al emperador Don Carlos, denunciando la lala
administracion de licenciado Vaca de Castro.   Cuzco.   9 de
Marzo de 1543.   Lettre LXXV. of Cartas de Indias.   *Madrid.*   1877.   4°

MALTE–BRUN (CONRAD).   *See* BRUUN (MALTHE CONRAD).

n. d.   MAPS.   PERU.   Tabula Americæ specialis geographica
regna Peru per Homarianos Heredes.   *n. d.*

n. d.   —— —— Amstelodami Guiljelmus Blaenco axcudit.
n. d.

n. d.   —— —— Amstelodami apud Joaunem Janssonium.
n. d.

n. d.   —— —— Le Peru, par Pierre Vanderaa.   *Amsterdam.*
n. d.

n. d.   —— —— Carte de la terre ferme du Perou, *etc.*   By
Guillaume Del Isle.   *Amsterdam.*   *n. d.*

1656   —— —— Le Perou et le cours de la Rivière Amazone,
etc.   Par N. Sanson.   *Paris.*   1656.

1814   —— —— Charte der Provinz oder Audiencia von Lima
oder des alten Königreichs Peru.   *Weimar.*   1814.
(Verlage des Geograph. Instituts, Weimar.)

1775   —— (SOUTH AMERICA.)   Mapa geog. de America Merid.
By Juan de la Cruz Cano y Almedillo.   *London.*   1775.

1748   —— —— Map of South America by D'Anville.   *Paris.*
1748.

1775   —— —— (Another edition.)   D'Anville.   Improved
by Bolton.   1775.

1779 —— ——— (Another edition.) D'Anville and Bolton. *Venice.* 1779.

1780 —— ——— Map of South America. By Brion de la Lour. *Paris.* 1780.

1807 —— —— ——— By Louis G. Da. de la Rochette. 1807.

1825 —— ——— L'Amerique meridional. By J. B. von Spix and C. F. P. von Martius. *Munich.* 1825.

1890 —— ——— Mapa general del América meridional (con cartons: Parte central de Chile, Venezuela, Colombia, Ecuador y contornos de Lima....) por Enrique Kiepert. Edicion segunda emendado y publicado por Ricardo Kiepert. *Berlin.* 1890.

1564, *etc.* —— AND PLANS. CUZCO. *See* RAMUSIO, Vol. III., page 412; DE BRY, Pt. VI.; HERRERA (1728), Vol. III., page 161; MUNSTER: Cosmographia, 1572 and 1598; BRAUN and HOGENBERG: Civitates orbis terrarum; DU PINET: Plantz, Pourtraitz et Descriptions de plusieurs Villes, *etc. Lyons.* 1564.
(Views of Cuzco: *See* Vanderaa and Rycaut's transl. of Garcia Lasso de la Vega's Commentaries.)

1702 MARABAN (PADRE PEDRO). Arte de la lengua Moxa con su vocabulario i catecismo. *Lima.* 1702. 16°.

1859 MARCOY (PAUL). *Pseud (i. e.,* Laurent Saint Cricq.). Une cérémonie nautique au bord du lac Titicaca. *Paris.* 1859. 8°.
(Revue Contemporaine, 31st Jan. and 15th Feb., 1859.)

1860 —— Scénes et paysages dans les Andes: la dernière ascension de l'Urusayhua. *Paris.* 1860. 8°.
(Revue Contemporaine, 15th Sept. and 30th Sept., 1860.)

1861 —— Scénes et paysages dans les Andes, *etc.* (Series 1 and 2.) *Paris.* 1861. 12°.

1863-64 —— Voyage à travers l'Amérique du Sud (de l'Océan Pacifique à l'Ocean Atlantique). ——. 1863-64. 4°.
(Published in parts, *Le Tour du Monde.* 1863-64.)

1869 ——— Voyage à travers l'Amérique du Sud, de l'Ocean Pacifique a l'Ocean Atlantique. 2 vols. Illustré par E. Riou. 20 Maps. *Paris.* 1869. Fol.

1871–73 ——— A journey across South America from the Pacific Ocean to the Atlantic Ocean. Issued in parts. 2 vols. Maps and illust. *London, Glasgow.* 1871–73. 4°.

1875 ——— (Another edition.) Travels in South America, *etc.* 2 vols. *London.* 1875. 4°.

1875 ——— (Another edition.) Travels, *etc.* 2 vols. *New York.* 1875. 4°.

(Vol. I., pages 1–282, Islay to Cuzco.)

1856 MARKHAM (*Sir* CLEMENTS ROBERT). Cuzco: A Journey to the Ancient Capital of Peru, with an account of the History, Language, Literature and Antiquities of the Incas; and Lima: A Visit to the Capital and Provinces of Modern Peru, with a Sketch of its Government, History and Literature. Map and tinted plates. *London.* 1856. 8°.

(Appendix: Grammar, Vocabularies, Dialogue and specimens of Quichua.)

1859 ——— Expeditions into the Valley of the Amazon, 1539, 1540, 1639. Translated and edited, with notes, by C. R. M. Map. *London.* 1859. 8°. *See* PIZARRO (G.), Expeditions, *etc.;* ORELLARA (FRAS. DE), Expedition, *etc.,* 1540; ACURA (EL PAD. CHRIST. DE), New Discovery, *etc.*

1861 ——— The Province of Caravaya in Southern Peru. *London.* 1861. 8°.

(Jol. R. Geog. Soc., Vol. XXXI., pages 190–203.)

1862 ——— *See* GUZMAN (ALONZO ENRIQ.) The Life and Acts of A. E. G., *etc.* Translated and edited by C. R. M. from an original MS. *London.* 1862. 8°.

(Hakluyt Soc. Pub., No. 29.)

1862 ——— Travels in Peru and India, while superintendiug the collection of Chinchona plants and seeds in South America, and their introduction into India. Maps. Pedigree of the Incas, and woodcuts. *London.* 1862. 8°.

1880   —————— Peruvian Bark.   A popular account of the introduction of Chinchona cultivation into British India....with
maps and illustrations.   *London.*   1880.   8ᵛ.

1865   ———— Zwei Reisen in Peru.   *Leipzig.*   1865.   8°.

1864   —————— *See* CIEZA DE LEON (PEDRO).   The Travels of P.C. de
L., *etc.*   Translated and edited with notes and introduction
by C. R. M.   *London.*   1864.   8°.
(Hakluyt Soc. Pub., No. 33.)

1864   —————— Contributions towards a Grammar and Dictionary
of the Quichua, the language of the Incas of Peru.   *London.*
1864.   12°.

1865   —————— *See* ANDAGOYA (PASCUAL DE).   Narrative of the
proceedings of Pedrarias Davila, *etc.*   Translated and edited
with notes and introduction by C. R. M.   *London.*   1865.   8°.
(Hakluyt Soc. Pub., No. 34.)

1869   —————— *See* LASSO DE LA VEGA (GARCIA).   First part of the
Royal Commentaries, *etc.*   Translated, with notes, etc., by
C. R. M.   2 vols.   *London.*   1869.   8°.
(Hakluyt Soc. Pub., Nos. 44 and 45.)

1871   —————— On the geographical positions of the tribes which
formed the empire of the Yncas, with an appendix on the
name "Aymara."   *London.*   1871.   8°.
(Jour. Roy. Geogr. Soc., Vol. XLI., pages 281–338.)

1871   —————— Ollanta in Quichua and English, with an introduction and notes, by C. R. M.   *London.*   1871.   8°.

1883   —————— *See* LOPEZ (DR. DON V. F.).   Poesia dramatica de
los Incas.   Ollantay, por C. R. M. traducido....del Dr. Don
V. F. L.   *Buenos Ayres.*   1883.

1890   —————— *See* MIDDENDORF (E. W.)   Die einheimischen
Sprachen Perus. Vol 3.   Ollanta.... (.... Markham's)
Text, *etc.*   *Leipzig.*   1890.   8°.

1872   —————— Reports on the discovery of Peru.   Translated by
C. R. M.   *London.*   1872.   8°.
See ESTETE (MIGUEL).   The Narrative of....H. Pizarro,
etc.; PIZARRO (H.) Letter from H. P., *etc.*; XERES (FR.) A
true account, *etc.*
(Hakluyt Soc. Pub., No. 42.)

1873   ——— Narratives of the rites and laws of the Incas. Translated by C. R. M. *London.* 1873. 8˙.
See Avila (Fr. de), a narrative of the errors, *etc.*; Molina (Chr. de), an account of the Fables, *etc.*
(Hakluyt Soc. Pub., No. 48.)

1877   ——— *See* Hawkins (Sir John), *Rear Admiral.* Voyages, *etc.* Observations of Sir R. H. on his voyage, etc. With an introduction by C. R. M. *London.* 1877. 8°.
(Hakluyt Soc. Pub., No. 57.)

1878-9   —·—— *See* Acosta (Jos. de). The naturall and morall historie of the Indies....With notes by C. R. M. *London.* 1878-9. 8˙.
(Hakluyt Soc. Pub., Nos. 60 and 61.)

1880   ——·— Peru. Maps and illustrations. *London.* 1880. 12˙.
(Part of "Foreign Countries and British Colonies," edited by F. S. Pulling.)

1882   ——— The war between Peru and Chili, 1879-82. *London.* 1882. 8°.

1883   ——— (Another edition). *New York.* 1883. 12˙.

1883   ——— *See* Cieza de Leon (Pedro de). The second part of the Chronicle of Peru. Translated and edited, with notes and introd. by C. R. M. *London.* 1883. 8°.
(Hakluyt Soc. Pub., No. 68.)

1889   ——·— *See* Winsor (Justin). Narrative and critical history of America. 8 vols. *Boston.* 1889. 8˙.
(Vol. I., ch. 4, the Inca civilization in Peru, by C. R. M.; Vol. II., chap. 8, Pizarro and the conquest and settlement of Peru and Chili, by C. R. M.)

1892   ——— A history of Peru (Latin-American Republics). Maps and illus. *Chicago.* 1892. 8°.
(Chap. 1, Inca Civilization; Chap. 2, Inca Empire.)

1840   Marmochi (———). Raccolta de Viaggi. 1840. 8°. *See* Xeres (Frans. de) Relazione del Conquisto del Peru e della provincia de Cuzco, *etc.* Traduttore O. Piccini.

1777   Marmontel (Jean Francois). Les Incas ou la destruction de l'empire du Perou. 2 vols. Front. and 10 plates. *Francfort.* 1777. 12°.

1778   ——— (Another edition.) 2 vols. *Paris.* 1778. 12˙.

1809 —————— Nouvelle edition.   2 vols.   *Franckfort* and *Leipzic.* 1809.   8°.

1821 ————— (Another edition.)   2 vols.   *Paris.*   1821.   16°.

1822 ————— (Another edition.)   2 vols.   *Paris.*   1822.   12°.

1777 —————— The Incas ; or, the destruction of the empire of Peru.   2 vols.   *London.*   1777.   12°.

1893 MARQUEZ (C. CUERVO).   *See* RECLUS (J. J. E.) Colombia (being portion of *Nouvelle Geographie Universelle*) traducida ....(With an introduction by C. C. M.)   *Bogota.*   1893.   8°.

MARRIOTTI (L.)   *See* GALLENGA (ANTONIO).

1834 MARSDEN (WILLIAM), *F. R. S.*   Miscellaneous works.   3 parts.   *London.*   1834.   4°.
(Page 104.)

1604 MARTINEZ (FRAY JUAN).   Vocabulario en Lengua general del Peru, llamada Quichua y en la Lengua Española.   Nuevamente emendado y añadido de algunas cosas que faltaban, por el Padre Mtro. Fr. J. M.   *Los Reyes.*   1604.   8°.

1883 MASON (THEODORUS B. M.), *Lieut. U. S. N.*   The war on the Pacific coast of South America between Chili and the allied republics of Peru and Bolivia, 1879–81.   *Washington.*   1883.   8°.
(Office of Naval Intelligence.   Bureau of Navigation. Information from abroad.   War series, No. 11.)

—— MASTRILLO (P. NICHOLAS).   Sermones en lengua general de Peru.
(Leon Pinelo: Epitome t. ii. col. 731 ; Viñaza : Bibl. Españ. No. 1,162.)

1879 MATHEWS (E. D.)   Up the Amazon and Madeira rivers through Bolivia and Peru.   *London.*   1879.   8°.

1825 MATHISON (GILBERT FARQUHAR).   Narrative of a visit to Brazil, Chile, Peru and the Sandwich Islands during the years 1821 and 1822.   *London.*   1825.   8°.
(Chaps. X. and XI., Lima.)

—— MATIENZO (LIC. JUAN DE).   Gobierno del Peru.
(MS.   Additional MSS. 5469, Brit. Mus., folio page 274.)

[MATIENZO, Judge of the Royal Audience at Lima, and adviser of Viceroy Don Francisco de Toledo, 1556–1561. Treats of the condition of the people, particularly in relation to forced labor and tributes.]

1875   MAURY (L. F. ALFRED).   On the Distribution and Classification of Tongues, their relation to the Geographical Distribution of Races, *etc.* *Philadelphia.* 1875. 4°.
(Chap. I. of NOTT (J. C.) and GLIDDON (G. R.) Indigenous Races of the Earth. Quichua of Peru, page 83.)

1752   MAUVILLON (———). *See* ULLOA (JUAN J. and ANT. DE). Voyage historique de l'Amérique meridionale, *etc.*, translated by M. 2 vols. *Amsterdam and Paris.* 1752. 4°.

1829   MAW (HENRY LISTER). Journal of a passage from the Pacific to the Atlantic, crossing the Andes in the northern provinces of Peru and descending the River Marañon, or Amazon. Map. *London.* 1829. 8°.

1849   MAYNARDE (THOMAS). *See* DRAKE (SIR FRANCIS). His voyage, 1595, by T. M. Edited, *etc.* *London.* 1849. 8·

1871   MEIGGS (ENRIQUE). Los Ferrocarriles del Peru. *Lima.* 1871.

1873   ——— El Departamento de Ancachs poblic. por E. M. *Lima.* 1873. Fol. *See* RAIMONDI (A.) El Departamento de Ancachs y sus Riquezas minerales.

1857   MEIGS (J. A.) Catalogue of Human Crania in the Collection of the Academy of Natural Sciences at Philadelphia. (*Philadelphia.*) 1857. 8·

1857   MEIGS (J. AITKEN). The Cranial Characteristics of the Races of Men. *Philadelphia.* 1857. 4°. *See* NOTT (J. C.) and GLIDDON (G. R.) Indigenous Races of the Earth, *etc.* Chap. III.
(Peruvian Crania, pages 220, 254, 258, 337.)

1681–82   MELENDEZ (JUAN). Tesoros verdaderos de los Yndias en la historia de la gran Provincia do San Juan Bavtista del Peru, *etc.* 3 vols. Portrait, view and plan. *Roma.* 1681–82. Fol.
(Vol. I. general history of Peru in 16th century ; II. treats of "religious" subjects ; III. concerns the natives and their customs.)

1690   **MELGAR** (D. ESTEVAN SANCHO DE).   Arte de la lengua general del ynga llamada Qquechhua. *Lima.* 1690. 8°.

1823   **MELLET** (JULLIEN).   Voyage dans l'Amerique meridionale, a l'interieur de la cote-ferme, et aux iles de Cuba et de la Jamaïque, depuis 1808 jusqu 'en 1819. 1823. 8 .

    (Pages 110–271. Coast, Callao to Guayagil—Interior of Ecuador to Quito—Cauca Valley to Carthagena.)

1859   **MEMORIAS** de los Vireyes que han gobernado el Peru durante el tiempo del Coloniaje Español. Edited by Don Manuel Fuentes. 6 vols. Map and 12 plates. *Lima.* 1859. 4 .

1867   ———— (Another edition.)   6 vols. *Lima.* 1867. Fol.

1880   **MENDIBURU** (GENERAL).   Diccionario Historico—Biografico del Peru. *Lima.* 1880.

    (Account of the administrations of Viceroys Marquis of Cañete and Garcia de Castro. 1556-61, 1564-69.

1643   **MENDISTA** (ALONZO DE).   *See* CORDOVA Y SALINAS (FRAY DIEGO DE). Vida del Apostol del Peru, aug. por Al. de M. *Madrid.* 1643.

1860   **MENENDEZ** (BALDOMERO JOSÉ).   Enciclopedia Hispano-Americana. Manual de Geografia y estadistica del alto Peru ó Bolivia. *Paris, Besanzon* (printed). 1860. 12°.

1861   ———— Enciclopedia Hispano-Americana. Manual de Geografia y estadistica del Peru. *Paris, Besanzon* (printed). 1861. 12 .

— —   **MERCADO** (P. FR. JUAN).   Compendio del V. P. Fr. Luis de Grenada, en la lengua general del Peru.

    (MS. Viñazo: Bibl. Españ. No. 936.)

1760   **MERCIER Y GUZMAN** (P. FRANCIS). *See* BERTONIO (P. LUD.) Historia de lo cuatro Evangelios en la lengua Aymara.... dis à luz el P. F. M. y G. 1760. 8 .

1791-5   **MERCURIO PERUANO** de Historia, Literatura, y Noticias publicas que da a luz la Sociedad Academica de Amantes de Lima. 12 vols. *Lima.* 1791-5. 4°.

    (Of great rarity ; was suppressed by the Spanish government. The last volume says, "dado a luz por uno de los individuos de la Sociedad.")

1590–1634 MERIAN (MATHEO).   *See* BRY (TH. DE).   Collectiones pere-
grinationum, *etc.*   XXV. partibus comprehenso a . . . . M. M.
Francofurti.   1590–1634.   Fol.

1634   —— *See* BRY (TH. DE).   Historia America·, *etc.*, in XII.
distinctis partibus . . . . accessit Elenchus Sectionem et Index
Capitum, *etc.*   (Part XII. by M.M.)   *Francofurti.*   1634.   Fol.

1866–7   MESA (PIO B.)   Los anales de la Ciudad del Cuzco, o las
cuatro epocas principales de su historia, narradas breve y
seveillamente.   2 vols.   *Cuzco.*   1866–7.   4°.

1648   MEXIA Y OCON (DE JUAN ROXO).   Arte de la lengua general
de los Yndios del Peru   *Lima.*   1648.   8°.

1867   MICHELENA Y ROJAS (F.)   Exploracion oficial . . . . desde el
Norte de la America del Sur : siempre por rios . . . . hasta el
Atlantico.   Comprendiendo . . . de Venezuela, Guyana Inglesa,
Nueva Grenada, Brasil, Ecuador, Peru y Bolivia . . . . en los
años de 1855, hasta 1859.   Maps.   *Bruselas.*   1867.   8°.

1890–92   MIDDENDORF (E. W.).   Die einheimischen Sprachen Perus.
6 vols.   *Leipzig.*   1890–92.   8°.
    Vol. I.   Das Runa Simi oder die Keshua-Sprache, wie sie
gegenwärtig in der Provinz von Cusco gesprochen wird
(Formenlehre, Syntax).   1890.
    Vol. II.   Wörterbuch des Runa Simi oder der Keshua-
Sprache.   1890.
    Vol. III.   Ollanta, ein Drama der Keshua-Sprache
(Tschudi's und Markham's) Text, mit Uebers. und Amerkk.
nebst ein Einleit. über die religione und Staatl. Einrichtt.
der Inkas.   1890.
    Vol. IV.   Dramat. und lyrische Dichtungen der Keshua-
Sprache, gesammelt und übers.   1891.
    Vol. V.   Die Aimarà-Sprache.   Mit ein Einleit. über die
frühere Verbreit. der dieselbe redende Rasse und ihr Ver-
hältn. zu der Inkas.   1891.
    Vol. VI.   Das Muchik oder die Chimu-Sprache, mit ein
Einleit. über die gleichzeitig mit den Inkas und Aimariàs in
Süd amerika lebend. Kulturvölker und Anhang über die
Chibka-Sprache.   1892.

1893   ——Peru. Beobachtung und Studien über das Land und
seine Bewohner während eines 25 jähr. Aufenthalts.   I.
Lima.   32 Taf. and 21 Hobzs.   *Berlin.*   1893.   8°.

1822   MIER NORIEGA Y GUERRA (S. T. DE). *See* CASAS (BART. DE LAS) Brevissima relacion, *etc.* Edited by S. T. de M. N. y G. *Mexico.* 1822. 16°.

1826   MIERS (JOHN). Travels in Chile and La Plata. Maps and illus. *London.* 1826. 8°.
(Chap. XXIV. The Indians.)

1579   MIGGRODE (J. DE). *See* CASAS (BART. DE LAS) Tyraunies et cruautez des Espagnols, *etc.* Trad. par J. de M. *Anvers.* 1579. 8°.

1828   MILLER (JOHN), *General.* Memoirs of General Miller, in the service of the Republic of Peru. 2 vols. 4 portraits, maps and plans of battles. *London.* 1828. 8°.

1829   ——— (Second edition.) 2 vols. *London.* 1829. 8°.
(Written by a brother of General Miller from the letters and notes left by him.)

1829   ——— Memorias del General Miller al servicio de la República del Perú. Trad. del ingles al Castellano por el General Torrijós. 2 tom. *Londres.* 1829. 8°.

1844   MILLER (N.), *General.* On the state of the Peruvian Empire previous to the arrival of the Spaniards. Edinburgh, 1844. 8°. (Fraser's Magazine, Vol. 30, pages 37-47.)
(Gives a translation, probably from Calancha, of Mancio Serra de Lejesama's so-called "Confession.")

1881-2   MILLOUÉ (——— DE). Momie péruvienne de la nécropole d'Ancon au Musée Guimet. *Lyon.* 1881-2. 8 .
(Bull. Soc. d'Anthropologie de Lyon, t. i. (1881-2), page 41.)

1879   MITRE (BARTOLOMÉ). Las Ruinas de Tiahuanaco. (Nueva Revista de Buenos Ayres.) *Buenos Ayres.* 1879.

1881   ——— Ollantay: Estudio sobre el drama Quichua. *Buenos Ayres.* 1881.

1887-8   ——— Historia de San Martin y de la emancipacion Sud-Americana. 3 vols. Portraits and plans. *Buenos Aires.* 1887-8. 8 .

1890   ——— Historia, *etc.* Segunda edicion corregida. 4 vols. *Buenos Aires.* 1890. 8°.

1873   MOLINA (CHRISTOVAL DE).   An account of the Fables and Rites of the Yncas.   Translated from the original Spanish manuscripts, and edited with notes and introduction by Clements R. Markham.   *London.*   1873.   8°.
(Hakluyt Society's Publications, No. 48, pages 3-64.)

1840   —————— History of the Incas.   *See* BALBOA (M. C.) (Miscellanea Austral) Histoire du Perou.   *Paris.*   1840.   8°.

[CHRISTOVAL DE MOLINA, chaplain to the hospital for natives, Cuzco; wrote between 1570-1584.   Knew Quichua, intimate with native chiefs and learned men, and questioned priests at Cuzco.   Next to Blas Valera as authority on native religious ideas and institutions.]

1569   MONARDES (NICHOLAS).   Des libros, al uno que trata de todas las cosas que se traen de nuestras Indias Occidentales, que sirven al uso de la medicina, y el otro que trata de la Piedra Bezoar, y de la Yerva Escuerçonera, *etc.*   *Sevilla.*   1569.   8°.

1571   —————— Segunda parte del libro de las cosas, *etc.*   *Sevilla.*   1571.   4°.

1574   —————— Primera y seguinda y tercera partes de la historia medicinal de las cosas, *etc.*   *Sevilla.*   1574.   4°.

1580   —————— (Another edition.) Primera y segunda, *etc. Sevilla.*   1580.   4 ·

1574   —————— De Simplicibus Mendicamentis ex occidentali Indie delatis quorum in medicina usus est....interprete C. Clusio.   *Antverpiæ.*   1574.   8°.

1579   —————— (Another edition.)   Simplicium Mendicamentorum ....historia.   *Antuerpiæ.*   1579.   8°.

1582   (Another edition.)   *Antuerpiæ.*   1582.   8°.

1576   —————— Della historia de i semplici, aromati, et altre cose che vengono portare dell' Indie Occidentale, portinenti all' uso della medicina.   (*See* ORTA (G. DE) Due libri dell' historia del simplici, aromati, *etc.*)   1576.   4°.

1582   —————— (Another edition.)   1582.   8°.

1589   —————— (Another edition.)   1589.   8°.

1605   —————— (Another edition.)   1605.   8°.

1616   —————— (Another edition.)   1616.   8 ·

1577   Joyfull newes out of the newe founde worlde, wherein is declared the rare and singular virtues of diverse and sundrie hearbes, trees, oyles, plantes and stones.... Also the portraiture of the said herbes.... Englished by J Frampton. B. L. *London.* 1577. 4°.

1580   —— (Another edition.) Joyfull news.... whereunto are added three other books treating of the Bezoar Stone, the herb Escuerçonera, *etc.* B. L. *London.* 1580. 4°.

1596   —— (Another edition.) B. L. *London.* 1596. 4°.

1619   —— Histoire des simples Medicaments apportés de l' Amérique desquels on se sert en la medicine.... trad. par de l' Ecluse. 3 vols. (Orta (G. de) Histoire des Drogues, Espiceries, *etc. Lyon.*) 1619. 8.°

1683   Montalvo (Dr. Juan Francisco A. de). El Sol del Nuevo Mundi ideado y compuesto en los esclarecidas operaciones del Bienaventurado Toribio Arcobispo de Lima. *Roma.* 1683.

1754   Montenegro (A. de la Peña) *Obispo de S. Franc. del Quito.* Itinerario par Parochos de Indios, en que se tratan las materias mas particulares, tocantes à ellos, paru su buena administracion. *Ambéres.* 1754. 4.
(Much valuable information about the Indians.)

1747   Montero (D. Vitorina). Estado politico del reyno del Peru govierno sin leyes, ministros relaxados, thesoros con polreza, fertilidad sin cultivo, sabiduria desestimada, milicia sin honor, cindades sin amor patricii, la justicia sin templo, huertos por comercios, integridad tenida por locura, rey, el mayor de ricos dominos, pabre de thesores. (Madrid, 1747.) Fol. (46 leaves.).
(Sabin. Bibl. Amer. 61124.)

Montesinos (Fernandez). *See* Fernandez Montesinos.

1774   Morghen (Le P.) *See* Peru. Lettres édifiàntes XXXII. recueil, contient : Relation du Perou par le P. M. *Paris.* 1774. 12.

1877   Mortillet (Gabriel de) La Cimitiére d' Ancon au Pérou. Illust. *Paris.* 1877. 4.
(La Nature, No. 200, 31 March, 1877.)

1839   MORTON (SAMUEL GEORGE) Crania Americana ; or a com
parative view of the skulls of various aboriginal nations of
North and South America, *etc.*   Colored map and 72 plates.
Philadelphia.   1839.   Fol.

1840   —— Crania Americana. (Review by G. Combe.)   *New
Haven.*   1840.   8°.
(American Journal of Science and Arts, No. 2, Vol. 38.)

1844   —— An inquiry into the distinctive characteristics of
the aboriginal race of America.   Second edition.   *Philadelphia.*   1844.   8°.

1887   MOSCHEN (S.) *See* SERGI (GUIS.) Crani peruviani antichi.
Firenze.   1887.   8°.

1857   MOSSI DE CAMBIANO (FRAY HONORIO).   Gramatica de la
lengua general del Perú llamada comunmente Quichua.
Sucre.   1857.   Fol.

1857   —— Ensaya sobre las escelencias y perfeccion del idioma
llamada comunmente Quichua.   *Sucre.*   1857.   Fol.

1857   —— Gramatica y Ensayo sobre las escelencias y perfeccion del idioma llamada comunmente Quichua.   *Sucre.*
1857.   4°.

1859   —— Gramatica y Diccionario de la lengua general de
Peru, llamada comunmente Quichua.   *Sucre.*   1859.

1860   —— Diccionario Quichua-Castellano.   2 pt.   *Sucre.*
1860.   Fol.

1864   —— Clave harmonica, o' demonstracion de la unidad de
origen de los idiomas....Segunda edicion, publicado por D.
F. Garcia Guterriez, *etc.*   *Madrid.*   1864.   8°.

1889   MOSSI (DON MIGUEL ANGEL).   Manual del idioma general
del Perú ; gramàtica razonada de la lengua Quichua, com-
parable con las lenguas del antiguo continente ; con notas
especiales sobre la que se habla en Santiago del Estero y
Catamarca.   *Cordoba.*   1889.   4°.

1867   MUELLER (F. G.) Geschichte der Amerikanischen Urrelig-
ionen.   *Basel.*   1867.   8°.
(Die Peruaner, pages 293-413.)

1878   MULHALL (MICHAEL G.)   The English in South America.
Buenos Ayres.   (1878.)   8°.
(Relates chiefly to the wars of independence of Peru and
Bolivia.)

1881   ——— (M. G.) *Mrs.* Between the Amazon and Andes, or Ten Years of a Lady's Travels.... Maps and Illustrations. *London.* 1881. 8°.
(Page 115-7, Callavayas Indians; pages 137-146, the Inca's Bridge.)

1793   Muñoz (Juan Bautista). Historia del nuevo mundo. *Madrid.* 1793.
(Comes down to 1500; gives critical review of sources of information. His MS. in the Real Academia de la Historia de Madrid.)

1572-98   Munster Cosmographia. 1572 and 1598. (Map of Cuzco.)

1775-89   Murr (G. G. von) Journal für Kunst und Literatur. 17 vols. *Nurnberg.* 1775-89. *See* Byer (Wolfgang) Aymara cum versione Latina.

1618   Múrua (Friar Martin de). Historia general del Peru, origen y descendencia de los Incas, pueblos y ciudades.... 1618.

[Lost. Copied by Dr. Muñoz for his collection. According to Leon Pinelo contained portraits of Incas, and colored drawings of insignia, *etc.* Múrua was an eminent ecclesiastic of Peru, born at Guernica, Biscay.]

1817   Myers (*Captain* John). The life, voyages and travels of Capt. J. Myers, detailing his adventures....on the coast of South America, *etc. London.* 1817. 8°.
(Touched at Arica, Tumbes, *etc.*)

Nadaillac (Marquis de). *See* Du Pouget (J. D.), *Marquis de Nadaillac.*

1873   Narratives of the rites and laws of the Yncas. Translated from the original Spanish Manuscripts, with notes and introduction by Cl. R. Markham. *London.* 1873. 8°.
(Hakluyt Society's Publications, No. 48.)

Navarette (Martin Fernandez de). *See* Fernandez de Navarette (Martin).

1671   Navarro (P. Tiburceo). Life of the Ven. Fray Francisco Solano, the apostle of Peru (Latin). *Rome.* 1671.

1884   NEHRING (H).   Rassebildung bei den Inka-Hunden. *Stuttgart.* 1884.

1887 ·   —— Die Todtenfeld von Ancon in Peru.   Map and 3 plates. *Berlin.* 1887. Fol.

1888   —— Alt-peruan. Hausthiere. Plate. *Berlin.* 1888.

1578   NICHOLAS (THOMAS).   *See* LOPEZ DE GOMARA (FR.)   The pleasant historic, *etc.*; translated by T. N. *London.* 1578, *etc.*

1581   ——— *See* ZARATE (AUG. DE).   The strange and delectable history of the discoverie and conquest of Peru, *etc.*; translated by T. N. *London.* 1581. 4°.

——   NIZA (FRAY MARCO DE).   Conquista de la Provincia del Quito, ritos y ceremonias de la Indio, *etc.*
(A companion of Pizarro. MS. lost, but referred to by Juan de Velasco.)

——   NODAL (J. F.) *See* FERNANDEZ NODAL (JOSE).

1843   NORRIS (EDWIN).   *See* PRICHARD (J. C.), *M. D.*   The Natural History of Man. 4° ed.   Revised and enlarged by E. N. 2 vols. *London.* 1843. 8°.

1879   NOTICIAS sobre las prov. del Litoral corresp. al depart. de Lima i de la prov. del Callao por la offic. hidogr. Map. *Santiago.* 1879.

1875   NOTT (JOSIAH CLARK) and GLIDDON (GEORGE R.)   Indigenous Races of the Earth ; or new chapters of ethnological inquiry.   Illustrated. *Philadelphia.* 1875. 4°.
(*See* MAURY (L. F. A.) and MEIGS (J. A.)

1782   NUIX Y DE PERPINA (JUAN).   Reflexiones imparciales sobre la humanidad de los Espagñoles en las Indias, contra los pretendidos filosofos y politicos ; para ilustrar las historias de M. M. Raynal y Robertson.   Escritas en Italiano por....y traducidas con algunas notas por D. Pedro Varela y Ulloa. *Madrid.* 1782. 4°.

1513   NUÑEZ DE BALBOA (VASCO).   Letter to the Spanish government, dated January, 1513, Darien.   Written six months before his discovery of the South Sia. *See* FERNANDEZ DE NAVARETTE (MARTIN).   Colleccion de Viages, *etc.* Vol. III. Introd. to Andagoya.

—— OCAMPO (BALTASAR D'). Descripcion de la Provincia de San Francisco de Villcapampa.

(*MS*. Brit. Mus. Lib. Story by eye-witness of capture and execution of Tupac-Amaru by Viceroy Toledo.)

1863 ODRIOZOLA (MANUEL). Documentos historicos del Peru en las epocas del coloniage despues de la conquista y de la independencia hasta a presente, colectados y arreglados por el coronel M. O. *Lima*. 1863, *etc*.

1857 OLIVA (LE P. ARELLO). Histoire du Pérou, traduite de l'Espagnol sur le manuscrit inédit par H. Ternaux-Compans. *Paris*. 1857. 12 .

(Part of the "Bibliothique Elzévirrienne." This translation is only of the introductory portion of Oliva's work in four books, written before 1631.)

[OLIVA, born at Naples, 1593 : arrived in Peru, 1597 ; died at Lima, 1642.]

1883 OLIVARES (ADOLFO F.) *See* LOPEZ (DR. DON V. F.) Poesia Dramatica de los Incas. Ollantay.... traducida del Ingles por A. F. O., *etc*. *Buenos Ayres*. 1883.

1633 OLMOS (FRAY DIEGO DE). Gramatica de la lengua general del Cuzco. *Lima*. 1633. 4 .

1878 ONCHEN (W.) Allgemeine Geschichte, *etc*. *See* RUGE (SOPHUS). Geschichte des Zeitalters der Entdeckungen. 1878. 8 .

ONDEGARDO (POLO DE). *See* POLO DE ONDEGARDO.

1685 ORDENANZAS del Peru dirig. al Rey por Melchor de Navarra, virrey de estos reynos recog. y coord. por Th. de Ballesteros. Vol. I. *Lima*. 1685. Fol.

(No second volume. The original is of great rarety.)

1752 —— (Another edition.) *Lima*. 1752. Fol.

1752 ORDENANZAS que para el nuevo establecim. en la distribuc. y recaudac. de la Zimosna de la Santa Bula de Benedicto XIV., formadla J. A. Manso de Velasco, Virrey del Peru y Chile. *Lima*. 1752. Fol.

1887 ORDINAIRE (O.) Les Sauvages du Pérou. *Paris*. 1887. 8°.

(Rev. d'Ethnographie. Vol. VI. (1887), pages 265–322.)

1602   ORE (FRAY LUDOVICUM HIERONIMUM DE).   Ritual o' Manual de párracos por el Ilmo.   *Napoles.*   1602.

(Hervas: Cat. de las lenguas I., 244–45.)

1607   —— Rituale seu Manuale Peruanum...Et quæ indigent versione, vulgaribus idiomatibus Indicis, secundom diversos situs omnium provinciarum novi orbis Peru .... *Neapoli.* 1607. 4

1859   ORELLANA (FRANCISCO DE).   Expedition into the valley of the Amazons in 1540.   *London.*   1859.   8°.   *See* PIZARRO (G.) Expedition, *etc.*

[FRANCISCO DE ORELLANA accompanied Gonzalo Pizarro to explore forest country eastwards of Quito, Christmas, 1539. Sent forward in small vessel to obtain supplies, he abandoned Pizarro, and sailing on in search of gold, reached the Atlantic, passing through the "country of Amazons," from whom the river he thus discovered is named.   Left mouth of the Napo December 31, 1541; reached the sea August 26, 1542.   Returned to Spain and sailed May, 1544, with expedition to the Amazon, but died after wreck of his vessels about 100 leagues up the river.]

1711   ORRELLANA (P. ANTONIO).   Compendio de la Vida del el padre Cypriano Baraze....muerto d manos de los barbaros Moxos en la Provincia del Peru.   *Madrid.*   1711.   8 .

(Account of Moxos Indians.)

1576   ORTA (G. DE).   Due libri dell historia de semplici, aromati, *etc.   See* MONARDES (NICHOLAS).   Della historia de i semplici, aromati....portare dell' Indie occidentali, *etc.*   1576.   4 .

1619   —— Histoire des Drogues, Especeries, *etc.*   Comprise en six livres: dont il y en a cinq tirés du Latin de C. de L'Ecluse (translations of G. de Orta, C. de la Coste and N. Monard.)   1619.   8 .

——   ORTIGUERA (TORIBIO DE).   MS. National Library, Madrid.

[At Nombre de Dios, 1561.   Sent forces against Aguirre in Venezuela; account of expedition of Gonzalo Pizarro and Orellana.]

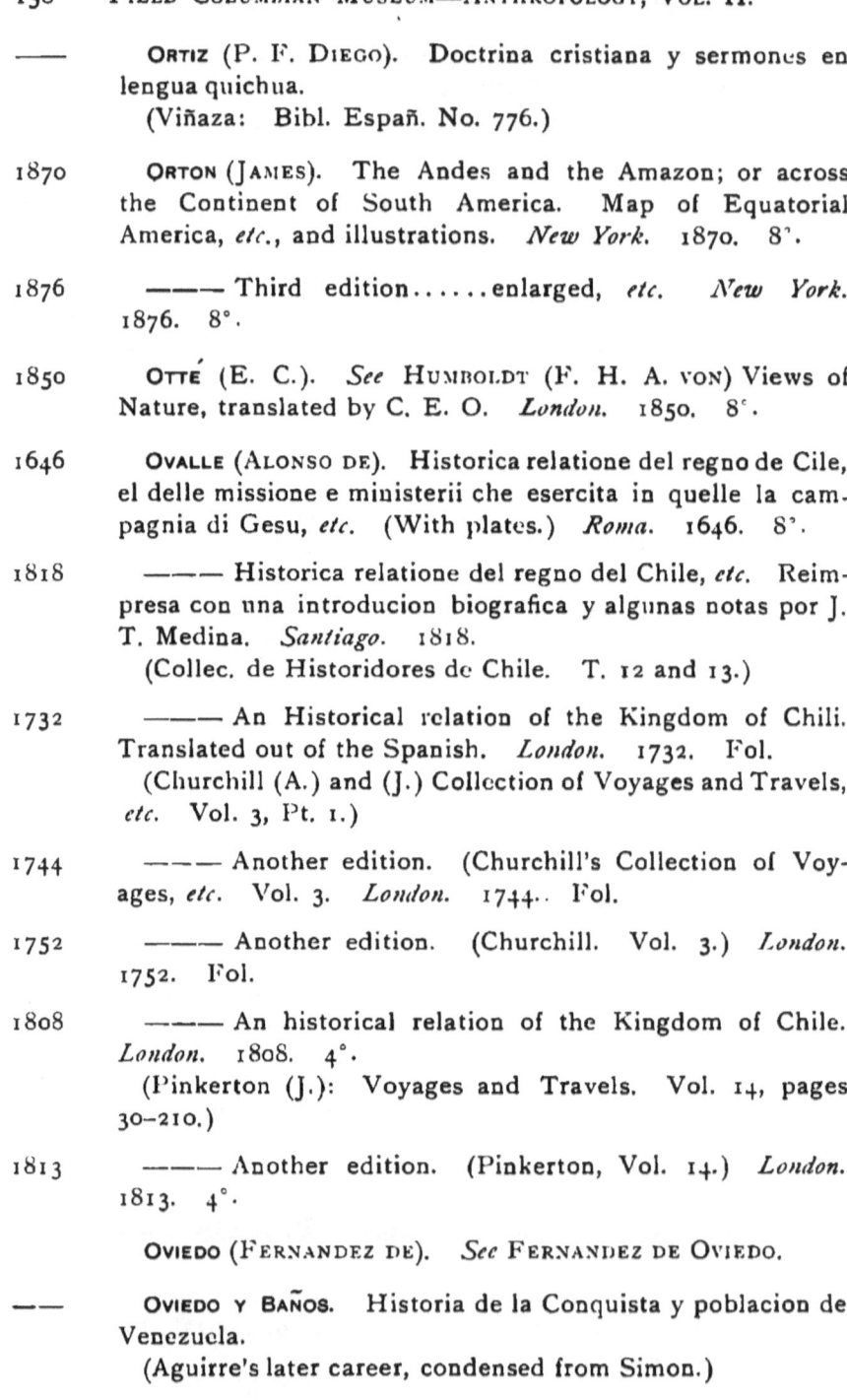

——   ORTIZ (P. F. DIEGO).   Doctrina cristiana y sermones en lengua quichua.
(Viñaza: Bibl. Español. No. 776.)

1870   ORTON (JAMES).   The Andes and the Amazon; or across the Continent of South America.   Map of Equatorial America, *etc.*, and illustrations. *New York.*   1870. 8°.

1876   —— Third edition......enlarged, *etc.*   *New York.* 1876. 8°.

1850   OTTÉ (E. C.).   *See* HUMBOLDT (F. H. A. VON) Views of Nature, translated by C. E. O. *London.* 1850. 8°.

1646   OVALLE (ALONSO DE).   Historica relatione del regno de Cile, el delle missione e ministerii che esercita in quelle la campagnia di Gesu, *etc.* (With plates.) *Roma.* 1646. 8°.

1818   —— Historica relatione del regno del Chile, *etc.* Reimpresa con una introducion biografica y algunas notas por J. T. Medina. *Santiago.* 1818.
(Collec. de Historidores de Chile.   T. 12 and 13.)

1732   —— An Historical relation of the Kingdom of Chili. Translated out of the Spanish. *London.* 1732. Fol.
(Churchill (A.) and (J.) Collection of Voyages and Travels, *etc.* Vol. 3, Pt. 1.)

1744   —— Another edition. (Churchill's Collection of Voyages, *etc.* Vol. 3. *London.* 1744. Fol.

1752   —— Another edition. (Churchill. Vol. 3.) *London.* 1752. Fol.

1808   —— An historical relation of the Kingdom of Chile. *London.* 1808. 4°.
(Pinkerton (J.): Voyages and Travels. Vol. 14, pages 30–210.)

1813   —— Another edition. (Pinkerton, Vol. 14.) *London.* 1813. 4°.

            OVIEDO (FERNANDEZ DE).   *See* FERNANDEZ DE OVIEDO.

——   OVIEDO Y BAÑOS.   Historia de la Conquista y poblacion de Venezuela.
(Aguirre's later career, condensed from Simon.)

1650?   PALAFOX Y MENDOÇA (JUANDE).   Virtudes del Indio, ó natu-
raleza y costumbres de los Indios de Nueva España.
(1650?)
(Appeal to the King on behalf of the Indians.)

1878   PALMA (R.).   Peru : Tradiciones.   *Lima*.   1878.   8ª.

——   PALOMINO (ALFONSO).   Informacion veridica de la obrado
en las provincias de Quito y Popayan.

[MS. lost; fragment of the work preserved in the "Breve
Informe" of Las Casas.   Palomino was a companion of Belalcazar.]

1868   PANCERI (P.).   La Mummia Peruviana del Museo Nazion.
di Napoli.   Plates.   *Napoli*.   1868.   4°.

1880   PANIAGUA (———).   Report to Pedro de la Gasca.   *See*
GASCA (PEDRO DE LA) Instructions to Lorenzo, *etc*.   *Revista de
Lima*.   1880.

1862   PARDO (———).   Estudios sobre la provincia de Janga,
No. 58.   1862.

1841   PARDO DE FIGUEROA (BALTHAZAR).   Mémoire présenté à Louis
XIV. pour l'engager à entreprendre la conquête de Pérou.
See Ternaux-Compans (H.) Archives des Voyages, *etc*.   Tom.
2.   (1841, *etc*.)   8°.

1880   PAYNE (EDWARD JOHN).   *See* HAKLUYT (RICHARD) Voyages
of the Elizabethan Seamen to America....selected and
edited....by E. J. P.   *London*.   1880.   8°.

1892   ——— History of the New World called America.   (Vol. 1.)
London.   1892.   8°.

1829   PAZOS-KANKI (V.) and SCIO (P.).   El Evangélio de Jesu
Cristo segun San Lucas en Aymara y Español.   Traducido
de la Vulgata Latina.   *London*.   1829.   8°.

1880   PAZ SOLDAN (C.).   *See* CARRERA (DON FERNANDO DE LA).
Arte de la lengua yunga, *etc*., edited by Dr. Gonzalez de la
Rosa.   Reimpresso (bajo la direccion de C. P. S.)   *Lima*.
1880.   8°.

1862   PAZ SOLDAN (MARIANO FELIPE).   *See* PAZ SOLDAN (MATEO)
Geografia del Perú, obra póstuma....corregida y aumentada por....M. F. P. S. (compendio de geografia, *etc*.)   1862,
etc.   4°.

1865   —— —— Atlas geografico del Pérú. 68 colored and other
plates. *Paris*. 1865. Fol.

1869   — - — (Nueva edicion.) *Paris*. 1869. Fol.

1865   —— —— (Another edition.) Atlas géographique et pittor-
esque de la République du Pérou. *Paris*. 1865. Fol.
(Published at the expense of the Peruvian government.
Pages 76–81, Peruvian bibliography.)

1868   —— —— Historia del Perú independiente. 3 vols. *Lima*.
1868. 8°.

1870   —— —— Historia del Perú independiente. Secundo Periodo,
1822–27. Tom. I. *Lima*. 1870. 8°.

1888   —— —— (Another edition.) Historia del Perú independiente.
Edited by C. Paz Soldan, with a biography of the author by
S. B. Camacho. *Buenos Aires*. 1888. 8°.

1868   —— —— Dos illustres sabios vridicados. Informe oral de
S. D. Er. Desjardins sobre las dos obras del S. Don S.
Lorente tituladas: Historia antigua del Peru e historia de la
conquista del Peru. *Apuntes* sobre la provincia de Loreto
por An. Raimondi. *Lima*. 1868. 4°.
(Spanish and French text side by side.)

1877   —— —— Dicionario geográfico estadistico del Perú: Contiene además la etimologia Aymará y Quechua de las principales pobliciones. *Lima*. 1877. 4°.

1862–3   PAZ SOLDAN (MATEO). Geografia del Pérú, obra postuma
D. D. M. P. S., corregida y aumentada por ...M. F. Paz
Soldan. (Compendio de geografia matemática, fiscica, y
politica.) 2 vols. *Paris*. 1862–3. 4°.
(Title page of Vol. II. reads: Compendia de Geografia
matemática, *etc*.)

1863   —- —— Géographie du Pérou. Corrigée....M. F. P. S.
Traduction française par P. Arséne Mouqueron. Portrait.
Paris. 1863. 8°.
(Treats of the history and customs of the Indians.)

             PAZ SOLDAN Y UNÁNUE (PEDRO). *See* ARONA (JUAN DE).

1874   PEABODY MUSEUM (HARVARD UNIVERSITY).   Report VII.
Cambridge. 1874. 8°.

1876   —— —— Report IX. *Cambridge*. 1876. 8°.
(Peruvian skulls.)

1848   **PENTLAND** (J. B.)   La Laguna de Titicaca and the Valleys of Yucay, Collao and Desaguadero, in Peru and Bolivia. Map and plate of Cuzco with key to Inca ruins, by J. B. P., H.M. Consul General to Bolivia. *Admiralty. London.* 1848.

1859   **PEREZ** (F.) El Carnero de Bogotá.   Edited by F. P. *Bogotá.* 1859. 8°. *See* RODRIGRUEZ FRÉSLE (JUAN) Conquista, *etc.*

1877   **PERTUISET** (E.) Le Tresor des Incas á la Terre de Feu. Aventures et voyages dans l' Amérique du Sud. *Paris.* 1877.   12°.

PERU.

———— La Conquista del Peru.
(4 leaves in British Museum Library.)

———— La conquista del Peru llamada la nueva Castilla La gl tierra por diuina vo luntad fue marauillosamente conquistada en la felicio sima ventura del Emperador y Rey nuestro señor: y por la prudencia y esfuerzo del muy magnifico y vale roso cavallero el Capitan Francisco pizarro Gouerna dor y adelanto de la neua castilla y de su herma no Hernando pizarro y de sus animosos capitans & fieles y esforzados compañeros q cō el se hallaron. Fol.   Title, 1 leaf. 8 unnumbered leaves.
(Sabin: Bibl. Amer. Vol. XIV. says: "The 'Bibliotheca Grenvilliana' states that it is identical with the ' Relatione d' un Capitano Spagnuolo della Conquista del Peru,' published by Ramusio, but with many variations.")

1795?   ———— Le Desespoir d' un Jeune Péruvien sur la destruction de l' Empire du Pérou.   (*Paris,* 1795?) 8°.
(A satire in verse.)

1828   — —— In the Valleys of Peru.   Wanderings on Four Continents. 1828.

1840   ———— Lettre sur les superstitions du Pérou, par un Religieux Augustin. *See* TERNAUX-COMPANS (H.)   Receuil de documents et mémoires, *etc.* 1840. 8°.

1534   ———— Nouvelles certaines de Isles de Perou. *Lyon.* 1534. 8°.
(An account of the conquest by Pizarro.)

1774   ———— Lettres édifiantes XXXIIe. recueil, contient: Relation du Pérou par le P. Morghen (description de Lima, de
Pisco, monumens de Chinca, Arica, situation d'Ylo, traditions des habitans, *etc.*, *etc.*) *Paris.*   1774.   12°.

1786   ——— The History of the Conquest of Peru. Plates.
London.   1786.   18°.

1796   ——— Habitans du Pérou, dessines par Grasset St. Sau-
veur.   1796.   4°.
(16 plates of nobles, warriors, ancient priest, and peasants.)

1838   ———— Peru before and at the Spanish invasion.   *London.*
1838.   8°.   (Dublin Review, Vol. V., pages 183–224.)
(Review of Vols. 1–6 of Ternaux-Compans' "Voyages.")

1879   ———— Relacion de las costambres antiguas de los naturales del Pirú.   *See* JIMÉNEZ DE LA ESPADA (M.) Tres relaciones de antigüedades peruanas.   1879.   8°.

1870   -   Relacion de Todo lo sucedido en la Provincia del
Pirú desde que Blaseo Nuñez Vela fue enviado por S. M. á
ser visorey della, que se embarco á primero de Noviembro del
año de MDXLIII.   *Lima.*   1870.   8°.

1753   ——— A voyage to Peru, etc.   *London.*   1753.   12°.   *See*
BLANCHARDERIE (ABBÉ COURTE DE LA).

1573   ——— De Wonderlycke ende warachtighe Historie vant
Conincrück vñ Peru, *etc.*   (Translated from the Spanish by
R. de Bacquere.)   *Thantwerpen.*   1573.   4°.

————   ——— Superstitions and Rites of the Incas.   Report by
Chaplain of Hospital for natives of Cuzco to Bishop Don
Sebastian de Artaum.
(MS. Library of Madrid, B. 35.)

——   (Attabalipa del) *pseud.   See* ATTABALIPPA.

1872   —   Le Perou et ses derniers événemens.   *Paris.*
1872.   8°.

1873   - ——— *See* MARKHAM (C. R.)   Reports on the discovery of
Peru.   Translated by C. R. M.   *London.*   1873.   8°.

1867   ——— (ANTHROPOLOGY OF).   Trephining in the days of the
Incas.   *London.*   1867.   8°.
(Anthropological Review, Vol. V., page 374.)

1884   —————— Contributions to North American Ethnology. *Washington.* 1884.
(Powell's Survey, 1882, Vol. V.   Plate of trephined Peruvian skull.)

——   ———— (Architecture of).   Ruins of Tiahuanaco.
(Revue d' Architecture de Travaux publies, Vol. 24.)

——   ———— (Art of).   Lyoux d'or péruviens.   1 Plate.
(Archives de la Soc. Amér. de France.   N. S. I. pl. v.
Emblems of royalty, colored.)

——   —————— Peruvian Pottery.   2 Plates.
(Mem. de la Soc. Antiq. du Nord.)

1868   —————— Ancient Art in Peru. *London.* 1868.   8°.
(Anthrop. Rev., Vol VI., page 120.)

1833   ———— (Languages of).   Vocabulario de la lengua de los
Campas, en la pampa del Sacramento en le Peru.   ("Copia
de un Vocabulario de la lengua de Campa ó Andes (Antis)
pertenciente á Don Manuel Ames, gobernador de Andamarca,
en 1833....").   4°.

    ———— (————).   *See* Quichua.

1791–95   ———— (Periodical Literature of) Mercurio Peruano de
Historia, Literatura, y Noticias publicas que da a luz la
Sociedad Academica de Amantes de Lima.   12 vols. *Lima.*
1791–95.

1837   —————— Museo Erudito, o los Tiempos y las Costumbres *Cuzco.*   1837, *etc.*

——   —————— Revista Peruana. *Lima.*

1752   **Phillippe de Pretot** (Étienne André).   Memoires sur l'
Amerique et sur l' Afrique.   1752.   4°.
(Article 2, Geography of Peru.)

1656   **Phillips** (J.)   *See* Casas (Bart. de las).   The tears of the
Indians, *etc.*, made English by J. P. *London.*   1656.   8°.

1723   **Picart** (Bernard).   Cérémonies et coutumes de tous les
peuples du monde, representées par des figures dessinées de
la maia de B. P., *etc.*   1723, *etc.*   Fol.

1733   ———— The ceremonies and religious customs of the various nations of the known world....translated into English,
etc.   1733, *etc.*   Fol.

1840   PICCINI (O.) *See* XERES (FRAN. DE) Relazione del Conquisto del Peru, *etc.*, traduttore, O. P.   Vol. V. of Marmochi's Raccolta de Viaggi. *1840.* 8°.

1844   PICKERING (CHARLES).   The geographical distribution of animals and plants. *See* WILKES (C.), *Commander U. S. N.* A narrative of the United States exploring expedition, *etc.* Vol. XV.   1844, *etc.*   4°.

1876   ——— The geographical distribution of animals and plants. Part II.   Plants in their wild state.   Maps. *Salem.* 1876. 4°. (Different from preceding item.   Chap. VI. Peruvian Regions.)

1844   ——— The Races of Man : and their geographical distri- bution. *See* WILKES (C.)   Narrative, *etc.* Vol. IX.   1844, *etc.*   4°.

1849   ——— New edition.   To which is prefixed an Analytical Synopsis of the Natural History of Man.   By J. C. Hall. (Illustrated.)   *London.*   1849.   8°. (Bohn's Illustrated Library.)

1850   ——— New edition. (Bohn, Illust. Lib.) *London.* 1850. 8 .

1851   ——— New edition.   *London.*   1851.   8°.

1840   PICKETT (JAMES C.) Letters and Dissertations upon sundry subjects.   *Washington.*   1840.   8°. (Ancient ruins in Peru, pages 15–22.)

1688   PIEDRAHITA (LUCAS FERNANDEZ).   Historia General de las Conquistas del Nuevo Reyno de Grenada.   *Amberes.*   1688.

[PIEDRAHITA was of Inca descent and native of Bogotá ; became priest, and died at Panama, 1688, aged 70. Only part of his *Historia* printed ; comes down to 1563.   Depends chiefly on Ximenes de Queseda, Castellanos, and Pedro Simon.]

1876 82   PINART (A. L.) Coleccion de linguistica y etnografica Amer- icanas. *Paris, San Francisco.* 1876–82. 4 . (Vol. IV. Bibliothéque de Linguistique et d'Ethnographie Américaines.)

1738   **Pinelo** (Antonio de Leon). Epitome de la Bibliotheca Oriental y Occidental, nautica y geografica de Don Antonio de Leon Pinelo....tomo seguendo. *Madrid.* 1738. Fol.

1802   **Pinkerton** (John). Modern Geography : a description of the Empires, States and Colonies, with the oceans, seas and islands in all parts of the world....with numerous maps. 2 vols. *London.* 1802. 4°.

1807   —— A new edition, greatly enlarged. 3 vols. *London.* 1807 4°.

1817   ——— New edition, with additions and corrections.. 1817. 2 vols. *London.* 1817. 4°.

1808–14   —— A general collection of the best and most interesting Voyages and Travels in all parts of the World, many of which are now first translated into English....with plates. 17 vols. *London.* 1804–14. 4°.

        (*See* Betaugh (Wm.), Vol. XIX.; Bouguer (P.), Vol. XIV.; La Condamine (C. M.), Vol. XIV.; Ovalle (Al. de), Vol. XIV.; Ulloa (G. J. & Ant. de), Vol. XIV.)

1533 ?   **Pizarro** (Francisco) *Marquis.* *See* **Cortes** (H.) Copia delle lettere del Prefetto (Hernando Cortes) della India, la Nuova Spagna detta, *etc.* (*Venice ?* 1533 ?) 8°.

        (Plaquette of two leaves. Account of the capture of Atabalipa by Pizarro.)

1534   —— Letter announcing the capture of Inca Atahualpa, November, 1532. Italian translation. *See* Benedetto. Libro di Benedetto. *Venice.* 1534.

1534   —— (German translation.) Newe Zeitung aus Hespanien. *Nuremberg.* Feb., 1534. (4 leaves.)

1534   —— (French translation). Nouvelles certaines des isles du Peru. 1534.

        (British Museum Library.)

1534?   —— Letera de la nobil cipta, novamente ritrouvata alle Indie...data in Peru adi.XXV.de novembre de M DXXXIIII. (1534?)

1535   —— (Another edition) "data in Zhanal." 1535.

——   *See* Peru. La Conquista del Peru. (Tractate of 4 leaves.)

1540   —— *See* **GUAZZO** (MARCO).   Historie di tutte le cose degne di memoria qual del ano MDXXXIIII.   1540, *etc.*

1534   —— *See* XERES (F. DE).   Verdadera relacion de la conquista del Peru, *etc.*   (1534).   Fol.

1547   —— —— (1547).   Fol.

1744   —— The History of the Discovery of Peru by F. Pizarro ....1748.   *See* **HARRIS** (JOHN) *D. D.*   Navigantium atque Itinerantium Bibliotheca, *etc.*   Vol. II.   1744, *etc.*   Fol.

1844   —— Relacion de los primeros'descubrimientos de F. Pizarro y Diego de Almagro, sacada del codice numero CXX. de la Biblioteca Imperial de Viena, 1844.   *See* FERNANDEZ DE NAVARETTE (M.)   Coleccion de documentos, *etc.*, tom. 5. 1842, *etc.*   8 .

1544   —— Relatione di un Capitano Spagnuolo del discoprimento et Conquista del Perù fatta da F. Pizarro et da H. Pizarro suo fratello.   Relatione di un secretario di F. Pizarro della conquista .... della Provincia del Peru, *etc.*   *See* RAMUSIO (G. B.)   Primo Volume .... delle navigatione et viaggi, *etc.*   Vol. 3.   1544, *etc.*   Fol.

1563   —— —— Vol. 3.   1563, *etc.*   Fol.

[MARQUIS FRANCISCO PIZARRO, illegitimate son of Gonzalez Pizarro, born about 1470 in Estremadura.   Could neither read nor write.   Went to Darien, 1509, with Alonzo de Ojeda's expedition.   Formed partnership at Panamá with Almagro and Luque for Southern exploration.   Sailed from Panamá Nov. 14, 1524, but had to return.   Sailed again, 1526, with Almagro and pilot Bartolomé Ruiz.   Returned to Panamá after visiting Atacames, Tumbez and other points on coast of Peru.   Expedition for conquest of Peru sailed Dec. 28, 1531.   Treacherously captured Atahualpa, November, 1532; Inca executed 29th August, 1533.   Entered Cuzco 15th Nov., 1533.   Founded Lima (Ciudad le los Reyes) Jan. 6, 1535.   Made written agreement, June 15, 1535, with Almagro, who set out to conquer Chili.   War between Pizarro and Almagro, who seized Cuzco 8th April, 1537. Almagro garotted at Cuzco, July, 1538.   Pizarro assassinated at Lima, by adherents of Almagro, 26th June, 1541.]

1859   PIZARRO (GONZALO), ORELLANA (F. DE) and ACUÑA (C. DE)). Expeditions into the Valley of the Amazons during the 16th and 17th centuries. Edited and translated (from the Royal Commentaries of G. J. de la Vega and the General History of Herrera) by C. R. Markham. *London.* 1859. 8°. (Hakluyt Soc. Pub., No. 24.)

[GONZALO PIZARRO, illegitimate brother of Francisco Pizarro, went with him to Panamá in 1530, and to Peru Dec., 1531. Led expedition against the Charcas, 1538. Explored forest region eastward of Quito, descending the Coca and Napo rivers, 1539–42. Headed revolt against Viceroy Blasco Nuñez Vela, 1544; declared by *Audiencia*, Governor and Captain-General of Peru. Surrendered to Pedro de la Gasca, 9th April, 1568; a few days afterwards executed at Cuzco.]

1535   PIZARRO (HERNANDO). La relatione del Vaggio che fece.... F. Piccaro....de la terra de Caxamalca fina a Parcama et de li a Xauxa (from the Spanish of M. de Sette). *See* XERES (F. DE) Libro primo de la conquista del Peru, *etc.* 1535. + ·

1872   ——— Letter from H. P. to the Royal Audience of Santo Domingo. Dated November, 1533. Translated by C. R. Markham. *London.* 1872. 8°.
(*See* MARKHAM (C. R.) Reports on the Discovery of Peru. Xeres' true account of the province of Cuzco, *etc.* Hakluyt Soc. Publ., No. 47, pages 113–27.)

[HERNANDO PIZARRO, eldest and only legitimate brother of Francisco Pizzaro: accompanied his brothers to Panamá, Jan., 1530. Went to Peru with Francisco, Dec., 1531. Headed expedition to Pachacamac, 1533. Returned to Spain with treasure, and on the voyage wrote his letter, dated November, 1533, to the *Audiencia* of Santo Domingo, covering the same ground as narratives of Xeres and Estete. Commanded Pizarro's army in the struggle with Almagro, whom he caused to be garroted, July, 1538. Returned, 1539, to Spain, where imprisoned 20 years.]

1639   PIZARRO Y ORELLANA (FERNANDO). Varones illustres del Nuevo Mundo. *Madrid.* 1639,
(Lives of Pizarro and his brothers and of Almagro. The author was a grandson of the daughter of Francisco Pizarro.)

1842   **PIZARRO** (PEDRO). Relaciones del descubrimiento y conquista de los Reynos del Peru. *Madrid.* 1842. 8°. *See* COLECCION DE DOCUMENTOS para la historia de España. Vol. V., pages 201–388.

[PEDRO PIZARRO, cousin of Francisco Pizarro, attended him as page on leaving Spain for Panamá, 1530, when 15. Eyewitness of the conquest and of the civil wars; lived at Arequipa after assassination of Francisco. His *Relaciones* completed, 1571.]

1876   **PLATZMANN** (JULIUS). Verzeichniss einer Auswahl Amerikanischer Grammatiken, *etc. Leipsic.* 1876.

1835-6   **POEPPIG** (EDUARD). Reise in Chile, Peru, und auf dem Amazonen strome, 1827–1832. 2 vols. Ob. fol. atlas of 16 plates. *Leipsig.* 1835–6. 4°.

1555   **POLEM** (J.). *See* FERNANDEZ DE OVIEDO Y VALDAS (GONZALES) L'Histoire naturelle et generalle des Indes....trad. ....by J. P. *Paris.* 1555. Fol.

1561-70   **POLO DE ONDEGARDO** (LIC.) Relaciones 1561 and 1570. (MS. at the Escurial, Madrid.)

1873   ——— Report....on the lineage of the Yncas and how they extended their conquests. Translated and edited by C. R. Markham. *London.* 1873. 8°. *See* MARKHAM (C. R.). Narrative of the Rites and Laws of the Incas, pages 151–71.

[POLO DE ONDEGARDO accompanied La Gasco in campaign against Gonzalo Pizzaro; Lawyer; Corregidor of Cuzco. Died at Potosi about 1580. Knowledge of native languages limited. Describes principles of Inca administration.]

1847   **PRESCOTT** (WILLIAM HICKLING). History of the conquest of Peru, with a preliminary view of the civilization of the Incas. 2 vols. *London.* 1847. 8°.

———   ——— Second edition.

———   ——— Third edition.

1850   —— Fourth edition.   3 vols.   *London.*   1850.   8°.

——   ———— Fifth edition.

——   ———— Sixth edition.

1854   ———— Seventh edition....revised.   *London.*   1854.   8°.

1855   ———— (New edition.)   2 vol.   *London.*   1855.   12°.

1872   ———— (New edition.)   1 vol.   *London.*   1872.   8°.

1874   —— New and revised edition, with the author's latest corrections and additions.   Edited by J. F. Kirk (Mr. Prescott's secretary).   2 vols.   *Philadelphia.*   1874.   12°.

1882   —— Author's authored version.   *London.*   (1882).   8°.

1885   —— Author's edition.   *London.*   (1885.)   8.

1887   —— New and revised edition, *etc.*   *London.*   1887.   8°.

1890   ———— (Another edition.)   3 vols.   *London.*   (1890.)   8°.

1893   —— New and revised edition....edited by J. F. Kirk (Biographical and Critical Miscellanies.)   *London.*   1893.   8°.

1847–8   ———— (Spanish translation.)   *Madrid.*   1847–8.

1848   —— Geschichte der Erorberung von Peru m. e. Uebers. des Bildungszustandes unter d. Inkas.   Aus. d. Englisch.   2 vols.   *Leipzig.*   1848.

1850   —— Historia de la conquista del Perú....Traducida al Castellano por J. Garcia Icazbalceta.   Con un appendice del traductor.   Segunda edicion.   (Relacion de la conquista del Perú escrita por S. Sancho, *etc.*)   2 tom.   *Mexico.*   1850.   8°.

1747–80   **Prevorst** (A. T.).   Histoire générale des Voyages.   Divers voyages au Pérou.   Vol. 16.   1747–80.

1873   **Price** (J. E.).   On the Peruvian pottery sent by Consul Hutchinson.   *London.*   1873.   8°.

        (Journal Anthropological Society, Vol. 3, pages 100–3.)

1883   —— On objects from ancient grave mounds in Peru.   *London.*   1883.   8°.

        (Journal of Anthropological Society, Vol. 13, pages 273-75).

1813   PRICHARD (JAMES COWLES), *M. D.*, *F. R. S.*   Researches into the physical history of mankind. *London*. 1813. 8°.

1826   ——— Second edition. 2 vols. Map. *London*. 1826. 8°.

1836-47   ——— Third edition. 5 vols. Map and plates (some colored.) *London*. 1836–47. 8 .

1843   ——— The natural history of man ; comprising inquiries into the modifying influences of physical and moral agencies on the different tribes of the human family. Plates. *London*. 1843. 8°.

1845   ——— (Second edition.) With supplement. 49 colored plates. *London*. 1845. 8°.

———   ——— Third edition.

1855   ——— Fourth edition, revised and enlarged by Edwin Norris, *etc.* 2 vols. 62 colored plates and 100 wood engravings. *London*. 1855. 8°.

1840-8   ——— Naturgeschichte des Menschengeschlechts.... Nach der dritten auflagert des englisches originals, with Amerkungen und Zusätzen herausgegeben von....R. Wagner....(und....J. G. F. Will). 4 vols. *Leipzig*. 1840–8. 8°.

1825   PROCTOR (ROBERT). Narrative of a journey across the Cordillera of the Andes, and of a residence in Lima and other parts of Peru, in the years 1823 and 1824. Map. *London*. 1825. 8 .

1824   PROPRIAC (CHEVALIER DE). Beautés de l' Histoire du Péru. Plates. *Paris*. 1824. 8°.

1827   PROSPECTUS of the Quipola, or an explanation of the Quipoes, now open for public opinion. *London*. 1827.
(Reviewed in Westminster Review, Vol. XI., page 228.)

1613   PURCHAS (SAMUEL) THE ELDER. Purchas his pilgrimage : or, Relations of the World and the Religions observed in all ages....in foure parts. This first containeth a.... historie of Asia, Africa and America, with the islands adjacent.... With briefe descriptions, *etc.* *London*. 1613. Fol.

1614   ——— (Second edition, enlarged.) *London*. 1614. Fol.

1617   ——— (Third edition, much enlarged.) *London*. 1617. Fol.

1626   ——— (Fourth edition, much enlarged with additions....) *London*. 1626. Fol.

1625 ——— Purchas his Pilgrimes. In five bookes. The first contayning the voyages....made by ancient kings....and others, to and thorow the remoter parts of the knowne world, *etc.* 4 pt. *London.* 1625. Fol.

(Vol. V. is the 4th edition of the "Pilgrimage." *See* Casas (Bartolomé de las) A brief narrative of the destruction of the Indies by the Spaniards, 1625. Fol.; Fernandez de Oviedo y Valdes (Gonzalo) Decades of the new world. 1625. Fol.; Lasso de la Vega (Garcia) Observations.... out of the first part of the Commentaries Royall, *etc.* *London.* 1625. Fol.)

1860–80 Quaritch (Bernard). A general catalogue of Books. 7 vols. 1860–80. 8°.

1887 ——— Supplement. 1887, *etc.* 8°.

1873–82 Quatrefages de Bréau (Jean Louis Armand de) and Hamy (Ernest T.). Crania Ethnica; les crânes des races humaines décrits et figurès d'apres....les principales collections de la France et de l'etranger, *etc.* 10 parts. Atlas with 100 plates. *Paris.* 1873–82. 4°.

Quesada (Ximenes de). *See* Ximenes de Quesada.

—— Quichua. Arte de la lengua general del Inca, llamada Quichua. 8°.
(MS., Viñaza: Bibl. Epañ. No. 1,106.)

—— ——— Arte de la lengua general del Cuzco, Qquichua. 4°.
(MS. Bibl. de Colegio de los Jesuites de Quito. Viñaza: Bibl. Españ. No. 841.)

1760? ——— Arte de la Lengua General del Inga llamada Qquechuea (Quichua). (Circa, 1760.) 8°.
(MS. Brit. Mus. Lib. Viñaza: Bibl. Epan. No. 998.)

1586 ——— Arte y Vocabulario en la lengua general del Peru llamada Quichua, y en la lengua española. El mas copioso. ....impresso. Por Antonio Ricardo. *Los Reyes.* 1586. 4°.

1608 ——— (Second edition.) *Los Reyas.* 1608. 4°. *See* Gonçalez Holguin (Pad. Diego).

1753 ———— Breve instruccion o arte para entender la lengua comun de los Indios, segun se habla en la Provincia de Quito. *Lima.* 1753. 12°.

———— ———— Vocabulario en la langue castellana, la del Ynga y Xebera. 8°.
(MS. Brit. Mus. Lib. Viñaza: Bibl. Españ. No. 1,018.)

———— ———— Vocabularios de las lenguas Lulé, Guarani, Caribe y Quichua. 4°.
(MS. Bibl. Imp. Berlin. Viñaza: Bibl. Españ. No. 1,081.)

1845 ———— Cartilla y catecismo de la doctrina cristiana en castellano y qquechua. *Cuzco.* 1845. 4°.

1773 ———— Catecismo tercero y exposicion de la doctrina cristiana por sermones (en quichua y en castellano).... Conforme á lo que se proveyo en el Santo Concilio Provincial de Lima, año de 1583. Mandado reimprimir por el Concilio provincial. *Lima.* 1773. 4°.

1866 ———— (Another edition.) Catecismo breve y exposicion de la doctrina cristiana, *etc.* Conforme á lo.... de 1,583. *Paris.* 1866.

1603 ————Catecismo en lengua española y Quichua del Peru. Ordenando por auctoridad del concilio Provincial de Lima. *Roma.* 1603. 12°.

———— ———— Confessionario en lengua Quechua. 4°.
(MS. Brit. Mus. Lib. Viñaza: Bibl. Españ. No. 1,003.)

1584 QUICHUA Y AYMARA. Doctrina christiana y catecismo para instruccion de los Indios.... con un confessionario.... traduzido en las dos lenguas generales, de este Reyno, Quichua y Aymara. Impreso.... por Antonio Ricardo. *Los Reyes.* 1584 (1583?). 4°.

1585 ———— Confessionario para los curas de Indios. Con la Instruccion contra sus Ritos: y Exhortacion para ayudar á bien morir: y summa de sus Privilegios: y forma de Impedimentos del Matrimonio. Compuesto y traduzido en las lenguas Quichua y Aymara. Impresso.... por Antonio Ricardo. *Los Reyes.* 1585.

——   QUINTANA (———).   Vidas de Españoles celebres.
(Best life of Pizarro; text of agreement between Pizarro,
Almagro and Luque; Pedro Sancho's Note on the distribu-
tion of the ransom of Atahualpa, *etc.*)

1872-80   RADA Y DELGADO (JUAN DE DIOS DE LA).   Museo Español
Antiguedades bajo la direccion del doctor Don J. de la R. y
D., *etc.*   11 vols.   *Madrid.*   1872-80.   8°.   Fol.

1883   ——— Les Vases peruviens du Musée Archeologique de
Madrid.   *Copenhague.*   1883.   8°.
(Compte-rendu der Congres de Americanistes.   5th Ses-
sion, pages 236-246.)

1856   RADIGUET (M.).   Souvenirs de l'Amérique espagnole: Chile,
Pérou, Brésil.   *Paris.*   1856.   12°.

1862   RAIMONDI (ANTONIO).   Apuntes sobre la provincia litoral
de Loreto.   2 maps.   *Lima.*   1862.   8°.

1868   ——— *See* PAZ SOLDAN (M. F.).   Dos illustres sabios vindi-
cados.   *Lima.*   1868.   4°.

1867   ——— On the rivers San Gavan and Ayapata, in the province of Carabaya, Peru.   *London.*   1867.   8°.
(Journ. of the R. Geographical Society, Vol. 37, pages
116-51.)

1873   ——— El Departamento de Ancaches y sus riquezas minerales.   *Lima.*   1873.   Fol.

1874-80   ——— El Peru.   3 vols.   *Lima.*   1874-80.   8·
(Vol. I. (1874), Preliminar; II. and III. (1876-80), Historia de la geografiá del Perú.)

1875-9   ——— Historia de la geografiá del Perú.   O relacion
cronologica de los viajes, descubrimientos, fundaciones de
ciudades y pueblos, cambios notables en las divisiones ter-
ritoriales que se verificaron en el Perú desde la ipoca de la
conquista hasta el dia.   2 vols.   Maps and engravings.
Lima.   1875-9.   4°.

1863   ——— *See* BOLLAERT (WILLIAM).   On the Indian tribes of
the great district of Loreto in Northern Peru ; translated by
W. B.   *Anth. Rev.*   Vol. I. (1863), pages 33-43.

1871   —— Peruvian Inca skulls. Anthrop. Notes and Journal of Anthropology (1871), page 363.

1756   RALT (RICHARD).   A new and accurate history of South America : containing, etc. London. 1756. 8°.
(Peru, Chap. III.)

RAMOS (PADRE ALONZO). See GAVILAN (FRAY ALONZO RAMOS).

1554-9   RAMUSIO (GIOVANNI BATTISTE).   Navigatione et Viaggi, etc. Edited by G. B. R.   Venetia. 1554-9. Fol.
(Terzo Volume (1556) forms part of the second edition, and is devoted to American voyages. See ANGLERIUS (P. M.) Sommario, etc., and FERNANDEZ DE OVIEDO (AL.)

1563   (Another edition. 3 vols.) Vol. 3. Venetia. 1563. Fol.

1565   (New edition. 3 vols.) Vol. 3. Venetia. 1565. Fol.

1590?   (Another edition. 3 vols.) Vol. 3. Venetia. (1590?). Fol.

1606   (Another edition. 3 vols.) Vol. 3. Venetia. 1606. Fol.
(Ramusio's Italian translations, in his third volume, were formerly the chief source of information on American voyages.   Most of them are given in English dress in Richard Hakluyt's Voyages, Navigations, Traffiques and Discoveries, Vol. III.)

1827   RANKING (JOHN).   Historical researches of the conquest of Peru, Mexico, Bogota, Natchez and Talomeco, in the thirteenth century, by the Mongols, accompanied with elephants; and the local agreement of history and tradition, with the remains of elephants and mastodonites found in the new world : containing invasion of Japan from China. A violent storm.   Mongols, with elephants, land in Peru and in California.   Very numerous identifications.   History of Peru and Mexico, etc. Maps and illust. London. 1827. 8°.

1885-88   RATZEL (FRIEDRICH). Volkerkunde. 1885-88.

1897   —— The History of Mankind. Translated from the second German edition by A. J. Butler, with Introduction by E. B. Tylor.   Colored plates, maps and illustrations. 3 vols. London and New York. 1897. 8°.
(The Americans. Vol. II. Book II. D.)

1876, etc.   RECLUS (JEAN JACQUES ELISÉE). Nouvelle Géographie universelle.   La Terre et les Hommes . . . Cartes et . . gravures sur bois. 13 vols. Paris. 1876, etc. 8°.

1876 ———— The Earth and its Inhabitants.   English translation of La Terre, *etc.*   Edited by E. G. Ravenstein.   13 vols. *London.*   1876, *etc.*   8°.

1894-5 ———— The Earth and its Inhabitants.   South America. Edited by A. H. Keane, B.A.   2 vols.   Maps and illustrations.   *New York.*   1894-5.   8°.

(Vol. I.   The Andes Region—pages 220–264, Colombia ; pages 265–273, Ecuador ; pages 354–96, Peru ; pages 397–477, Bolivia ; pages 478–96, Chile ; *Peruvian aborigines*, pages 301–16.   Vol. II.: Amazonia and La Plata ; the *Coyos* or *Coyas*, descendants of Quichuas in Argentina, page 408.)

1893 ———— Colombia (being a portion of "Nouvelle Géog. univ.") Traducida y anotada....por F. J. Vergara y Velasco (with an introduction by C. Cuervo Márquez).   *Bogotá.* 1893.   8°.

1597 REGNAULD (R.).   Histoire naturelle et morale des Indes.... traduite par R. R.   *Paris.*   1597.   8°.

1600 ———— (Another edition.)   *Paris.*   1600.   8°.

1889 REISS (WILHELM).   *See* UHLE (M.)   Kultur und Industrie sudamerikanischen Völker, nach dem....Sammlungen von ....W. Reiss, *etc.*   2 vols.   1889, *etc.*   Fol.

1880-7 REISS (WILHELM) and STÜBEL (A.)   Das Todtenfeld von Ancon in Peru.   Ein Beitrage zur Kultur und Industrie der Inca-Reiches.   Nach dem Ergebnissen eigener Ausgrabungen.   141 Taf. in Fahbendruch mit Text.   3 Bde.   *Berlin.* 1880-7.   Fol.

(A monumental work.   Vol. III. contains memoirs on the craniology of the ancient Peruvians, by Prof. R. Virchow, and on their alimentary plants and domesticated animals, by Prof. Whittmach and A. Nehring respectively.)

1880-7 ———— ———— The Necropolis of Ancon in Peru, a contribution to our knowledge of the culture and industries of the Empire of the Incas, being the results of excavations made on the spot.   Translated by A.H. Keane.   3 vols.   141 plates in colors.   *Berlin.*   1880-7.   Fol.

———— ———— ———— Die Schädel des Todtenfeldes von Ancon in Peru.   9 plates.   *Berlin.*   Fol.

(Part XIV. of Das Todtenfeld von Ancon.)

1886 ———— ———— Reisen in Sud-Amerika. *Berlin.* 1886, *etc.* 4°.

1879 RELACION ANONYMA de las costumbres antiguas de los naturales del Peru. Edited by M. Jiménez de la Espada. *Madrid.*
1879. 8°.
(Pages 135–227 of Tres relaciones de Antiguadades Peruanas, edited by M. J. de la E.)

1879 RENAUD (J.). La céramique péruvienne de la Société d'études
américaines de Nancy. *Bruxelles.* 1879. 8°. Atlas of
plates. 4°.
(Compte-Rendu de la trois. session du Congrés interna-
tionale des Americanistes.

1883 REVILLE (ALBERT). Histoire des Religions. *Paris.* 1883,
etc. 8°.
(Vol. II. Religion du Mexique, de l'Amérique centrale, et
du Pérou.)

1884 ———— Lectures on the origin and growth of religion as
illustrated by the native religions of Mexico and Peru.
Delivered at Oxford and London in 1884. Translated by
Philip H. Wicksteed. *London.* 1884. 8°.

1886 RICCORDI (PAOLO). Crani e oggeti de glé antichi Peruviani
appartenenti al Museo civico di Modena el al Museo di ana-
tonia umana de lar. Università di Modena. 3 plates. *Firenze.*
1886.
(Archivio per l'Anthropologia e la Ethnologia di Firenze,
XVI., 305–405.)

1832 RICH (OBADIAH). A catalogue of books relating principally
to America, arranged under the years in which they were
printed (1500–1700). *London.* 1832.

1863 RICHARD (MAJOR F. IGNACIO). A Mining Journey across the
Great Andes. *London.* 1863. 8°.
(South American Mines and Miners, pages 201–221.)

RICHARDERIE (BOUCHER DE LA). *See* BOUCHER DE LA RICH-
ARDERIE.

1835–46 ———— Bibliotheca Americana nova. 2 vols. *London.*
1835–1846.
(Supplement to the catalogue of 1832. I. (1701–1800),
1835. II. (1801–1844), 1846.)

1865   RISING (*Lieut.*) On the artificial eyes of certain Peruvian mummies, with notes by Francis Galton. *London.* 1865. 8°. (Trans. Eth. Soc., Vol. IV., pages 59-60.)

1827   RIVERO Y USTARIZ (MARIANO EDUARDO DE). Memoria sobre las aguas minerales de Yura y otros puntos erranos a Arequipa.... Vargas y Arve. *Lima.* 1827. 8°.

1851   ———— and TSCHUDI (JUAN DIEGO DE). Antiguedades Peruanas. Folio Atlas of colored plates. *Viena.* 1851. 4°. (Relations between the two hemispheres before the discovery by Columbus ; the ancient inhabitants of Peru and their institutions ; the Quichua language.)

1853   ———— ———— Peruvian antiquities translated into English from the original Spanish by F. L. Hawkes, *etc.* *New York.* 1853. 8°.

1859   ———— ———— Antiquités Péruviennes. *Paris.* 1859. 8°.

1851   ———— ———— La Lengua Quichua. *Vienna.* 1851. 4°. (Antiguedades Peruanas, Chap. IV., pages 86-115.)

1777   ROBERTSON (WILLIAM), *D. D.* The history of America. 2 vols. Map. *London.* 1777. 4°. (Book VII., Mexico and Peru.)

1778   ———— Second edition. 2 vols. *London.* 1778. 4°.

———— Third and fourth editions.

1788   ———— Fifth edition. 3 vols. *London.* 1788. 8°.

1790   ———— New edition. 3 vols. *Basil.* 1790. 8°.

1796   ———— Seventh edition. 3 vols. *London.* 1796. 8°.

1800-1   ———— Eighth edition. 3 vols. *London.* 1800-1. 12°.

1800   ———— Ninth edition, in which is included....the history of Virginia and of New England. 4 vols. *London.* 1800. 8°.

1803   ———— Tenth edition. 4 vols. *London.* 1803. 8°.

1808   ———— Eleventh edition. 4 vols. *London.* 1808. 8°.

————   ———— Twelfth edition. 4 vols. *London.*

1817   ———— Thirteenth edition. 4 vols. *London.* 1817. 8°.

1777   ———— W. Robertson's....Geschichte von Amerika. aus dem Englischen ubersetzt von J. F. Schillen. 2 vols. L.P. *Leipzig.* 1777. 8°.

1845   ———— Histoire de l' Amerique par W.R.   Traduction de J. B. Suard et Morellet.   Sixiéme edition, avec les notes de Humboldt, Bullock, Warden, Clavigero, Jefferson, etc., receuillies par de la Rouette.   2 vols. *Paris.* 1845. 8°.

1775   ———— *See* Roxas (Jos. Ant. de).   Descripcion de las provincias del Peru, *etc. Madrid.* 1775. 12°.

1807   ROCHETTE (Louis G. D. de la). *See* Maps.   South America. 1807.

1684   RODIGRUEZ (Manuel), *Jesuit.*   El Marañon y Amazonas: Historia de las descubrimientos, antradas, y reduccion de naciones, tribajos....assi temporales como espirituales en las dilatadas montoñas y mayores rios de la America, *etc. Madrid.* 1684. Fol.

1688?   ———— Compendio historial e Indice cronológico Peruana y del nuevo Regno de Granada. *Madrid.* (1688?)

1819   RODNEY (C. A.) and GRAHAM (John).   Report on the present state of the United provinces of South America, laid before the Congress of the United States. Map. *London.* 1819.

1859   RODRIGRUEZ FRESLE (Juan).   Conquista i descubrimiento del nuevo reino de Granada de las Indias Occidentales del mar océano, i fundacion de la ciudad de Santa Fe de Bogotá, *etc.* (also known as "El Carnero de Bogotá," edited by F. Pérez.) *Bogotá.* 1859. 8°.

1884   ———— Nueva edicion (corregida). *Bogotá.* 1884. 8°.

1878   ROJAS (D. Aristides).   Estudios Indigenas.   Contribuciones a la historia antigua de Venezuela. *Caracas.* 1878. 4°.

1878   ———— La belle frase en las lenguas americanas. *Caracas.* 1878. 4°.
        (Estudios Indigenas, pages 67–87.)

1878   ———— La silaba gua ó hua, como interjeccion, articulo, verbo, adjectivo, radical, afijo y particula en las lenguas americanas. *Caracas.* 1878. 4°.
        (Estudios Indegenas, pages 89–110.)

1878   ———— Las radicales del agua en las lenguas americanas. *Caracas.* 1878. 4°.
        (Estudios Indegenas, pages 111–134.)

1891   ———— Historia patria. Estudios historicos.   Origenes Venezolanas. *Caracas.* 1891, *etc.* 8°.

ROSA (M. GONZALEZ DE LA). *See* GONZALEZ DE LA ROSA (DR. M.).

1870 ROSNY (LEON DE). Les Écritures figuratives et hieroglyph-iques des differens peuples anciens et modernes. 2nd edi-tion augmenteé de planches nouvelles, *etc.* *Paris.* 1870. 4°.

(Another edition of " Recherches sur l' écriture des differ-ens peuples anciens et modernes," published in 1857.)

(Figure of a Quipu.)

1882 ———— Les documens écrits de l' antiquité américaine. Compte-rendu d' une mission scientifique en Espagne et en Portugal, 1882. *Paris.* 1882. 4°.

(Mémoires. Soc. d' Ethnographie Americaine et Orien-tale. No. 3. 1882.

1847 ROSS (THOMASINA). *See* HUMBOLDT (F. H. A. VON). Per-sonal Narrative, *etc.* Translated and edited by T. R. *Lon-don.* 1847. 8°.

1859 · ———— (Another edition.) *London.* 1859. 8°.

1847 ———— *See* TSCHUDI (J. J. VON). Travels in Peru, *etc.* Translated by T. R. *London.* 1847. 8°.

1845 ROUETTE (———— DE LA). *See* ROBERTSON (WILLIAM), *D. D.* Histoire de l' Amérique. Sixiéme edition, avec notes de Humboldt, *etc.*, receuilliés par de la R. 2 vols. *Paris.* 1845. 8°.

1775 ROXAS (JOSEF ANTONIO DE). Descripcion de las Provincias del Peru que van puestas por orden de sus obispados. Faltan los de Buenos Ayres y los dos de Chile. La embia al Sr. Robertson por man del Sr. Lowes. 2 vols. *Madrid.* 20 de Junio, 1775. 12°.

(Spanish manuscript.)

1878 RUGE (SOPHUS). Geschichte des Zeitalters der Entdeckun-gen. *See* ONCKEN (W.) Allgemeine Geschichte, *etc.* Haupt. ii. The. 9. 1878, *etc.* 8°.

(Tiahuanacu basreliefs, pages 430-31.)

1892 ———— Die Entdeckungs–Geschichte der Neuen Welt. (Komité für eine Hamburgische Amerika Feier–Hamburg-ische Festschrift zur Erinnerung an die Entdeckung Ameri-kas, *etc.* 1892. 8°.

1892   —— Die entwickelung der Kartographie von Amerika bis 1570. Zeitschrift zur 400 jährigen seier der Entdeckung Amerikas. Mit 32 Kärtchen auf 2 Tafeln. *Gotha*. 1892. 4°.

   (Mitteilungen aus Justus Perthes' Geographischen Anstalt, *etc*. 1892. No. 106.)

1639   RUIZ DE MONTOYA (A.). Arte de la Lengua Guarani (Vocabulario de la lengua guarani. Tesoro de la lengua Guarani). 2 pt. *Madrid*. 1639. 4°.

1876   —— *Viena. Paris*. 1876. 8°.

1722   —— (Without Vocabulary and Tesoro). *S. Maria la Maya*. 1722. 4°.

1724   —— (Another edition.) *S. Maria la Maya*. 1724. 4·

1890   —— (Latin version.) *Stuttgardiæ*. 1890. 8°.

1892   —— (Another edition.) *Stuttgardiæ*. 1892. 8°.

1893   —— (Another edition.) *Stuttgardiæ*. 1893. 8·

1640   —— Catecismo de lengua Guarani. *Madrid*. 1640. 8·.

1876   —— Arte, Bocabulario, tesoro y catecismo de la lengua Guarani (1640). Publ. neuv. sin alteracion alguna por J. Platzmann. 4 vols. *Leipzig*. 1876. 4·.

——   RUIZ (R. GASPAR). Gramática de la lengua Gorgotoquiense, en le Peru.

   (Léon Finelo : Epitome, t. ii., col. 721.   Viñaza : Bibl. Españ. No. 955.)

1834   RUSCHENBERGER (W. S. W.). Three Years in the Pacific, including Notices of Brazil, Chili, Bolivia and Peru. By an officer of the U. S. Navy (W. S. W. R.) *Philadelphia*. 1834. 8·.

1835   ———- (Another edition.) 2 vols. *London*. 1835. 8°.

1890   RUSSELL (WILLIAM HOWARD), *L. L. D*. Visit to Chile and the Nitrate Fields. Illustrated. *London*. 1890. 8·.

   (Peru, pages 268-79 and 289-338.)

1688   RYCAUT (SIR PAUL). *See* LASSO DE LA VEGA (GARCIA). The Royal Commentaries of Peru, *etc*. Rendered English by Sir P. R. *London*. 1688. Fol.

1867   SABIN (JOSEPH). A Dictionary of Books relating to America, from its discovery to the present time. *London.* 1867, *etc.*

1868   —— *New York.* 1868, *etc.* 4 .

1869   —— American Bibliopolist. *London.* 1869, *etc.*
(New Books, with literary miscellanies.)

1870   —— A list of the printed editions of the works of Fray Bartolomé de Las Casas, Bishop of Chiapa, extracted from a Dictionary of Books relating to America. *New York.* 1870. 8 .

1877   —— A Bibliography of Bibliography, or a handy book about books which relate to books, being an alphabetical catalogue of the most important works descriptive of the literature of Great Britain and America, *etc. New York.* 1877. 8°.

1849   SABINE (MRS.) *See* HUMBOLDT (F. H. A. VON). Aspects of Nature, translated by Mrs. Sabine. *London* and *Philadelphia.* 1849.

1850   SAHUARAURA YNCA (DR. JUAN JUSTO). Recuerdos de la Monarquia Peruana. 16 portraits. *Paris.* 1850.
(The author, a canon of Cuzco, claims descent from the Incas.)

1870   SAMANEZ Y OCAMPO (J. B.) Exploracion de los rios peruanos. *Lima.* 1870. 8 .

1850   SANCHO (PEDRO). Relacion de la conquista del Perú.... Publicada en Italiano.....traducida.....al Castellano por J. Garcia Icazbalata. *See* PRESCOTT (W. H.) Historia de conquista del Peru, *etc.* Tom. 2. 1850. 8 .

1872   —— Report on the distribution of the ransom of Atahualpa. *London.* 1872. 8 .
See Xeres' Relacion. Hakluyt Society, Pub. No. 48. Reports on the Discovery of Peru. pages 131–143.

1860   SANS (FR. RAFAEL). *See* GAVILAR (FRAY ALONSO RAMOS). Historia de Capacabanca y de su milagrossa imagen. Edited by Fr. R. Sans. *La Paz.* 1860.

1652   SANSON (NICHOLAS). L'Amerique en plusieurs cartes, et en divers traités de Géographie, *etc. Paris.* 1652. 4 .
(Map and description of Peru, No. 13.)

1656   ————— *See* MAPS. Le Perou et el cours de la Rivière Amazone, *etc. Paris.* 1656.

1667   ————— Tables de Geographie ancienne et nouvelle ou methode pour s' instruire avec facilité de la Geographie et connoistre les empires, monarchies, royaumes, estats, republiques et peuples....de toutes les parties du monde, *etc. Paris.* 1667. Fol.

    (Engraved throughout.)

1879   SANTA CRUZ PACHACUTI YAMQUI SALCAMAYHUA (JUAN DE). Relacion de Antigüedades deste Reyno del Péru. Edited by Marcos Jiménez de la Espada. *Madrid.* 1879. 8°.

    (Pages 230–328 of *Tres Relaciones de Antigüedades Peruanas.* Publicadas el Ministerio de Fomento.)

1873   ————— An account of the Antiquities of Peru. Translated from the original Spanish by Clements R. Markham. *London.* 1873. 8°.

    (Hakluyt Society, No. 48; Narrative of the Rites and Laws of the Incas, pages 67–123.)

    [DON JUAN DE SANTA CRUZ PACHACUTI YAMQUI SALCAMAYHUA, son a chief of the Callao, wrote about 1620. Had intimate knowledge of native language and preserves traditions handed down to third generation after conquest.]

1879   SANTILLAN (FERNANDO DE). Relacion del origen, descendencia, politica y gobierno de los Incas por el licenciado F. de S. Edited by Marcos Jiménez de la Espada Publicadas el Ministerio de Fomento. *Madrid.* 1879. 8°.

    (Pages 3–135 of Tres Relaciones de Antigüedades Peruanas.)

    [FERNANDO DE SANTILLAN, appointed Judge of the Royal Audience for Peru, 1550, afterwards took orders; died, Lima, 1576, while on way to bishopric of La Plata. His *Relacion* is an official report on the administrative system of the Incas: relates chiefly to collection of tribute. Shows the evils inflicted by Spanish misrule.]

—— **SARAVIA** (MELCHOR BRAVO DE). Antigüedades del Peru.

> [Referred to by Juan de Pelasco, but lost or inaccessible. Melchor Bravo de Saravia was Judge of the Royal Audience. Cieza de Leon mentions his work as having been perused by Saravia and Santillan.]

1836   **SARDON** (FRANCISCO CIPRIANO). Doctrina cristiana traducida en aymara. *Paz de Ayacucho.* 1836. 4°.

—— **SARMIENTO DE GAMBOA** (DON PEDRO). History of the Incas. (MS. lost).

1572   —— Memorial (dated at) Cuzco, March 4th, 1572.

> [DON PEDRO SARMIENTO DE GAMBOA, a distinguished sailor and cosmographer, superintended the preparation of the map accompanying the pedigree of the Incas sent to Spain by Viceroy Don Francisco de Toledo. Accompanied, in 1567, Mandana's Expedition in search of South Sea islands discovered by Tupa Yupanqui; made Report of Voyage to Viceroy. Captured by Sir W. Raleigh, 1586, and taken to England.]

1872   **SAUNDERS** (TRELAWNEY). Map of Peru. *London.* 1872. (Journal R. Geogr. Soc., Vol. 43 (1872), p. 513. Illustrative of Markham's "Empire of the Incas.")

1888   **SAWYER** (C. M.), *Mrs.* The Civilization and Religions of Ancient Mexico, Central America and Peru. *Boston.* 1888. (The Universalist Quarterly, Vol. 25, n. s., pages 479–90.)

1838   **SCARLETT** (HON. P. CAMPBELL). South America and the Pacific. 2 vols. *London.* 1838. 8°. (Peru, Vol. II., pages 80-173.)

1777   **SCHILLEN** (VON J. F.). *See* ROBERTSON (WILLIAM) *D. D.*, W. R.'s....Geschichte von Amerika, aus dem Englischen ubersetzt von J. F. S. 2 vols. L. P. *Leipzig,* 1777. 8°.

1875   **SCHOEBEL** (CHARLES). Les Antiquités Americaines du Musée ethnographique à Saint Petersbourg. *Nancy.* 1875. 8°. (Compte-rendu du Congrés des Americanistes, Nancy, 1875, pages 271–74.)

1851-60   SCHOOLCRAFT (HENRY ROWE).   Historical and Statistical
Information respecting the history, condition and prospects
of the Indian tribes of the United States: collected....by
H. R. S. 6 vols. *Philadelphia.* 1851-60. 4°.

(Vol. V., Sec. iii., pages 86-95. Antiquities: Illustrations
of houses, implements, *etc.*, by J. N. Gillis.)

See EVANS (W. W.). Peruvian Antiquities.

1883   SCHÜTZ (DAMIAN VON), *Freiherrn.* Der Amazones. Wan-
derbilder aus Peru, Bolivia und Nord-brasilien. Mit 10
Vollbildern und 31 Textilluste. *Freiburg.* 1883.

(19 years in South America. Bibliography, pages 427-38.)

1895   ———(Second edition.) Enlarged. *Freiburg.* 1895.

1747-74   SCHWABE (JOHANN JOACHIM).   Allgemeine Historie der
Reisen zu Wasser und Lande, *etc.*, durch eine Gesellschaft
gelehrter Männer....ins Deutsche übersetzet. Edited by
J. J. S. 21 Bde. *Leipzig.* 1747-74. 4°.

Vol. IX. ULLOA (JUAN G. and A. DE). Reise nach dem
Königreiche Peru.

Vol. XV. FREZIER (A. F.). Reise an den Kusten von
Peru. 1713-47.

——— LA CONDAMINE (C. M.). Reise nach Peru.
1735-42.

Vol. XVI. ACUÑA (CRISTOVAL DE). Reise auf dem Amazonen flusse. 1637-40.

——— LA CONDAMINE (C. M.). Reise in Quito. 1747.

1829   SCIO (P.) AND PAZOS-KANKI (V.). *See* PAZOS-KANKI (V.).
El Evangelio de Jesu Christo segun San Lucas en Aymara y
Español. Traducida, *etc.* *London.* 1829. 8°.

1892   SEARS (ALFRED E.). The Republic of Peru. Illustrated.
Boston. 1892.

(New England Magazine, Vol. 7. n. s., pages 441-64.)

1893   SELER (EDUARD). Peruanische Altertümer, insbes. altperuanische Gefässe und Gefässe der Chibcha und der Tolima-
und-Cauca-Stämme. Goldschmuck, *etc.* Herausg. von der
Verwaltung des Kon. Museums für Völkerkunde zu Berlin. 64 Lichtdrucktafeln mit erläut. Text. In mappe.
Berlin. 1893. Fol.

1884.   —— See DU POUGET (J. F. H.), *Marquis de Nadaillac*.
Die ersten Menschen....herausgegeben von W. Schlösser
und E. Seler, *etc.*   1884.   8°.

1887   SERGI (GUISEPPE) AND MOSCHEN (L.).   Crani peruviani
antichi del Museo antropologico nella Università di Roma.
Firenze.   1887.   8 .

          (Archiv. p. l'Antrop.   Firenze, Vol. 17. (1887), pages
5–26.)

1828   SETIER (——).   *See* STEVENSON (W. B.).   Voyage....au
Pérou, *etc.*, traduite....par S.   3 vols.   *Paris*.   1828.   8°.

1859–62   SHEA (DR. JOHN GILMARY).   Library of American Lingu-
istics.   Edited   by   Dr.   J.   G.   S.   13 vols.   *New York*.
1859–62.   4°.

1817   SHILLIBEER (JOHN), *Lieut.*   A narrative of the Briton's voyage to Pitcairns island.   Etchings.   *Taunton*.   1817.   8°.

          (Chap. VII., Peru.)

1818   —— (Third edition.)   *London*.   1818.   8°.

1841   SILVESTRE (JOSEPH BALTHAZAR).   Paléographie universelle.
Collection de facsimile d' écritures de tous les peuples et de
tous les temps....dessinées et peints par M. Silvestre....et
accompagnés d' explication historiques et descriptives, par
M. M. Champollion-Figeac et A. Champollion.   4 pt.   *Paris*.
1841.   Fol.

          (Gives figure of Peruvian quipu.)

1850   ——— Universal Palaeography ; or facsimiles of writings
of all periods and nations....accompanied, *etc.*   Translated
....and edited, with corrections and notes, by Sir F. Madden.   2 vol.   *London*.   1850.   8°.

1627   SIMON (PEDRO).   Primera parte de las Noticias historiales
de las conquistas de Tierre Firme en las Indias Occidentales.
Cuenca.   1627.

          [Pedro Simon, born in Spain, 1574 ; visited Bogotá 1604 :
began to write 1623.   Gives Francisco Vasquez's account of
Ursua and Aguirre's expedition, translated by Bollaert (Hakluyt Society, 1862).   Two other parts of Simon's *Noticias*
unprinted.   *See* ACOSTA (COL. J.) Compendio historico, *etc.*]

1886   SIMSON (ALFRED). Travels in the wilds of Ecuador and the exploration of the Putumayo river. Map. *London.* 1886. 8°.

(Natives, Chaps. 7, 8, 12, 13 and 14.)

1883   ———— Notes on the Napo Indians (of Ecuador). *London.* 1883. 8°.

(Journal Anth. Inst., Vol. 12, pages 21–27.)

1805   SKINNER (JOSEPH). The Present State of Peru: comprising its Geography, Topography, Natural History, Mineralogy, Commerce, the Customs and Manners of its Inhabitants.... embellished by 20 engravings of costumes, *etc.* Map. *London.* 1805. 4°.

(Principally compiled from Mercurio Peru.)

1806   ———— Gegenwärtiger Zustand von Peru. Aus. d. Engl. *Hamburgh.* 1806.

1839   SMITH (ARCHIBALD), *M. D.* Peru as it is; a Residence in Lima and other parts of the Peruvian Republic, comprising an account of the social and physical features of that country. 2 vols. *London.* 1839. 8°.

1836   SMYTH (W.), *Lieut.*, and LOWE (F.). Narrative of a journey from Lima to Para, across the Andes and down the Amazon, undertaken with a view of ascertaining the practicability of a navigable communication with the Atlantic by the rivers Pachitea, Ucayali and Amazon. 3 maps and illustrations. 1836. 8°.

(Eight months' expedition; notices of Indians, silver mines, natural history, *etc.*)

1857   SMYTH (W. H.), *Admiral. See* BENZONI (GIROLAMO). History of the new world, by Girolamo Benzoni, *etc.,* translated and edited by Admiral W. H. S. *London.* 1857. 8°.

SOBRON (D. FELIX C. Y). *See* C. Y SOBRON (D. FELIX).

1648   SOLARZANO (JUAN DE). Politicia Indiana. *Madrid.* 1648.

[Juan de Solarzano, member of the Council of the Indies and learned jurist; gives ordinances and decrees of the Spanish authorities, civil and ecclesiastical, in Peru.]

1862   SOLDARI (M. P. and M..F.).   Geografía del Peru.   *Paris.*
1862.

(Vol. I. contains a bibliography of Peru.)

1821   SOUTHEY (ROBERT).   The expedition of Orsua and the crime
of Aguirre.   *London.*   1821.

(Written for Southey's *History of Brazil*, but first published
in Edinburgh Annual Register, Vol. III., pt. 2.)

1816–21   SOUZA (DR. JOSÉ MARIANO BERISTAIN DE).   Bibliotheca
Hispano-Americana.   3 vols.   *Mexico.*   1816-21.

1880   SPILSBURY (REV. J. H. GYBBON).   Apunchis Santa Yoan-
cama Ehuangelium, Quichua cayri Ynca siminpi quilkcasea.
El Santo Evangelio de N. S. Jesu-Christo segun San Juan,
traducido del original a la lengua Quichua o del Ynca. *Buenos
Aires.*   1880.

1825   SPIX (J. B. VON) and MARTIUS (C. F. P. VON).   *See* MAPS.
L' Amerique meridional.   *Munich.*   1825.

1853   SQUIER (EPHRAIM GEORGE).   Ancient Peru, its people and
its monuments.   Illustrated.   *New York.*   1853.   8°.

(*See* Harper's New Monthly Mag., Vol. 7, p. 7–38.)

1860   ———— Collection of Rare and Original Documents and
Relations concerning the Discovery and Conquest of America,
chiefly from the Spanish Archives, in the original, with
Translations, Notes, Maps and Sketches.   *New York.*   1860.

(Printed only 100 copies, small paper, and 10 copies, large
paper.)

1868   ———— The Andes of Peru and Bolivia.   Illust.   *New York.*
1868.   8°.

(*See* Harper's New Monthly Mag., Vols. 36 and 37.)

1871   ——— The primeval monuments of Peru compared with
those in other parts of the world.   *Salem.*   1871.   8°.

(American Naturalist.   Vol. IV., pages 1–17.)

1877   ——— Peru.   Incidents of Travel and Exploration in the
Land of the Incas.   Illustrated.   *New York.*   1877.   8°.

1883   ——— Peru.   Reise-und Forschungs-Ergebnisse, in dem
lande der Incas.   Ins deutsche übertragen von Prof.
Schmick.   Illustrated.   *Leipzig.*   1883.   8°.

1874   STANFORD (——). Compendium of Geography and Travel based on Hellwald's Die Erden und ihre Völker, translated by A. H. Keane. *See* BATES (HENRY WALKER). Central America, the West Indies and South America, edited....by H. W. B.. *etc. London.* 1874. 8°.

1882   —— *See* BATES (H. W.). Central America, *etc.* Second and revised edition. *London.* 1882. 8°.

1885   —— —— New edition. *London.* 1885. 8°.

1869   STANLEY (H. E. J.). *See* CORREA (G.). The three voyages of Vasco de Gama and his viceroyalty .... translated with original documents, notes and introduction by H. E. J. S. *London.* 1869. 8°.

1883   STEFFEN (MAX). Die Landwirtschaft bei den Altamericanischer Kulturvölkern. *Leipzig.* 1883.

1535   STETTE (M. DE). *See* PIZARRO (HERNANDO). La relatione del Vaggio che face....F. Picciarro, *etc.* 1535. 4°.

1870   STEVENS (EDWARD THOMAS). Flint Chips. A guide to prehistoric archæology, as illustrated by the collection in the Blackmore Museum, Salisbury. Illustrated. *London.* 1870. 8°.

    (Peru, pages 269-75.)

(1857-62)   STEVENS (HENRY). .Historical Nuggets : Bibliotheca Americana, or a descriptive account of my collection of rare books relating to America. 2 vols. *London.* (1857) and (1862). 8°.

1885   —— (Continued). 1885.

1861   ——— Bibliotheca Americana. *London.* 1861. (Sale catalogue.)

1870   —— Bibliotheca Historica. *Boston.* 1870. (Sale catalogue of Henry Stevens' Library.)

1870   —— Schedule of Two Thousand American Historical Nuggets, taken from the Stevens Diggings in September, 1870, and set down in chronological order of printing from 1490 to 1800, described and recommended as a supplement to my printed Bibliotheca Americana. *London.* 1870.

1708   STEVENS (JOHN) *Captain.   See* CIEZA DE LEON (PEDRO DE). The seventeen years of Travels of Peter de Cieza through the kingdom of Peru and the provinces of Carthegena and Popayan in South America ; translated from the Spanish by J. S. *London.* 1708. 4°.

1709   ——— (Another edition.) *London.* 1709. 4°.

1711   ——— (Another edition.) *London.* 1711. 4°.
(A new Collection of Voyages and Travels.   Vol. I.)

1711   ——— A new collection of voyages and travels into several parts of the world....2 vol. *London.* 1711.
(Apparently a collection of pieces published separately.)

1725   ——— *See* HERRERA TORDESILLAS (A. DE).   The general history of....America....translated by....J. S., *etc.* 1725, *etc.* 8°.

1825   STEVENSON (W. B.).   A historical and descriptive narrative of twenty years' residence in South America....containing travels in Arauco, Chile, Peru, and Columbia, with an account of the Revolution.   Plates.   3 vols. *London. Liverpool* (printed).   1825.   8°.
(Notices of the Indians, Vol. II., Pisco to Guayaquil.)

1829   ——— (Another edition.)   3 vols. *London.* 1829. 8'.

1828   ——— Voyage en Araucanie, au Chili, au Pérou et dans la Colombie, ou relation historique et descriptive d' un séjour de vingt ans dans l' Amérique du Sud....traduite de l' anglais et augmentée de la suite des révolutions des colonies, depuis 1823, jusqu'à ce jour, par Sétier. 3 vol. *Paris.* 1828.   8'.

1831   STEWART (CHARLES SAMUEL).   A visit to the South Seas in U. S. ship Vincennes during the years 1829 and 1830, *etc.* 2 vols. *New York.* 1831.   12°.
(Pages 121-183.)

1832   ——— (Another edition.)   2 vol. *London.* 1832,   12 ·

1833   ——— (Another edition.)   2 vol. *New York.* 1833.   8

1832   ——— (Another edition.)   Edited and abridged by W. Ellis. *London.* 1832.   8'.

1838   STEWART (J.). Bogotá in 1836-7. Being a narrative of an expedition to the Capital of New Grenada, and a residence there of 11 months. *New York*. 1838. 8°.

——   STOCKLEIN (——). Reise Beschreibungen.

(Collection of letters by Jesuits in all parts of the world. Gives Samuel Fritz' map of the Amazons.)

- —   STRONG (AL.). History of the Quipos or Peruvian Knot-cords as given by the early Spanish historians, with a description of a supposed specimen.

(Assigned to Al. Strong by Leclerc, No. 2413.)

1886   STUEBEL (ALPHONS). Skizzen aus Ecuador. Katalog ausgestellter Bilder, mit zahlr. Abbildd. (Landschaften, Volkstypen.) *Berlin*. 1886. Fol.

1888   —— Ueber altperuanische Gewebemuster und ihrer analoge Ornamente der altklassichen Kunst. *Dresden*. 1888.

1888   —— and REISS (WILHELM). Indianen-Typen aus Ecuador und Colombia. 28 Lichtdruckbilder. *Berlin*. 1888.

1889   —— and REISS (W.) and KOPPEL (B.). Kultur und Industrie südamerikanischer Völker. Nach den im Besitze des Museums für Völkerkunde zu Leipzig befindlich Sammlungen. Text und Beschreibung der Tafeln von Max Uhle. 55 chromolithographic and other plates. 2 vols. *Berlin*. 1889. Fol.

(Vol. I. ancient art, ceramic, stone implements and ornaments, metal work and textiles. Colombia, Ecuador, Peru, Bolivia, *etc.*)

1893   —— and UHLE (M.). Die Ruinenstätte von Tiahuanaco im Hochlande des alten Peru. Kulturgeschichten Studien nach selbständigen Aufnahmen. Map and 42 plates. *Breslau*. 1893. Fol.

1845   SUARD (J. B.) and MORRELLET. *See* ROBERTSON (WILLIAM), *D. D.* Histoire de l' Amerique par W. R. Traduction de J. B. S. et M. Sixième edition avec notes....2 vols. *Paris*. 1845. 8°.

1613   SUAREZ DE FIGUEROA (DON CRISTOVAL). Hechos de Don Garcia Hurtado de Mendoza, cuarto Marques de Cañete. 1613.

1864 —— Hechos de Don Garcia Hurtado de Mendoza. *See* ARANA (DON DIEGO BARROS). Coleccion de Historiadores de Chile, edited by D. B. A. 7 vols. *Santiago.* 1864.

[Don Garcia H. de Mendoza, Governor of Chili, 1555-61 ; Viceroy of Peru, 1590-96. Son of Viceroy Andrea Hurtado de Mendoza, Marquis of Cañete.]

(1841) SUTCLIFFE (THOMAS). Sixteen years in Chile and Peru, from 1822-39. By the retired Governor of Juan Fernandez (T. S.). Map, portraits and plates. *London.* (1841). 8°.

1830 TEMPLE (EDMUND). Travels in various parts of Peru. Including a year's residence in Potosi. 2 vols. Map and illustrations. *London.* 1830. 8°.

1833 —— (Another edition.) 2 vols. *Philadelphia.* 1833. 12°.

1837 TERNAUX-COMPANS (H.). Bibliothèque Américaine ou Catalogue des ouvrages relatifs à l'Amérique qui ont paru depuis sa découverte jusqu'à l'an 1700. *Paris.* 1837. 4°.

1837-41 —— Voyages, Relations et Mémoires originaux pour servir à l'histoire de l'Amérique. 20 vols. *Paris.* 1837-41. 8°.

(Vol. 4. *See* XERES (F.). Relation de la conquête du Perou et de la province du Cuzco, *etc.* *Paris.* 1837. 8°.

(Vol. 16. *See* BALBOA (MIG. CAV.). Histoire du Perou. *Paris.* 1840. 8°.

(Vols. 18 and 19. *See* VELASCO (DON JUAN DE). Histoire du Royaume de Quito. 2 vols. *Paris.* 1840. 8°.)

1838 —— *See* PERU. Peru before and at the Spanish invasion. 1838. 8°.

(Dublin Review. Vol. V. Notice of "Voyages, *etc.*," by T-C.)

1840 —— Recueil de documents et mémoires, *etc.* *Paris.* 1840. 8°.

See PERU. Lettre sur les superstitions du Perou, par un Religieux Augustin.

—— TERUEL (LUIS DE).   Gramatica de la lengua tabalosa del Peru.
(León Pinelo: Epitome, t. ii. col. 722 ; Viñaza : Bibl. Epañ., No. 973.)

- —— ——— Tratado de las idolatrias de los Indios del Peru. (Not printed.   Referred to by Pinelo.)

[LUIS DE TERUEL, priest and companion of Francisco de Avila.   Discusses origin of coast people.]

- — THOMPSON (T. P.).   Knot Records of Peru.
(Westminster Review.   XI., p. 228.)

1685   TOLEDO (DON FRANCISCO DE) *Viceroy.   See* BALLESTEROS (DON THOMAS DE).   Ordenanzas del Peru recogidas y coordenades por Don F. de T.   *Lima.* 1685.   Fol.

1752   ——— (Another edition.) *Lima.* 1752.   Fol.

1882   ———*See* FERNANDEZ MONTESINOS (EL LIC. DON).   Memoiras antiguas, *etc.,* hechas por mondado de D. F. de Toledo (1570-72), edited by Don M. J. de la Espada. *Madrid.* 1882.   8°.

1882   ——— Imformaciones acerca del Senorio y Gobierno de los Ingas hechas, por mandado de Don F. de Toledo (1570–72), edited by Don M. J. de la Espada. *Madrid.* 1882.
(Vol. 16, Coleccion de libros Españoles raros ó curiosos. Series of Reports on the origin of Inca soverignty to prove the right of the Spaniards to treat Incas as usurpers.)

—— ——— Libro de Tasas (Code of Laws, relating particularly to tribute payable by natives, and forced labor in the mines.)

[DON FRANCISCO DE TOLEDO entered Lima as Viceroy 26 November, 1569; confiscated property and privileges of Incas, and caused youthful Inca Tupac Amaru to be beheaded on false charge of conspiracy.   Based his legislation on the system of the Incas, and his *Libro de Tasas* was followed by all subsequent Viceroys.   Inquisition introduced into Peru during his government, but natives exempted as catechumens.   Returned to Spain 1580 ; was coldly received by Philipp II., who said he had not been sent to Peru to kill kings. |

1603   **Torres Rubio** (Diego de).   Grammatica y Vocabolario en
la lengua general del Peru, llamada Quichua y en la lengua
Española,....*Sevilla*.   1603.   12°.

(Very rare.   Sometimes referred to as the first edition of
the work published by Francisco del Canto, Lima, 1614, and
ascribed to Diego Gonçalez Holguin.)

1619   —————— (Another edition.)   *Lima*.   1619.   8 .

1700   —————— Arte de la lengua Quichua.   *Lima*.   1700.   8°.

(With vocabulary of the Chinchaysuyu dialect by Juan de
Figueredo.)

1754   —————— (Another edition.)   Correg. y aumentado.   *Lima*.
1754.   12°.   (With Figueredo's Vocabulary.)

1603   —————— Grammatica y Vocabulario en lengua Quichua,
Aymara y Española.   *Roma*.   1603.   8°.

1616   —————— Arte de lengua Aymara.   *Lima*.   (Francisco del
Canto.)   1616.   8°.

1619   —————— (Another edition.)   *Lima*.   (Franc. Lasso).   1619.
8°.

1603   —————— Relacione Breve del P. D. de T.   By F. Vucz.
Milano.   1603.

1604   —————— Brevis Relatio Historica rerum in Provincia Peruana apud Indios a Patribus Societatis Jesu gestarum A. R. P.
Jacobo Torrensi....conscripta....Accessere, *etc. Moguntiæ*.
1604.   12°.

[Diego de Torres Rubio, born 1547, near Toledo, Spain.
Went to Peru 1577.   Rector of college at Potosi : became
missionary at Chuquiasca, where died, 1638, aged 91.   Studied Quichua, Aymara and Guarani languages.]

1850   **Traill** (T. S.).   On a Peruvian musical instrument like the
Syrinx of the ancients.   Plate.   *Edinburgh*.   1850.   4°..

1879   **Tres Relaciones** de Antigüedades Peruanas.   Edited by
Don Marcos Jiménez de la Espada.   Publicadas el Ministerio
de Fomento.   *Madrid*.   1879.   8 .

1830   **Trueba y Cosio** (Joaquin Telesforo).   History of the Conquest of Peru by the Spaniards.   *Edinburgh*.   1830.   16°.

1858   **TRUEBNER** (NICHOLAS). *See* LUDEWIG (HERMAN ERNST).
The literature of American aboriginal languages, with addi-
tions and corrections, by Prof. Wm. M. Turner.   Edited by
N. T. *London.* 1858. 8°.

1882   —— Truebner's Catalogue of Dictionaries and Gram-
mars of the Principal Languages and Dialects of the World.
Second edition. *London.* 1882. 4°.

——   **TRUXILLO** (DIEGO DE).   Relacion de la tierra que descubrio
Don Francisco Pizarro.

    [MS. lost.   Truxillo was a companion of Pizarro.]

1846   **TSCHUDI** (J. J. VON). Peru. Reiseskizzen in die Jahre,
1838-42. 2 vols. *St. Gallen.* 1846.

1847   —— Travels in Peru during the years 1838-42, on the
Coast, in the Sierra, across the Cordilleras and the Andes,
into the Primeval Forests.   Translated from the German by
Thomasina Ross. Plate. *London.* 1847. 8°.

1847   —— (Another edition.) *New York.* 1847. 12°.

1849   —— Die Huanulager an die peruanischen Küste.   7
plates. *Wien.* 1849. 4°.

1853   —— Die Kechua Sprache. Sprachlehre. Sprachproten.
Wörterbuch. 2 vols. *Vienna.* 1853. 8°.

1866   —— Reisen durch Südamerika.   5 vols.   Maps and
illustrations. *Leipzig.* 1866.

1875   —— Altperuanisches Drama. Kechua und deutsch mit
Einleitung und Commentar. *Wien.* 1875. 4°.

1876   —— Ollanta ein alt peruanisches Drama aus die Kes-
chua-sprache übers und commentirt. *Wien.* 1876. 4°.

1890   —— *See* MIDDENDORF (E. W.). Die einheimischen
sprachen Perus. Vol. 3. Ollanta, ein Drama des Keschua-
sprache (Tschudi's....) Text. *Leipzig.* 1890. 8°.

1884   —— Einleitung zu Organismus der Khetsua-Sprache.
Leipzig. 1884. 8°.

1885   —— Das Lama. Zeitschrift für Ethnologie. *Leipzig.*
1885. °.

1891   —— —— Cultur historische und sprachliche beiträge zur kenntuiss des alten Peru. *Wien.* 1891. 4°.
(Denkschriften der Kaiserlichen Academie der Wissenschaften. Vol. 39., pp. 1–220.)

1884   —— —— On the ancient Peruvians. *London.* 1884. 8°.
(Journal of the Ethnological Society, Vol. I., pages 79–85.)

1851   —— —— *See* Rivero y Ustariz (M. Ed. de) and T. (J. J. de). Antiguëdades Peruanas. *Vien.* 1851. 4°.

1853   (English translation.) *New York.* 1853. 8°.

1859   (French translation.) *Paris.* 1859. 8°.

1851   —— —— —— La Lengua Quichua. *Vienna.* 1851. 4°.
(Antiguëdades Peruanas, Chap. IV., pages 86–115.)

1858   TURNER (Wm. M.). *See* Ludewig (H. E.). The literature of American aboriginal languages, with additions and corrections, by Prof. W. M. T. *London.* 1858. 8°.

1878   TYLOR (Edward Burnet). Early history of mankind. *New York.* 1878. 8°.
(Quipu, page 156.)

1889   UHLE (M.). Kultur und Industrie sudamerikanischer Völker nach dem.... Sammlungen von....W. Reiss, *etc.* 1889, *etc.* Fol.

1892   —— —— und Stübel (Alphons). Die Ruinenstätte von Tiahuanaco im Hochlande der alten Peru. 42 plates. *Breslau.* 1892. Fol.

1772   ULLOA (Antonio). Noticias Americanas: entretenimientos fisico-historicos sobre la America Meridional, y la Septentrional oriental.... con una relacion particular de los Indios ....y de las antigüedades. *Madrid.* 1772. 4°.

1748   ULLOA (Jorge Juan) y ULLOA (Antonio). Relacion historica del viage a la America Meridional hecho de orden de S. Mag. para medir algunos grados de meridiano terrestre, y venir por ellos en conocimiento de la verdadera figura y magnitud de la Tierra, con otras varias Observaciones astronomicas, y phisicas. Maps and plates. 5 vols. *Madrid.* 1748. 4°.
(Manners and customs of the Kingdom of Quito ; abridged history of the origin and rites of the Incas (14) from Manco-Capac to Atahuallpa, with portraits.)

1751 —————— Reise nach dem Königreiche Peru. Aus dem Spanische. Plates and maps. *Leipzig.* 1751. 4°.
(9 Vol. of *Allgemeine Historie den Reisen zu Wasser und zu Lande.*)

1752 —————— Voyage historique de l'Amerique Meridionale fait par ordre du Roi d'Espagne. Translated by Mauvillon. 2 vols. Maps and plates. *Amsterdam and Paris.* 1752. 4°.
(The history of the Incas taken from French translation of Garcia Lasso de la Vega's Commentaries.)

1758 —————— Voyage to South America, describing at large the Spanish Towns, Provinces, *etc.*, with the Genius, Customs. Manners and Trade of the Inhabitants, *etc.* Seven plates. 2 vols. *London.* 1758. 8°.

1772 —————— (Another edition.) *London.* 1772. 8°.

1807 —————— (Fifth edition.) *London.* 1807. 8°.

1813 —————— (Another edition.) *London.* 1813. 4°.
(Pinkerton's Voyages and Travels. Vol. 14., pages 313–696.)

1771 —————— (Dutch translation.) Historical Relation, *etc.* 2 vols. 1771.

1773 —————— Observaciones astronomicos y phisicas, hechas de orden de S. M. en los reynos del Peru. Plates. *Madrid.* 1773. Fol.

1787 —————— Memoires philosophiques, historiques, physiques, concernant le découverte de l'Amerique. *Paris.* 1787.

1826. —————— Noticias secretas de America....presentadas en informe secreto á Fernando VI., sacadas á luz por Don David Barry. 2 vols. Portrait. 1826. Fol.
(Report on the conduct of the Spanish officials and priests.)

1851 —————— (Noticias Secretas de America.) Abridged. English version. "By an American." *Boston.* 1851.

1563 ULLOA (S. A.). *See* ZARATE. (AUGUSTIN DE). Le Historie del Sig. A. di Z......dello scoprimento et conquista del Peru......nuovamente di lingua Castigliano traddota dal S. A. U. *Vinegia.* 1563. 4°.

————— UNANUE (DR.). Guia Politica, Ecclesiastica y Militar del Virreynato del Peru para al ano de 1794. 12°.

1824 —————— Nuevo dia del Peru. 1824.

1854   **Uricoechea (Ezequiel).** Memoria sobre las Antigüedades Neo-Granidinas. Plates. *Berlin.* 1854. 4°.

1854   —— Noticias sobre la lengua chibcha y particularmente sobre les nombres numerales. *Berlin.* 1854. 4°.

(Pages 6–10, Memoria sobre les Antigüedades Neo-Granidinas.)

1860   —— Mapoteca Columbiana. Coleccion de los titulos de todos las mapas, planos, vistas, *etc.*, relativos a la America Espagñola, Brezil é islas adjacentes, arregeada cronologicamente i precidida de una introduccion sobre la historia cartografica de America. *Londres.* 1860. 12°.

(Peru Sec. 15.)

1871   —— Grammatica, vocabulario, catecismo i confessionario de la lengua Chibcha segun antiguos manuscritos anónimos e inéditos aumentados i correjidos. *Paris.* 1871. 4·

1879   **Ursel (Charles)** *Comte d'*. Sud Amerique. Séjours et Voyages au Brésil, a la Plata, au Chili, en Bolivie, et au Perou. Map and illust. 2d edition. *Paris.* 1879. 12°.

1880.   —— (Third edition.) *Paris.* 1880. 12°.

1862   **Ursua (Pedró de).** *See* Bollaert (Wm.). Expedition of P. de Ursua and Lope de Aguirre in search of El Dorado and Omagua, 1560-61. *London.* 1862. 8°.

[Pedro de Ursua, nephew of Armendariz, Judge of New Granada, went to Bogotá, 1542; led several expeditions in search of Eldorado. About 1558 went to Lima, in 1557 sent by Viceroy Cañete on expedition down the Huallaga to find Eldorado and the Omaguas. Murdered Jan. 1, 1561, near Machiparo by conspirators under Lope de Aguirre and Fernando de Guzman.]

1877   **Vaca de Castro (Cristobal).** Carta del licenciado Vaca de Castro al emperador Don Carlos, refiriendo las penalidades de la navegacion hasta aportar en la Isla Española, Santa Domingo, 4 *de enere* de 1541. *Madrid.* 1877.

(Letter 80 of Cartas de Indias.)

1877   ———— Carta del licenciado V. de C. al emperador Don Carlos, participándale el asesinato del Marquis Don Francisco Pizarro y la rebelion de Don Diago de Almagro, el mozo. *Quito*, 15 de Noviembre de 1541. *Madrid.* 1877.
(Letter 81 of Cartas de Indias.)

1877   ————Carta del licenciado V. de C. al emperador Don Carlos, dandale cuenta de la sublevacion y castigo de Don Diego de Almagro, el mozo, y de atros importantes asuntos. Cuzco 24 de noviembre, 1542. *Madrid.* 1877.
(Letter 82 of Cartas de Indias.)

[CRISTOBAL VACA DE CASTRO, Governor of Peru, 1542; defeated Diego Almagro; imprisoned by Gonzalo Pizarro and sent to Spain, 1544; imprisoned 12 years, but finally acquitted of charges against him.]

————   VANDERAA (PIERRE). *See* MAPS. Le Peru. *Amesterdam. n. d.*

1727   ———— Ontdekking Van West Indien Sliftig ondersogt, nangetreckend door J. D.' Acosta....1592 nyt het Spaans verladd M. P. Van de Aa., *etc.* Deil 8. 1727. Fol.
(Borrows from Acosta, Herrera, Purchas, De Bry, *etc.*)

1873   VARELA (H. T.). Le Perou devant les pays d'Europe. *Havre.* 1873. 8°.

1782   VARELA Y ULLOA (D. PEDRO). *See* NUIX Y DE PERPINA (JUAN). Reflexions imparciales sobre la humanidad de los Espagndes en las Indias.... traducidas con agunas notas por D. P. y M. *Madrid.* 1782. 4°.

1879   VARIAS RELACIONES del Peru y Chile y Conquista de la isla de Santa Catalina, 1535–1658. *Madrid.* 1879.
(Vol. 13 of Coleccion de libros que tratan de America raros y curiosos.)

1876   VARNHAGEN (————). L'origine Tourancen des Américains Tubis–Caribes et des anciem Egyptiens montrée par la philologie comparée. *Vienne.* 1876.

1627   VASQUEZ (FRANCISCO). Expedition of Ursua and Aguirre. *See* SIMON (PEDRO). Primera parte de las Noticias historiales, *etc.* *Cuenca.* 1627.
(MS. Royal Library, Madrid. Vasquez was a companion of Ursua and Aguirre.)

1806, 9–17 **VATER** (JOHAN SEVRAIN) and **ADELUNG** (J. C.). Mithridates, oder allgemeine Sprackenkunde mit dem Vater-Unser als sprach-probe in beynahe fünfhundert Sprachen und Mundarten von J. C. Adelung and J. S. Vater. *Berlin.* 1806, 1809–17. Fol
> Vol. I. (Adelung.) *Berlin*, 1806; Vols. II., III. and IV. (Vater). *Berlin*, 1809–17.
> (Quichua, Vol. III., pages 522, 537, 538, 547 and 571; Aymara, Vol. III., Pt. 2, pages 537, 538 and 547.)

1854 **VAUX** (WALTER SANDYS WRIGHT). The World Encompassed, by Sir Francis Drake, by Francis Fletcher. Edited by W. S. W. V. *London.* 1854. 8°.
> (Hakluyt Society Pub.. No. 17.)

1858 **VEDIA** (———). Histoire prim. de Indias. 1858.
> (Vol. I. contains the Spanish text of Oviedo y Valdes' De la natural hystoria de las Indias.)

——— **VEGA** (JUAN DE). Arte ó Rudimentos de Gramatica en lengua indigena del Peru. (Lima.)
> (Viñaza. Bibl. Españ., No. 818.)

1844 **VELASCO** (JUAN DE). Historia del Reino de Quito en la America Meridional escrita por el Presbitoro Don Juan de V., nativo del mismo Reino (de Reobamba) año de 1789. 2 vols. *Quito.* 1844.

1840 ——— Histoire du royaume de Quito, translated from the Spanish MS. *See* TERNAUX-COMPANS (H.). Voyages, *etc.* Vols. 18 and 19. *Paris.* 1840. 8°.

> [JUAN DE VELASCO, native of Riobamba; Jesuit priest for forty years in Kingdom of Quito. His *Historia* completed 1789. Quotes from works of Fray Marco de Niza and Jacinto Collahuaso now lost, and relates traditions of early kings of Quito.]

1893 **VERGARA Y VELASCO** (F. J.). Colombia: traducida y anotada. ....por F. J. V. y V. *Bogotá.* 1893. 8°. *See* RECLUS (J. J. E.) Nouvelle Geographie Universelle.

——— **VICTORIA** (F. MARTIN DE). Arte y Vocabulario de la Lengua del Inca por Fr. M. de V....el primero que redujo á reglas dicho idioma.
> (Pinelo: Epit. t., ii., col. 721–22.)

1825   VIEW of South America and Mexico, comprising their history, the political condition, geography, agriculture, commerce, *etc.*, of the republics of Mexico, Guatemala, Colombia,
Peru, the United Provinces of South America and Chile,
with a complete history of the revolution in each of these
independent states.   By a citizen of the United States.
New York.   1825.
(Peru, chap. 8.)

1887   VILLAR (LEONARDO), *Dr.*   Lexicologia Keshua uiracocha.
Lima.   1887.   Fol.
(First published in the Lima *El Comercio.*)

——   VILLASANTE (SALAZAR DE).   Relacion general de las pobla-
ciones espagnoles del Peru.

1563   VILLOA (S. ALFONSO).   *See* ZARATE (AUG. DE).   Le historie.
....dells scoprimento et conquista del Peru, *etc.*, tradotte
dal S. A. V.   *Vinegia.*   1563.   4°.

1892   VINAZA (EL CONDE DE LA).   Bibliografia Española de Lenguas indigenas de America (obra premiada por la Biblioteca
Nacional....e impresa á expensas del Estado).   *Madrid.*
1892.   Fol.

1890   VINCENT (FRANK).   Around and about South America.
Twenty months of quest and query.   Maps, plans and illustrations.   *New York.*   1890.   8°.

VIRCHOW (RUDOLPH).   Crania Ethnica Americana.   Samm-
lung auserlesener amerikanischer Schädeltypen.   Mit 26
Tafeln und 29 Text-Illustrationen.   *Berlin.*   1892.   Fol.
(Peruvian skulls.   Plates 8. 9, 25, 26.)

1886   —— Ueber Krankhaft veränd. Knocken alter Peruaner.
Berlin.   1886.   4.

1887   —— Die Schädel des Todtenfeldes von Ancon in Peru.
9 plates.   *See* REISS (WILHELM) and STUBEL (A.).   Das
Todtenfeld von Ancon in Peru, Vol. 3 (Pt. 14).   *Berlin.*
1887.   Fol.

1818   VOSS (J. VON).   Der sterbende Mönch in Peru.   Ein
Geschichte a. der südamerikanische Revolutionskriege.   2
parts.   *Berlin.*   1818.   12°.

1840–48   WAGNER (R.).   *See* PRICHARD (J. C.).   Naturgeschichte des Menschengeschlechts....mit Anmerkungen und Zusätzen herausgegeben von....R. W., *etc.*   4 vols.   *Leipzig.*   1840–48.   8°.

1877   WAITZ (THEODOR).   Anthropologie. der naturvölker.   6 vols.   *Leipzig.*   1877.   8°.
(Die Peruaner, Vol. IV., pages 378–502.)

1878   WAKE (C. STANILAND).   The Evolution of Morality, being a history of the development of moral culture.   2 vols.   *London.*   1878.   8°.
(Peru: Uncivilized tribes, Vol. I., pages 218–22 ; Inca civilization, Vol. II., pages 11–21.)

1849   WALPOLE (FREDERICK), *Lieut. R. N.*   Four years in the Pacific in her Majesty's ship "Collingwood," from 1844–48.   2 vols.   Illustrated.   *London.*   1849.   8°.
(Peru, Lima, Pachacamac, Payta.   Vol. II., pages 1–81.)

1820   WARDEN (DAVID B.).   Bibliotheca Americo-Septentrionalis.   *Paris.*   1820.

1869   WARREN (THOMAS ROBINSON).   Dust and Foam ; or, three oceans and two continents ; being ten years' wanderings in Mexico, South America, and Sandwich Islands.   *New York.*   1869.   16°.
(Peru, pages 92–123.)

1884   WATSON (ROBERT GRANT).   Spanish and Portuguese South America during the colonial period.   2 vols.   Maps.   *London.*   1884.   8°.
(Peru, Vol. I., pages 105–141, 169–208 ; Vol II., 126–145.

1850–61   WEDDELL (H. ALGERNON).   Voyage dans le Sud de la Bolivie.   *See* CASTELNAU (F. DE).   Expedition dans les parties centrales de l' Amerique du Sud.   Vol. VI.   *Paris.*   1850–61.   8°.

1853   —— Voyage dans le Nord de la Bolivie.   Map and illust.   *Paris.*   1853.   12°.

1808   WEYLAND (——).   *See* BERTUCH (VON F. J.).   Peru nach seinem gegenwärtigen Zustande.   2 vols.   *Weimar.*   1808.   8°.

1892   WHYMPER (EDWARD).   Travels amongst the Great Andes of the Equator.   Illustrated.   *London.*   1892.   8°.

1897 ——— *See* DALTON (O. M.). An ethnographical collection from Ecuador. *London.* 1897. 8°.

1874 WIENER (CHARLES). Pérou et Bolivie, Récit de voyage, suivi d'études archéologiques et ethnographiques, et de notes sur l' écriture et les langues des populations indiennes. Maps, plans and engravings. *Paris.* 1874. 8°.

1880 ——— (Another edition.) *Paris.* 1880. 8°.

1874 ——— Essai sur les Institutions politiques, religieuses, economiques, et sociales de l' Empire des Incas. *Paris.* 1874.

1874 ——— Notice sur le comunisme des Incas. *Paris.* 1874.

1879 ——— La Ville morte du Gran-Chimu et la Ville de Cuzco. Plans. *Paris.* 1879. 12°.
  (Bulletin de la Soc. de Geographie, October, 1879.)

1844 WILKES (CHARLES), *Comm. U. S. N.* Narrative of the United States Exploring Expedition in the years 1838, 1839, 1840, 1841 and 1842. 6 vols. and Atlas. *Washington.* 1844, *etc.* 4°. and fol.

1840-48 WILL (J. G. F.). *See* Prichard (J. C.). Naturgeschichte des Menschengeschlechts....mit Anmerkungen und Zuzätzen herausgegeben von....J. G. F. W. 4 vols. *Leipzig.* 1840-48.

1814 WILLIAMS (HELEN MARIA). *See* HUMBOLDT (F. H. A. VON). Researches concerning the....ancient inhabitants of America....translated....by H. M. W. 2 vols. *London.* 1814. 8°.

1822-29 ——— *See* HUMBOLDT (F. H. A. VON). Personal narrative of travels, *etc.*, translated by H. M. W. 7 vols. *London.* 1822-29. 8°.

1835. WINDERMANN (———) and HAUFF (———). Reisen und Länderbeschreibungen. 1835. 8°. *See* XERES (FR. DE). Geschichte der Entdeckung und Eroberung Peru's.

1889 WINSOR (JUSTIN). Narrative and Critical History of America. Edited by J. W. 8 vols. *Boston.* 1889, *etc.* 8°.
  (Vol. I., chap. 4, The Inca Civilization in Peru, by C. R. Markham ; Vol., II., chap. 8, Pizarro and the Conquest and Settlement of Peru and Chili, by C. R. Markham.)

1885   **Wright** (Bryce). Description of the Collection of Gold Ornaments from the "Huacas" or Graves of some Aboriginal Races of the Northwestern provinces of South America, belonging to Lady Brassey. Illustrations in gold. *London.* 1885. 8°.

1872   **Wuttke** (Heinrich).   Geschichte der Schrift und des Schriftums. *Leipzig.* 1872.
(Quipuschrift, pages 79–190.)

1534   **Xeres** (Francisco de). Verdadera relacion de la conquista del Peru y provincia del Cuzco. *Sevilla.* 1534. Fol.

1547   —— (Another edition.) *Salamanca.* 1547. Fol.

1547   —— (Another edition.) *Madrid.* 1547. Fol.
(Published with Oviedo y Valdez' Chronica de las Indias. *Valladolid.* · 1557.)

1556   —— Relatione della conquista fatta de F. Pizarro del Perù. *See* Ramusio (G. B.). Navigationi et Viaggi. Vol. 3. *Venetia.* 1556, *etc.* Fol.

1563   —— (Another edition.) 1563. Fol.

1749   —— (Another edition.) Conquista del Peru. *See* Barcia (D. A. G. de). Historiadores primitivos de las Indias occidentalas. Vol. 3. *Madrid.* 1749. Fol.

1849   —— (Another edition). Verdadera Relacion, *etc.* Edited by B. C. Aribau. *Madrid.* 1849. 8°.
(Vol. 26, Bibliotheca de Autores Espagnoles.)

1891   —— (Another edition.) *Madrid.* 1891.
(Coleccion de libros que tratan de America, raros y curiosos.)

1534   —— Libro Segunda delle Indie Occidentali. *Vinegia.* 1534. 4°.

1535   —— Libro primo de la conquesta del Peru et provincia del Cuzco de la Indie Occidentali. (Translated by Domingo de Gaztelu.) *Vinegia.* 1535. 4°.

1840   —— Relazione del conquisto del Perù e della provincia del Cuzco, *etc.*, traduttore D. Piccini. 1840. 8°.
(Vol V., Marmochi's Raccotta di Viaggi.)

1547   ———— L'histoire de la terre nueve du Péru en l'Indie occidentale, translated by Jacques Gahory. *Paris.* 1547.

(Pretends to be a summary of Oviedo's work, but is a translation of Xeres.)

1837   ———— Relation véridique de la conquête du Pérou et de la province de Cuzco nommée Nouvelle Castille, *etc.* (*Salamanque,* 1547). *Paris.* 1837. 8°.

(Vol. IV. Ternaux-Compans, Voyages, *etc.*)

1836   ——— Geschichte der Entdeckung und Eroberung Piru's. 1836. 8°.

(Windermann and Hauff, Reisen und Länderbeschreibungen.)

1843   ——— Geschichte der Entdeckung und Eroberung Peru's, translated by P. H. Kulb. *Stuttgart.* 1843. 8°.

1613   ———— 1613, *etc.* Fol.

1872   ——— A true account of the province of Cuzco, called New Castile, conquered by Francisco Pizarro, captain to his majesty the emperor, our master. (*Salamanca, 1547.* 2d ed.) Translated by C. R. Markham. *London.* 1872. 8°.

(Hakluyt Soc. Pub., No. 48. Reports on the Discovery of Peru.)

[FRANCISCO DE XERES left Spain for America 1530, with Pizarro, whom he accompanied as secretary on Peruvian expedition. His *Relacion,* written on the spot by Pizarro's order, March, 1533. Returned to Spain 1534. Gives Miguel Estete's narrative of Hernando Pizarro's expedition to Pachacamac.]

———— XIMINES DE QUESADA. Compendio (Conquest of New Granada).

(Work lost ; made use of by Lucas Fern. Piedrahita in his Historia General de las Conquistas del Nuevo Reyno de Granada.)

1890   YDIAQUEZ (A. DE). Le Perou en 1889. *Havre.* 1890. 8°.

——   YNCA (DR. JOHN JUSTO SAHUARAURA). *See* SAHUARAURA YNCA (DR. JOHN JUSTO).

1555   **Zarate** (Augustin de). Historia del Descubrimiento y
Conquista del Peru, con las cosas naturales que señalada-
mente alli se hallan, y los successos que ha avido. *Anvers.*
1555. 12°.

1557   —— Second edition. *Sevilla.* 1557. Fol.

1577   —— (Another edition.) *Sevilla.* 1577. Fol.

1749   —— (Another edition.) *Madrid.* 1749. Fol. *See*
Barcia (D. Andres Gonz. de). Historiadores primitivos de
las Indias occidentales. Vol. 3.

1853   —— (Another edition.) *Madrid.* 1853. 8°. *See*
Aribau (B. C.). Biblioteca de autores Españoles. Vol. 26.

1563   —— Le historie....dello scofrimento et conquista del
Peru, nelle quali si hapiena et particular relatione delle cose
successe in quelle bande, *etc.* Nuovamente di lingua cas-
tigliana tradotte dal S. Alfonso Villoa. *Vinegia.* 1563. 4°.

1564   —— De Wonderlycke ende warachtige historie vaut
coninck rijck van Peru, *etc.* *Hantwerpen.* 1564. 4°.

1573   —— (Another edition.) *Hantwerpen.* 1573. 4°.

1596   —— (Another edition.) Conqueste van Indien, *etc.*
Map. *Amsterdam.* 1596. 4°.

1598   —— (Another edition.) *Amsterdam.* 1598. 4 .

1623   —— (Another edition.) *Amsterdam.* 1623. 4°.

1581   —— The strange and delectable history of the discoveries and conquest of Peru, *etc.* Translated out of the Spanish tongue by T. Nicholas. *London.* 1581. 4°.

1700   —— Histoire de la découverte et de la conquête du
Pérou (transl. by de Broë?). 2 vols. *Amsterdam.* 1700. 8°.

1706   —— (Another edition.) Traduite de l' Espagnol d'
Aug. de Z. par S. D. C. (de Broë, seigneur de Citry et de la
Guëtte). 2 vols. *Paris.* 1706. 16°.

1716   —— (Another edition.) 2 vols. *Paris.* 1716. 16 .

1717   —— (Another edition.) *Amsterdam.* 1717.

1718   —— (Another edition.) *Amsterdam.* 1718.

1719   —— (Another edition.) *Amsterdam.* 1719.

1742   —— (Another edition.) *Paris.* 1742. 8°.

1752-4 —— (Another edition.) *Paris.* 1752-4.

1774   —— (Another edition.)   2 vols.   Maps and plates. *Paris.* 1774. 12°.

1830   —— (Another edition.)   2 vol.   *Paris.*   1830.   8°.

[AUGUSTIN DE ZARATE went to Peru, in 1543, with Viceroy Blasco Nuñez, as royal treasurer, and remained several years. In 1554 went to England with Philip, to whom as "King of England" his work is dedicated. A shrewd observer, but ignorant of the native languages. Gives good description of the Inca roads.]

1875   ZEGARRA (GAVINO PACHECO). Alphabet phonétique de la langue Quéchua. *Nancy.* 1875. 8°. (28 pages.)

1878   —— Ollanaï, drame en vers quechuas du temps des Incas. Texte original écrit avec les caractères d' un alphabet phonétique spécial pour la langue quechua ; précédé d' un appendice en deux parties et d' un vocabulaire de tous les mots contenus dans le drame. Trad. et commenté par G. P. Z. Portrait. *Paris.* 1878. 8°.

——   ZEIVELA (ROQUE DE CEJUELAÓ DE). Catecismo en lengua yunga o' quichua y española.
(Vinaza : Bibl. Espan. No. 895.)

1884   ZOELLER (H.). Pampas und Anden. Sitten-und Kultur-Schilder. *Berlin.* 1884.
(Uruguay, Argentine, Paraguay, Chile, Peru, Ecuador, Columbia.)

1874   ZOJA (G.) Di un Teschio Boliviano Microcefalo. 4 plates. *Milano.* 1874. 4°.